THE SWEET SHOP OF SECOND CHANCES

HANNAH LYNN

Boldwood

First published in 2021. This edition first published in Great Britain in 2023 by Boldwood Books Ltd.

Copyright © Hannah Lynn, 2021

Cover Design by Alexandra Allden

Cover photography: Shutterstock

The moral right of Hannah Lynn to be identified as the author of this work has been asserted in accordance with the Copyright, Designs and Patents Act 1988.

All rights reserved. No part of this book may be reproduced in any form or by any electronic or mechanical means, including information storage and retrieval systems, without written permission from the author, except for the use of brief quotations in a book review.

This book is a work of fiction and, except in the case of historical fact, any resemblance to actual persons, living or dead, is purely coincidental.

Every effort has been made to obtain the necessary permissions with reference to copyright material, both illustrative and quoted. We apologise for any omissions in this respect and will be pleased to make the appropriate acknowledgements in any future edition.

A CIP catalogue record for this book is available from the British Library.

Paperback ISBN 978-1-80549-583-3

Large Print ISBN 978-1-80549-579-6

Harback ISBN 978-1-80549-578-9

Ebook ISBN 978-1-80549-576-5

Kindle ISBN 978-1-80549-577-2

Audio CD ISBN 978-1-80549-584-0

MP3 CD ISBN 978-1-80549-581-9

Digital audio download ISBN 978-1-80549-575-8

Boldwood Books Ltd
23 Bowerdean Street
London SW6 3TN
www.boldwoodbooks.com

To Nina

1

Given that Holly Berry had left London in such a hurry, she hadn't really put much thought into the clothes she had packed. And 'packed' was using the term very loosely. After hurling several shoes at her now definitely ex-boyfriend, she had hauled the suitcase from the top of the wardrobe and thrown in a half dozen armfuls of clothes. Meanwhile Dan (said ex) had been attempting to rescue some of his own things which were getting caught in the mix. A task that was hindered somewhat by the fact that he seemed unsure whether he should be trying to appease Holly, his girlfriend, who had just caught him butt-naked in a compromising positioning in their new Ikea bed – a bed she had paid half for – or comforting the sobbing woman who was still on said bed, also without a stitch on and desperately trying to cover herself.

'Hols. Hols, just wait. Please, wait. Listen.'

'I heard enough, thanks. Trust me, those noises are going to be hard to forget.'

Her hands were shaking as she grabbed another dress and ripped it off the hanger. Six years. Six years of her life had been all about him. Six years she had put her plans on hold for *their* plans. What a bloody fool.

'Please let me explain.' The moment his hand touched her shoulder, she span around and flung it away from her.

'Don't you dare. Don't you dare touch me, or speak to me, or even look at me.'

'But you don't understand...'

'No. No, I don't. You're completely right about that. I do not understand how the hell you could do this to me.'

'I just... we just...'

'We had a plan, Dan. You and I. We had everything planned out. We were looking at houses last weekend. *Last weekend*.'

'I just... I just...'

'Slipped?' she questioned.

Her eyes moved involuntarily to where the woman was now wrapped up in the bed sheet. She had definitely paid for that. She remembered being particularly impressed with the 75 per cent discount she'd got during the sales. Her attention left the sheet and returned to the woman. Dark hair, dark eyes. Dan clearly had a type, that much was obvious. Apparently, he had gone for the oldest cliché in the book and traded her in for a younger model.

'Please,' he whined, trying to pull the pity card now, his eyes watery and pathetic.

Unable to take any more, she zipped up the case and marched out of the room, down the stairs and out of the front door.

While driving away from Dan and London, her mind was filled with questions. How could he have done it, after all they had been through? She had been there for him, through everything. And why? Why would he do it? And why hadn't she seen it coming?

Despite having been at the same university for three years, the pair had never even laid eyes on each other until the day of their graduation. Ceremonies over, and celebration dinners concluded, she had headed out to a club with her old house mates.

It was on a brief respite away from the dance floor, when she had gone to the bar to grab them all drinks, that she saw him. His deep-brown eyes had caught her attention straight away. And the way he had struggled hopelessly to get the barman's attention. After watching him get pushed in front of several times – clearly too polite to say anything about it – she had sidled up next to him and, on getting served first, had ordered drinks for both of them, which he had then gratefully paid for. She'd later learned that he had played the part of the helpless man in need of rescuing in the hope of attracting her attention. She had thought it was sweet. They'd laughed about it over dinner with friends. Now she saw the truth: he'd been manipulating her from day one.

It wasn't until she'd turned off the M4, the sun long since set, that Holly actually thought about where she was driving to. She realised she was automatically heading towards her parents, but did she really want to face them? Of course, they would be supportive, but deep down she knew they'd never been that keen on Dan.

'He just seems a bit beige,' she recalled her mother saying once.

'Beige?'

'You know. Plain. Unexciting.'

'There's nothing wrong with someone who's sensible, Mum.'

'No, but do you have fun together?'

'Of course we do.'

Her mother hadn't look convinced. 'What about that house you were talking about last month. I thought you were going to buy it?'

'We were, but we've decided to wait. Save a little longer. Get a bigger deposit together.'

'You were saving last year, weren't you? And the year before. You've got a steady job. You don't have to always be worrying about money, you know.'

She had gritted her teeth. 'Yes, but houses are expensive, and the bigger the deposit we have, the less we'll have to pay back in the long run.'

'But you need to have some fun too, Holly darling. It can't all be about saving money and working hard.' Then her mum had tutted in a way that suggested her desire to be financially secure was the most irresponsible thing she'd ever heard of. How would she respond to *this* news? She'd be devastated that Holly was upset, that was for certain, but beyond that it was impossible to tell.

As she reached the turnoff for her parents' home, she kept going. She would talk to them later. She still had a spare key and could sneak in when they were asleep, if she wanted. Or maybe she'd just splash out and get a room somewhere for the night. It wasn't like she needed her savings for a house deposit now, was it?

She was travelling down a long, straight road. If you looked on your satnav, this particular road was now called the A429, but to anyone who lived locally, it was the Fosse Way. The full length of this Roman road extended for miles, going as far north as south Leicester. Holly never travelled that far, though. She continued on past Northleach, then the little Cotswold village of Cold Aston, until she reached the bottom of a low hill, where she flicked on her indicator and turned left. This took her right alongside the river and led straight to the heart of Bourton-on-the-Water.

* * *

Even the most cynical visitor to Bourton would struggle to argue with the claim that it was one of the most idyllic villages in Britain. With its shallow river flowing gently next to the High Street, complete with quaint little bridges, it is Instagram heaven, whatever the season. In the autumn, it's time to don your woollen coat against the chilly air and enjoy watching the flurries of amber and gold leaves cascading from the trees at every hint of a breeze. And during the festive season, when thousands of twinkling white lights adorn the shop fronts, a fifteen-foot Christmas tree stands smack in the middle of the river. It really is a little slice of countryside paradise.

However, for residents, particularly a teenaged Holly, this was something of a double-edged sword. Any day with remotely pleasant weather resulted in traffic that backed up all the way from the High Street to the nearest A road, half a mile away. When said vehicles finally managed to get into the village, they would inevitably park in the first available spot they saw, regardless of whether it was an actual, designated space or who they blocked in. It was generally impossible to find a seat in any of the cafes – which were mostly overpriced – and the whole village was overrun with screaming children, irate parents and hikers, not to mention the busloads of tourists who visited just to pose for a photo, ice cream in hand, ankle deep in the river, before hopping back onto the bus for their next destination.

It hadn't been all bad growing up there, though. Cycle rides on her rusty, old bike, up hills so steep her legs wanted to give up a third of the way there, were seared vividly into her memory. Hikes across the surrounding fields to one of the more hidden streams where, armed with jam jars and fishing nets, she and her friends would catch newts all afternoon. Traipsing up and down the riverside, searching for various flowers and herbs to take back and place in homemade, ceramic vases. A simpler time, before iPads and phones.

But there were other memories, too. Ones she didn't recall quite so fondly. Like the bedroom window that didn't close properly so that, in winter, her breath fogged the air when she was in bed. Or dry cereal days, when they had run out of milk and were saving the last few coins to feed the electric meter (Cold showers were one thing. Cold showers in a freezing house were altogether another). The day her father was made redundant. Then when it happened again... and yet again.

It was difficult to pinpoint her exact age when Holly realised her family was poor. She suspected it was around the start of secondary school. While other children would start each new term with their brand-new, designer shoes – Kickers, Doc Martens, Air Jordans, or whatever the fashion at the time dictated – her feet would be squeezed into whatever pair of black lace-ups her mother had sourced. Her uniform was always either too big or too small, the window of time when it would actually fit comfortably seeming narrower each year.

While other parents bought their children the latest fad toy or favourite doll for their birthday, Holly received cookery books, often dog-eared, with stained proof of their previous owner's attempt at culinary skills. On her birthday morning, after tearing off the wrapping paper, she would choose a recipe to make, usually something sweet and, no matter what, her parents would somehow always manage to scrape together the ingredients she needed: vanilla pods, dark chocolate, double cream, whatever. It wasn't until she was in her twenties that she realised the weeks that followed were always filled with more frugal meals, like lentil soup, or Welsh rarebits made with homemade bread and the thinnest slithers of cheese.

For the longest while, it hadn't bothered her. She had counted her blessings for her loving family, and despite their lack of wealth they were happy. But, on her fourteenth birthday, that all changed.

She had made little attempt over the previous few months to hide what she really wanted. She'd had enough of the recipe books and the cooking. After all, she was fairly accomplished already, always preparing her own lunch box and often the family evening meal, too. It no longer felt like a treat and certainly not something worthy of a birthday present. What she'd really wanted was a pair of Levi 501s.

She had hoped that Christmas would yield the illusive garment but instead had received a tie-died T-shirt. But she didn't lose faith; after all, there was still her birthday in March.

'Now, I hope they fit okay,' her mother said, stepping into the room and placing the parcel down on the bed next to her. 'If they don't, I'm sure Maureen at the pharmacy will take them up for you. She's far better at hemming things with an overlocker than I am.'

When Holly ripped off the wrapping paper to reveal a neatly folded pile of denim, emblazoned with the Levi 501 badge, her heart leapt. She gazed at the jeans in her hands. Was it really possible that, after months and months of completely ignoring every request she'd made, her parents had finally listened to what she'd been saying? Her hands shook with excitement as she picked them up and flicked them outwards.

Her jaw had dropped.

'Are they okay? I know they're not the fancy make you keeping banging on about and they aren't brand new, but they've got a lot of life left in them. The seams are strong, and there are only small holes under those patches.'

Patches. Much of the denim was lost beneath a hideous array of multi-coloured, multi-patterned fabric, stitched haphazardly all the way from the waist to the hems. Later, on reflection, she realised there couldn't have been more than five or six squares, but to her teenage eyes it looked like there were thousands strewn across the jeans. It mightn't have been so bad if they had all been one colour. But half of them looked like they'd been stolen from a children's nursery and at least one had teddy bears on it.

'Why don't you try them on?' her mother asked. 'We need to make sure they fit.'

Holly continued to stare at the monstrosity. What could she do?

The last thing she wanted was to hurt her mother's feelings. Knowing her luck, she'd probably spent the last six months sourcing the materials for the patches. But she just couldn't try them on. She couldn't bear to even look at them without wanting to cry. Forcing herself to smile, she folded the jeans neatly back up and dropped them down behind her on the bed.

'I'll just have a shower first,' she said.

As her mother's face fell, guilt churned in the pit of Holly's stomach, but she just couldn't put them on. She couldn't. If they fitted, then she would insist on her wearing them out in public and that was more than she could take. At least, this way, she could pretend they were far too small, and her mum would be none the wiser.

'Oh, okay then.'

Silence filled the room as her mother rose to her feet, her lips strained upwards in a smile. Holly's guilt intensified. Even at fourteen, she couldn't fail to recognise the sadness in her eyes. But she'd forget about it soon enough, she reasoned. They were only jeans.

'Well, you try them on when you're ready then,' she said, crossing to the door. 'I'm going to put some porridge on for breakfast.'

'Sounds good,' she replied.

It was not until that evening, after a full day at school with friends questioning her about what presents she'd received, that Holly got a knock on her bedroom door for the second time that day. This time it was her father.

A man of few words, Arthur Berry was a six-foot two, gentle giant who'd had little luck when it came to employment. After the closure of the factory he'd worked in since his teenage years, when Holly was only two, it was one short-term position after another. Always last in, first out. He had now been working a steady position for a couple of months, but they never took anything for granted.

After hearing the knock, she called that it was open. He waited until he'd walked across the room and taken a seat at her desk before speaking.

'So your mother thinks you don't like your present.'

It was said as a statement, not a question. Her dad had an annoying habit of doing that. Making statements and then leaving it to her to be the next to speak. He gave her a look at the same time, too, as if puzzled, brows down. It was an impressive skill that ensured she'd feel as guilty as possible in the shortest time. She held her tongue, determined not to fall into his trap. But the look just kept going, stretching the tension in the air.

'She can't seriously expect me to wear them.' she said, unable to restrain herself for even half as long as she had hoped. 'There are teddy bears on them, Dad. No one over five wears jeans with teddy bears on.'

'Is that right?'

'Yes,' she nodded emphatically. 'It is. People wear normal jeans. Blue jeans. Light blue jeans. Occasionally black jeans. But they don't wear ones with nursery characters on. Just like they don't wear sweaters knitted with multi-coloured wool, or socks with hundreds of darns in that they've done themselves.'

Her father steepled his fingers and put them against his top lip. This was his 'thinking' pose, which Holly knew well. Both she and her mother had lost many an hour with her father like this, as he'd internally debated various decisions, from what to have for dinner, to which politician to vote for in an upcoming election.

'I know it's difficult,' he said, finally removing his fingers. 'I'm sure I didn't appreciate my parents at your age either.'

Holly felt the anger rising.

'That's not fair. I do appreciate her. I appreciate you both.'

As the words came out, all whiny and high-pitched, she was fully aware of how petulant she sounded, but she wasn't going to be accused of something that wasn't true. Yes, she was a child, but she had always worked hard at school and done far more chores than any of her friends had ever had to do. She mended her own clothes, cooked family meals. Not to mention the other stuff, like traipsing along to seed-swap parties with her mother and unpicking jumpers so that the wool could be re-used. Other children got to spend their Saturday mornings watching cartoons while they lazed around in bed, whereas she had to travel ten miles on the bus to get a tomato plant someone was giving a way.

'I just wanted a normal pair of jeans, that's all. I don't see what the big deal is.'

'Holly, those jeans you want cost a fortune. More than we spend on food for the entire week. Do you have any idea how many hours your mum spent patching those for you?' With a heavy sigh, he pushed his glasses to the top of his head and rubbed the bridge of his nose. 'I'm sorry,' he said. 'I'm sorry that we can't afford to spend money on all the things you wish we could. I'm sorry that you're disappointed by the gift.'

'Dad...' The churning guilt in her gut intensified.

'No, I understand. I do. We've never had enough money to save, Hols. I wish we had, of course I do, but we've been lucky in lots of other ways. We're healthy, and we're happy. At least I hope we are?'

His weary look had now transferred to her, as her shoulders slumped down in a huff.

'I'm sorry,' she said, moving from the bed and wrapping her arms around his shoulders. 'I am. And I'll wear the jeans, I promise. But maybe if she could change the teddy bear patches?'

'I'm sure we can see to that. You'll talk to her, then? She's worried she ruined your birthday.'

Together they headed downstairs and her parents sang 'Happy Birthday' over a homemade lemon cake her mother had baked that afternoon.

Later that night, when she was tucked up in bed considering the events of the day, a thought tumbled through her mind. Her father was right; her parents had never had much money, but they had always made sure she was loved and well. Still, if she ever had children, she would make sure they could have everything they wanted, and that meant money. Money she was going to start earning as soon as possible.

2

There was no competition for a parking space at this late hour and Holly could take her pick as she slowed her car on the empty street and turned into a spot by the river. She thought she would just sit there for a while and ponder what a mess her life had become. But no sooner had she cut the engine than she found herself unbuckling her seatbelt and crossing to other side of the road. A moment later and she was standing outside the grubby window of Just One More, her gaze lost in its dark interior until a high-pitched meow drew her attention away.

A lithe, black-and-white cat with scruffy fur snaked its way between her ankles, pressing its head against her calves as it meowed again for attention.

'What are you doing?' she asked, as she knelt down to stroke it and it immediately started purring at her. 'If you're out hunting, I'm afraid you'll only find chocolate mice in there.'

With a final, plaintive meow, it sauntered to the front door of the shop where it paused for just a moment before continuing on down the High Street.

The night air was chilly as she stood up and peered back into the shop. Spring was on its way, but it definitely hadn't arrived yet. The sign above the door looked worn, the paint chipped and peeling, and the awning had also seen better days, with rust along the edge. Apart from that, it was exactly the same as it had been when she'd first gone through the door. Her heart swelled as she cupped her hands around her eyes, pressed them to the glass and was just able to make out the jars filled with sweets inside. One by one, memories from days gone by seeped into her consciousness and slowly, as the seconds ticked by, a smile crept across her face for the first time since she'd arrived home early from work to surprise Dan.

'Are you lost?'

She jumped, banging her head against the glass.

'Crap,' she said, rubbing her forehead and turning back to the street. Considering the road had been empty only moments earlier, she was surprised to find herself face to face with a very serious-looking man.

'Are you lost?' he asked again.

'Uhm. No. I'm not lost,' she replied.

'Then would you care to tell me what you're doing here so late in the evening?'

As the temperature continued to fall, Holly locked eyes on this stranger who, despite being smartly dressed, not unattractive and probably only in his mid-thirties, wore the suspicious frown of a busy-body pensioner. Having been torn from her reverie, she was in no mood to accommodate his nosiness.

'Are you with the police?' she asked.

He bristled slightly. 'No.'

'Neighbourhood Watch then?'

'No.'

'Well, if you're not with the police or Neighbourhood Watch, why is it any of your business?'

He shuffled his feet. 'Well, it is rather late, and you've been staring into that window for nearly ten minutes.'

'So you've been watching me? Spying on me?'

'Yes... no. I mean, I watched you... I saw you... but I wasn't spying.'

Her initial annoyance was rapidly passing through indignation and now transforming into something decidedly more like anger.

'I was merely questioning your intentions here,' he stuttered.

'My intentions?' Her eyebrows disappeared under her fringe. After the day she'd been having, pompous, village do-gooders were the last thing she was in the mood for. She pulled back her shoulders and placed her hands squarely on her hips. 'Firstly, as you're not a police officer, you have absolutely no right to ask me what I am doing. Secondly, are you implying that I might be about to rob a sweet shop? Seriously? There's a jewellers three doors down, and the shop next to it sells antiques. Not to mention all the holiday homes on Sherborne Street that are empty during the week. If I were going to rob a place, I think there are far better options for me in the village than this little place, don't you?'

The man, who now looked not only confused but also somewhat fearful, took a step back.

'You're from the village?' he asked.

'Well done. Now, if you don't mind, my intention is to stand here, minding my own business and stare at these jars of sweets,' she said. 'Do you have a problem with that?'

His Adam's apple bobbed up and down, all of his previous bravado gone, although a bristle of mistrust remained.

'Sorry, I didn't recognise you. I'll wish you a good evening then,' he said and, without a final word or apology, strode off down the High Street and out of view.

'A good evening, yeah right,' she said out loud, turning her attention back to the shop.

* * *

Two days after her fourteenth birthday, Holly found herself walking along the riverfront, heading into each of the cafes in search of employment. If she had her own money, it would solve so many problems. They wouldn't have to worry about buying her things to start with. Not to mention the fact that she could help them out, too. Pay for some groceries occasionally. Treat them to decent birthday and Christmas gifts. Getting a part-time job would be an all-round win. So when she left the house that morning, the teddy bear patches on her jeans having been swapped for more subtle, green ones, she was full of optimism.

'Do you have any experience?' the first cafe owner asked her when she enquired if there was anything going.

'No, but I'm a quick learner.'

'I've already taken on two new staff this month. Come back in the summer when you know the ropes and I'm sure we'll find you something then.'

She could already see the flaw in this plan. After all, if she had a job already or got one somewhere else, why would she leave it? She knew enough from her dad's redundancies that you didn't walk away from guaranteed work. Unfortunately, it was the same story at the second place, then the third and the fourth. Whatever type of establishment she walked in to – bakery, mini-mart, souvenir shop – they all said the exact same thing. She needed experience. Classic catch-22. By the time she'd reached half way down the High Street, she'd already received a dozen rejections. Her feet were aching and her good mood was utterly demolished. She was about to abandon the idea when she looked up and found herself outside Just One More. Taking it as a sign, she pushed open the door.

There were two sweet shops in the village at the time, although Holly wasn't a frequent visitor to either of them. Sweets were a luxury, and on the few times she had decided to spend her pocket money on a packet of Polo mints or a Mars Bar, both the Co-op and the Post office were closer to home.

However, once inside, she discovered that Just One More was not a shop of Mars Bars and Polo mints, or any of the sweets she was used to seeing stacked next to the supermarket checkout. It was something else entirely. First of all, the smell hit her, so sweet her mouth immediately started to water. After that, it took her a full minute to take in the rainbow of confectionary on offer. Glass jars everywhere she turned, shelves packed from floor to ceiling. Aniseed twists and liquorice allsorts. Love hearts, wine gums and strawberry laces. Sugar mice, chocolate mice, all manner of marzipan animals. Not to mention the array of fudges, coconut ices and a selection of exceptionally expensive-looking boxes of choco-late too. Obviously, at the time, she had no idea of all the names, but they were soon to become as familiar to her as the letters of the alphabet. Transfixed, she slowly turned in a circle, absorbing as much as her senses could take in.

'Can we help you?'

Shaking her head clear, she looked towards the counter, where two women stood, side by side. The pair looked similar in age and wore the same light-blue apron, each with a brass name tag, although that was where the similarity ended.

The woman who had spoken – Agnes, according to her badge – wore a floaty linen dress with white flowers embroidered on the collar and a selection of colourful bangles jangled on her wrist. The other lady – Maud – wore a pair of jeans and a sharply ironed, navy shirt. Where Agnes wore her blonde hair loose and flowing, Maud kept her curly dark hair scraped back. Of course, initial judgements can be misleading. As the years went by, Holly learned that the women were two sides of the same coin, two souls more destined to be together than any two people she had ever known. But, at the time, the only thing she knew was that she had walked into a wonderland.

Maud cleared her throat.

'Is everything all right? Is there something in particular you're looking for?'

A moment of silence followed. Holly's standard spiel about looking for a job and being hardworking and a quick learner, et cetera, et cetera, had disappeared somewhere into the back of her head. Instead what she said was, 'I want to stay here... forever.'

The two women grinned, first at her, then at each other, at which point Holly realised what an idiot she sounded and straightened herself back up.

'Sorry. What I mean to say is, I'm looking for some part-time work. On Saturdays. Or Sundays. Or after school. Any time, really. I wouldn't mind. I can do school holidays too.'

Rambling when panicking was a habit she wished she could kick, but her brain was working triple time, trying to think of anything else she could say that would make her sound more appealing.

'I'm very punctual,' she added. 'And I don't live a far away. And I really like sweets. And chocolate. I probably like chocolate more than sweets, actually.'

Praying that one of the women would say something soon, she clamped her mouth shut. But it was no use.

'I don't mind early mornings,' she prattled on, quite unable to stop. 'And am very tidy. I'm good at darning too and fixing things. Not that I think anything would need darning or fixing here. It's just perfect.'

She had headed out intending to get a weekend job, anything to give herself a little bit of money. But now she wanted this one. She wanted to be here all the time, among the rosy apples and the rhubarb and custards. She wanted to spend every minute she could straightening up those glass jars and using the massive, brass, weighing scales that stood on the counter. At that point she would have offered to work for free, or near enough. She just didn't want to go back outside, to face the rest of the world, not now she knew a place like this existed. Then came the question she'd been dreading.

'Do you have any experience?' asked Maud.

Her heart sank as she dipped her head and took a deep breath. Her voice came out as a mutter, the shy, unintelligible one which made her teachers ask her to speak up.

'N-no,' she stammered. 'No experience.' The sadness of the day's rejections was pushing down on her shoulders with such a force that she found herself unable to look up. Maybe next year, she thought. Maybe if she was a year older, it wouldn't matter so much that she hadn't worked before. Maybe. When she finally raised her eyes back up to thank the ladies for their time, the blond woman was beaming at her.

'Well, it shouldn't take that long to train you up, should it Maud?' she said, a smile glinting in her eyes. 'When can you start?

* * *

A breeze rustled the leaves on a nearby tree and sent a shiver down her spine. It had been late afternoon when she'd slammed the door in Dan's face and started driving. At some point, she would have to make a plan. Not just for tonight, but for the future. The lease on the flat was in both their names. Maybe he'd leave and let her stay there. She'd saved enough money to pay the rent herself if she had to. But she'd never want to sleep in that bed again. No, he could keep the bed and the flat. She'd figure something else out. She had to.

She felt the heat building in her eyes again. She had trusted him completely, but what was worse was that she had trusted her judgment too, thought she had found someone who would make her happy and be content with her and the steady life she'd envisioned. And now look where she had ended up.

She was debating whether to slump to the ground and cry, or pick up the nearest rock and hurl it into the river, when a small cough echoed behind her.

'I'm going, all right? I'm going,' she said, simultaneously spinning around and wiping her cheeks.

'Maud?' She blinked, doing one double take and then another. 'Maud!'

3

It had been four years since Holly had last seen her friend and former employer, in a situation that had been less than ideal: a funeral. When she'd heard the news of Agnes' death, it had come like a knife to the heart. The women had been together for over forty years and never had she or anyone else ever doubted that *'til death do us part* would apply to them. The occasion, whilst so very sad, had been beautiful. The church had been packed full to bursting and, in a pre-arranged act of thoughtfulness, jars of sweets had been placed on every pew for mourners to enjoy during the service. Only Agnes could have dreamt up something like that.

The wake had been in the tiny cottage that the two women had called home as long as Holly had known them. Dan had come with her for support, but they'd needed to get back to London for work the next day, so hadn't stayed long. They would visit again soon, Holly had promised.

A hundred times, if not more, she had thought about popping in to see how Maud was bearing up. Maybe spend the night at her cottage and reminisce about the good old days over a sherbet fountain or a takeaway, but there had never been quite enough time. Of course she'd known the loss of Agnes would have been tough on her; however, judging by the additional creases on the old lady's face and the grey hair that had replaced her tight, dark curls, she felt a deep pang of guilt for having not kept her promise. She was still recognisable, of course, with her arched brows and delicate, almond eyes, but she had changed. Her once proud, erect posture had gone and, in its place, her slumped shoulders curved inwards, as if to protect herself from the world. A couple of phone calls. An email now and then. Would it really have taken that much on Holly's part?

'It's me. Holly. Holly Berry.'

The old woman's eyes widened. 'No! Holly, I barely recognised you. Well, this is a wonderful surprise.' Maud broke into a smile that somehow rolled back the years. 'What on earth are you doing here? How've you been? Oh, it's so good to see you. So very good to see you.'

The old women's smile caused an ache to spread through Holly's chest, making it difficult to speak. The prickly heat had returned to her eyes and a thick lump wedged itself in her throat. And then, with the pressure of a hundred thoughts weighing on her heart, Holly Berry burst into tears.

For a full minute, she stood there, burying her head in her hands as huge tears escaped through her fingers. When she finally got herself under control, she looked up to find her old friend regarding her with a look of deepest concern carved into her features.

'Well then,' Maud said, attempting to straighten herself up and pulling down the hem of her jacket. 'I think we probably both need a drink. What do you say to that?'

While The Seven Hounds wasn't the closest pub to either the shop or Maud's cottage, the ones in the centre of the village tended to cater more for the tourist trade. They were the ones with the fancy menus and mood lighting, nice for special occasions, like birthdays or other celebrations, but not the type of place you'd ever be a regular, mainly because of the price. The Seven Hounds, by contrast, was the epitome of a local pub for locals. The seating was old, the décor dated and somehow, even after so many years since the smoking ban had come into place, it still held a faint aroma of stale tobacco and cigar smoke, particularly if you moved about too much on the cushioned seats, but the drinks were cold, and the reception warm.

They had found themselves a corner seat. Holly swilled the drink in her glass thoughtfully.

'So, it sounds like a bit of a mess,' Maud said, taking a sip from her soda and lime. 'I'm sorry. I really am. What a terror. I'm glad I never got to the meet the man.'

Holly opened her mouth to speak. Maud had met Dan a few times, the last time being the funeral.

'I'm so angry at myself,' she said, instead. 'For not spotting something sooner. I mean, he didn't just wake up one day and turn into a cheat, did he? I've had so many friends get married recently. People who've only been in a relationship for a year or two. Sometimes even less. But I kept thinking I was being sensible, you know? We were doing things the right way. We didn't blow a load of money on a big wedding day. We were thinking long term. Thinking about the future. Our future. Smug, that's what I was. A bloody, smug fool.' Holly knew she ought to let it go and talk about something else, but she was just so angry. 'I feel like everything I thought I knew about life was wrong. Does that make sense? Probably not. I've just got so many regrets.' They were swirling around and around in her head. So many years of living a safe, sensible life. She had thought she'd found her perfect match in Dan, someone who wouldn't buy a train-station pastry without putting it into his budget-planning app. 'Do you know something? I haven't even bought a new pair of shoes in nearly two years?'

'Why's that?' Maud asked.

'Because this entire time I've been saving, trying to get this big deposit for a house that we'd live in and raise our kids. Because I wanted them to grow up never missing out on anything. Because I wanted us to be secure. *Secure*. What does that even mean? Honestly, how could I have been such a fool? I'm the one who's missed out.'

'Don't be so hard on yourself. You were in love. And there's nothing wrong with being sensible.'

'Is there not? Then why aren't I happier? Even before this, if I was doing everything right, why weren't we happier? Surely we should have been?'

Wishing she could answer her own question, Holly picked up her glass and finished the rest of her wine. She'd certainly never been a person to believe in The One. So many of her friends were still out there searching for Mr Right, or even Mr He'll Do, but she knew that love didn't have to be all that. To her, it was about having someone there every evening that she could talk to and who would do the washing up without being asked when she'd made dinner. But, over the last few years, Dan hadn't even been that.

'I remember him now,' Maud said, placing her hand firmly on the table in front of her. 'You brought him to the cottage once, didn't you? Weak chin. That's what Agnes said. Should have trusted her. She was always the most wonderful judge of character.'

'Is a weak chin a measure of character?'

'It was to Agnes.'

Holly chuckled sadly as a new silence filled the air. One in which she suspected a thousand memories were flitting through Maud's mind now.

'I still can't believe she's gone,' Holly said, breaking the silence before it settled in too deeply. 'I guess it's because I haven't been back.'

'Four years. Four years, two months and nine days, to be exact. Honestly, sometimes it feels like she's barely been gone a day. Others, I feel like I've been lost for decades without her. Nothing seems to work right without her here. I know I certainly don't.'

Holly didn't have the words she needed. She didn't think it was possible to find them. Still, she tried.

'I'm so sorry. I can't imagine what it's been like for you.'

Maud nodded. There were no tears in her eyes. Not even a sheen to them, just pure, undiluted sadness.

'It hasn't faded, you know. People tell you that it does, with time. That it gets easier. But I still think I hear her talking. Sometimes, when I'm downstairs in the shop, I swear I hear her voice calling from upstairs. Occasionally, when I'm in the cottage, I speak to her because I've forgotten for a moment that she's gone. It doesn't get any easier. You just get used to the pain.'

'I'm sorry,' Holly said again, the words sounding even more futile than before. 'I should have visited.'

With a shake of her head, Maud attempted a small smile. 'Nonsense, Life goes on and you've been living yours. Although, you know, it's funny you turning up today of all days,' she said, gesturing to the barmaid to bring them each another drink.

'Really? Why is that? What's special about today?'

Maud took her time answering.

'To be honest, I'm not normally out this late at night. Not any more. But I came out to say goodbye.'

'Say goodbye? To what?'

'To the shop. I've decided its time.'

'Time for what?'

'To move on. To sell up.'

It felt like a physical blow to her stomach. First Dan, now this.

'Why? Why would you do that?' she asked, unable to hide the horror in her voice. 'And to whom? Who's buying it?'

Before she could get an answer, the barmaid arrived with their fresh drinks. Maud took a long draw of hers, placed it down on the table and then folded her hands on her lap.

'Obviously, it won't happen immediately, but I'm going to sell it to developers,' she said. 'It's just got too much. The whole thing. I've let it go to pot.'

'I don't believe that.'

'Oh, I wish it wasn't true, but it is. I just can't keep it going. I've been trying, you know, because it was always her baby, wasn't it? I mean it was ours, both of ours, but it was her dream first. And I've let her down, Holly. I couldn't keep it up. I can't keep that place going, not without her there. But these developers, they've been after it for years. They'll give me a good-enough price. There's too much work that needs to be done to keep it as it should be. They'll fix it up properly, I guess, before selling it on again. Probably just strip it bare and turn it into a blank canvass.'

'But it doesn't need stripping. It's perfect.'

Maud gave a small, sad laugh before sipping again at her drink. She seemed so calm about it all. So matter of fact. Holly, on the other hand, was not.

'But what can they want with it? The building is tiny.'

'Oh, everything goes to developers, nowadays. They even took the old care home on Station Road. Did you know that?'

Another pang of sadness hit her. As a schoolchild, she had gone carolling at the home each Christmas. The old people always came to life then, singing along with the classics. It was a shame to think they didn't get the opportunity to do that now.

'I didn't know that, no.'

'Oh, well, it caused quite the uproar. The other homes in the village had no spaces, so most of the folk were shipped off elsewhere. Morton, Northleach. Some even ended up as far away as Cirencester. Was a terrible mess for lots of people. So, I know everything you're going to say about selling Agnes' shop to these people. I've already said it all to myself, but what can I do? I'll have to sell up at some point. I can't still be working there in my nineties. My nephew's just got married and he and his new wife could do with a bit of money to help set themselves up. Besides...' She paused.

'What? You can tell me.'

With a slow nod, Maud's eyes met with Holly's.

'When I finally made up my mind this evening, when I decided I was going to let it go, it honestly felt like the first right decision since she's been gone. Really, I need to let it go. When I realised I wouldn't have to worry about it any more, I felt... I felt... relieved. Happier than I've been since I lost her, in fact.'

Holly could see clearly in the old woman's eyes that it was the truth. She needed to do this. She had to let go of Agnes' dream while she still had time to live her own life. But still, Bourton needed Just One More. It was an institution in the village. It couldn't just go to developers to be gutted.

'I'll take it,' she said.

'What?'

'Sell the shop to me.'

Even as she was speaking, she could hardly believe the words coming out of her mouth, yet at the same time she knew she absolutely meant it.

Despite her enthusiasm her former employer didn't look convinced.

4

Maud frowned, creating an exceptionally large ridge between her brows, which stayed in place for a full five seconds before she burst into laughter.

'Oh Holly, you can't be serious. You don't want to take on the shop.'

'Yes, yes I do. It's exactly what I do want. You know how much I love that place.'

'You're young. You're a city girl now, with a steady job. Trust me, you do not want it.'

It should have been disheartening how Maud's face remained crumpled in amusement, but Holly could feel a new energy pumping through her.

'This is perfect, absolutely perfect. I've got money sitting in my account for a deposit on a house I will never buy. And I hate my job, I really do, and I think it's the first time I've actually said the words out loud. I'm fed up with staring at computer screens and listening to people whine all day. It is a steady job with good pay, but that's the only reason I stayed so long. I want to do something that makes people happy.'

Despite her enthusiasm, her former employer didn't look convinced.

'It's so much work and we haven't had a good year in, well...' She let out her breath in a puff of air. 'It's been a long time. Trade is not like it used to be. I'm not sure you understand what you'd be getting yourself into.'

Holly grinned. In fact, she was grinning so much, her cheeks were starting to ache.

'Yes, I do. I know exactly what I'd be getting myself into. You don't want the place to go to property developers any more than I do. This is the answer to everything.'

Maud had stopped laughing now and although the furrow had returned to her forehead, it wasn't quite so deeply etched as before.

'It's more work than people think, running a shop.'

'I know that. I was there, remember?'

'And there were two of us running it back then, three when you were around. Agnes took on the lion's share of the tasks, too, as you know.'

'You'll still be here,' Holly said.

Maud waved the comment away. 'No. I told you. I'm done with the place. Besides, I've promised Agnes's sister, Eleanor, I'd spend some time with her up in Scotland. They've been on at me about moving up there since she died. I rang her just before I saw you. There's no way she'd forgive me if I didn't go now.' She stopped, a new look clouding her face, a blend of sadness and disappointment. 'I need to be honest with you, Holly. I didn't do so well with Agnes gone. It's not that I stopped caring... It's just been hard. Too many memories, everywhere I look. To be honest, this deal with the developers, it feels like the simplest thing to do to make it all go away.'

A new silence fell between them. Holly reached out her hands across the table and rested them on one of Maud's. 'Look, however bad it is, I know I can make it work. I know I can. Honestly, how difficult could it be?'

Still, Maud didn't look convinced. 'I don't mean to sound patronising but what if you don't like it? If you don't like all the pressure of running it?'

'I will.'

A slight smacking sound came from the old woman's lips. 'How about this then. I've got a little bit of savings put away. Money from Agnes. I don't need to sell the shop immediately. What if you start running the place now, while you're waiting for the mortgage to come through? It would be all yours. I'd be backing away entirely. But if you change your mind before you sign on the dotted line, then there'll be no recriminations. You just let me know, and I'll ring those developers. How does that sound?'

How did it sound? It sounded like Maud was worried about what Holly was proposing and whether she actually knew what she was taking on. But, for once in her life, Holly wasn't worried at all. She was very, very excited.

'That sounds perfect,' she replied.

* * *

Despite having lived in Bourton for the first eighteen years of her life, Holly had never stayed in any of the hotels or B&Bs there, including The Seven Hounds. While the decor appeared to be out of the nineteen seventies, the quality of the mattress and the softness of the pillow were spot on and, had her alarm not blasted shrilly into the morning air, she could well have slept on until midday. Fortunately, she didn't as there were plenty of jobs to get on with.

Starting with an email to work.

Could she really do it? Could she hand in her notice just like that? Working data entry probably wasn't anyone's dream job, but it had given her a solid income for the best part of six years. Could she really just give it up? After ten minutes composing a suitable resignation letter, she deleted it and sent instead:

I'm ill. Sorry.

Calling in sick wasn't something she did, even when she actually wasn't well. She was the person who turned up with a large box of tissues, wearing extra jumpers and kept typing away at her computer come what may. The one who kept a stash of not only ibuprofen, but paracetamol, Imodium and antihistamines in her top drawer, just in case. As such, she was left with a fair amount of guilt over the phoney email.

After this, she composed another to the mortgage broker that she and Dan were going to use when they found their potential forever-home. In it, she explained her change in circumstances, her new source of independent income and asked if he would be able to help her secure a commercial mortgage.

With these rather formal steps towards her new life out of the way, it was time to deal with the messages from Dan.

First came the texts:

Hol, please. Let me explain. It was a mistake, that's all.

We need to talk about this.

You know I love you. I've just been going through a really difficult time.

This isn't fair now, you can't just ignore me.

It was a onetime thing.

Next came the voice messages:

'Can you at least call me, so I know where you are?'

'Fine. Be like this. This is so you.'

'You know what? Screw you! If this is how you want to behave, I'm done.'

Holly's jaw dropped.

'How I *want to behave*,' she said out loud, her finger hovering momentarily over the reply button, before hurling the phone onto the bed. She had bigger fish to fry. Like a sweet shop to buy.

A wide smile spread involuntarily across her face. It was ridiculous, she thought, crossing from her bed and opening up her bag to find something to wear. The serendipity of it. Just as she thought that everything had gone wrong, this happened. She recalled the sappy poster in the cubical of the girl next to her at work. *Sometimes things aren't falling apart at all. They are falling into place.* It accompanied a picture of a kitten falling off a shelf into a fancy cat bed. She'd ridiculed things like that before, but this time it really felt it could be true. Although clothes were an issue.

Given that buying a new business and completely starting her life over hadn't been on the agenda when Holly had stuffed her holdall and rushed out of the house, her selection of garments was, to put it kindly, somewhat eclectic. She had managed to pack several pairs of knickers, one clean bra and one worn one, two pairs of gym socks and one pair of black jeans. That was where the practicalities had ended. In her frenzied state, she had pulled other items randomly off their hangers. Things which included: her favourite, sparkly, halter-neck dress that hadn't fitted properly in the best part of three years; two blouses: one sheer and one with such a hideous print she couldn't even fathom why she'd bought it in the first place; one pair of linen trousers that she really liked but never could be bothered to iron, so didn't wear very often; and three summer dresses. All in all, it was not a great selection to keep her going.

Deciding to go with the jeans, she ran the shower on hot and hung her top from the previous day over the rail for a while in the hope of eliminating the stale smell. She would buy some more clothes, she thought, as she got under the shower and washed the aroma of the country pub from her skin. She'd spent enough years scrimping and saving and making things last. She was going to be a business owner now. An entrepreneur. She would need to at least try and look the part.

Once dried and dressed, she made the most of the pub's limited, complimentary breakfast before walking into the village to meet Maud. They had agreed that they would spend the day in the shop together so they could go over more details of the sale. She couldn't wait.

When she reached the High Street, the morning sun was a pale yellow, glinting off the river where, next to one of the bridges, a group of ducks was sleeping, their heads tucked under their wings. March. In a couple of months all the ducklings would be hatched and start waddling their way across the green. Morning was always the best time of day in Bourton, she remembered, when the village felt like a secret waiting to be discovered. As she continued down the road, a man in *short* shorts jogged past her and she felt an involuntary shudder. Joggers. You couldn't escape them, even in the countryside. Still, it was hardly a thing to put her off the place.

'Still as punctual as ever,' Maud said, as they both arrived at the same time.

'Well I do remember you saying you'd dock me the full hour if I ever turned up late,' Holly replied.

'I did no such thing. But if I did, it was only to make sure you'd grow up to be an excellent employee.' Her smile dropped by a fraction. 'So, have you changed your mind in the sober light of day?' she asked. 'Ready to head back to that fancy job in London?'

Holly tilted her head to the side a fraction, before grinning madly.

'No way. And, trust me, staring at a computer screen all day is not a fancy job.'

'All right then. Well, I rang the accountant first thing and asked him to send over the books.'

'Fantastic. I've contacted my mortgage broker and I don't think it'll take long to get an answer from the bank. Oh my God, this is really going to happen!'

There was no way of denying the tingle of anticipation that was buzzing through her as she stood waiting for Maud to open up. She could almost smell it already. The peppermint. The aniseed. The door didn't look in the best state, though. She hadn't spotted it the night before, but the paintwork was flaking off and the putty was crumbling away from the glass panes. After a moment, she finally heard the click she'd been waiting for.

'It's gotten stiff,' Maud said, as the familiar little bell jingled above their heads. 'Keeps on jamming and it gets worse every winter. I've had a mind to get it changed for a year or so now, but you know how it is; there are always other jobs to do. Besides, it's not the end of the world if you door sticks now and again, is it?'

'I'm sure it won't be that big an expense,' Holly said, inspecting the ancient lock. It was nice that it was traditional and engraved, but quaintness might need to be sacrificed for security and convenience.

She started a mental list of jobs that she needed to do once ownership was hers. Yet the moment she stepped past the jingling bell and into the shop itself, everything was forgotten. She was exactly where she was meant to be.

5

Inside was exactly as Holly remembered. The counter on the left was home to the large till – dated but not antique –a small cabinet filled with handmade chocolates to the left of that. The large, weighing scales were next to the till; these were genuinely antique and definitely the centrepiece of the counter. She brushed her fingers against the large, brass dish and watched as the needle danced along the measuring scale. A small, free-standing shelf unit on the far side of the room contained some of the pricier products – boxes of artisan fudge and chocolate pralines – while bars of Kendal mint cake sat next to chocolate hedgehogs and slabs of toffee. Behind the counter, though, was the pièce de résistance. The floor-to-ceiling shelves were jam-packed with glass jars, filled with every imaginable treat. Glistening spheres and paper-wrapped delicacies gleamed from within. Yellows, reds, blues, greens: every colour of the spectrum shone there. Her eyes immediately sought out her favourites: pear drops, strawberry bonbons, chocolate-coated almonds. Not to mention the crystallised ginger and sherbet lemons.

'I'm afraid I've not had a dust yet this week,' Maud said,

bringing Holly back from her trance. If she'd had her way, she would have gazed at every single jar individually, but there would plenty of time for that. Reminded of the task at hand, she considered some of the practicalities that needed to be addressed.

'What time do you normally open up now?' she asked, remembering all too clearly the early starts back in her teenage days. Early for a teenager, that was. Nowadays, nine o'clock seemed pretty lenient.

'To be honest, my joints don't like the early mornings all that much,' Maud replied. 'Depends on the weather, usually. I try to get here by ten, but trade's not what it used to be. Not with the supermarket staying open twenty-four-seven.'

Holly nodded slowly. That was a big change. In peak season, they would have had the doors open at eight. Maybe she would try starting early for a few weeks and see how it went. Then again, Maud knew the business far better than she did.

'Do you mind if I have a look upstairs?' Holly asked, edging further inwards. 'You know, just to see.'

'Course not. I'll come with you. Remember, you need to mind your head,' she said, as they passed under the low-hanging beam in the centre of the ceiling.

In the old days, she'd been too short for it to bother her, but she'd seen plenty of taller people come a cropper. She instinctively ducked as she followed Maud to the back of the shop and up the narrow staircase, to what she suspected was the smallest storeroom in the country.

'Oh, I forgot how much I loved it up here,' she sighed.

While in square footage it was exactly the same size as the shop downstairs, the sloping ceiling made it feel much smaller. A little sink, mini-fridge and kettle were positioned next to the staircase, just below the window which hadn't opened when Holly was last there, and she very much suspected still didn't. Boxes, most likely filled with fudge and rock, were stacked against the wall, and every spare corner was filled with bags of sweets.

'Mind the bucket,' Maud said, as Holly went to inspect the shelves.

'Bucket?' She glanced down at the small plastic container only inches from her feet, that was currently filled with a little over a centimetre of water. 'Where's that coming from?' she asked, scouring the ceiling above her and not seeing any signs of a leak.

'No idea,' Maud replied. 'It's been dripping like that since Agnes was here. Never fills up more than that. I think she got someone in to look at it once. Didn't seem to make any difference but it hasn't got any worse. Just one of those things: old buildings, you know.'

'I'm sure I can get it seen to.'

The now familiar frown lines reappeared on Maud's forehead.

'Holly love, I don't want to sound like I'm patronising you, really I don't, but are you sure you're thinking straight about this? Buying a business is not something you should do without thinking it through properly. I know you're obviously upset about this thing with Dan...'

'Nope.' Holly lifted her hand, bringing Maud to a stop. 'It's not about him. It's about me. For once, it's about me. He's not even the slightest factor in this.'

The frown didn't budge. 'It's not too late. That's all I'm saying. If you want to change your mind.'

'No. This place is not going to developers. I couldn't bear it. Not when I can stop it from happening. No, I'm not backing out of this now.' Holly lifted her hand again and stroked the wooden beams. 'This was fate.'

Pulling her hand away, she glanced down at one of the whole-sale bags of wine gums then, squinting, looked again a little closer before picking up the bag. These were one of the bulk buys they got from the suppliers before transferring them into the glass jars downstairs.

'Have you noticed this?' she asked, titling the bag towards Maud. 'They need to be used by the end of the month.'

'Do they?' Maud leaned in, adjusting her glasses as she read the numbers on the bottom. 'So they do.'

'We should get them down on the shop floor, straight away,' Holly said, placing them to the side so she could inspect what was beneath. 'These are the same,' she said, picking up a bag of aniseed jellies. 'And these toffee eclairs, too.' Never in all her time working there had she seen an item of stock get that close to its sell-buy date, let alone three. A sinking feeling told her those were unlikely to be the only ones.

'Like I said, business has been slow. Things just aren't moving as they use to.'

'It's fine.' Holly smiled, reassuringly. 'I'm sure if we put them on special offer, they'll be gone by the end of the week.'

She was still thinking about just how much she might to have to try and salvage amongst the stock when a jingle of the bell cut through from downstairs.

With a twinkle in her eye that Holly hadn't seen all day, Maud's lips pressed together in a smile.

'Think you can still remember how to serve?' she asked.

* * *

The slow start was exactly what Holly needed to get back into the rhythm of things. Stretching up to the shelves, she pulled down one jar of sweets and then another, before taking them over to the scales. Those scales. While she didn't know for certain, she wouldn't have been surprised if they'd been there even longer than Maud and Agnes. At least they were still polished and gleaming.

The delicate needle wavered back and forth before finally settling on the weight. Sometimes adding a few sweets, sometimes taking one or two out, she hadn't completely lost the knack, but she definitely wasn't as sharp as she used to be.

At lunch time, she headed over to the bakery to grab them both a roll. In the old days, they'd had to take it in turns to head up to the storeroom to eat, but given that the customers were fairly sporadic, they ate downstairs together, reminiscing over the past. So many memories, so many good times. Like the year the snow fell so deep, they had to dig out the front of the shop just to get inside. Or the time a mother duck and half a dozen ducklings waddled straight in through the front door, hopped up onto the bottom step of the staircase and fell fast asleep for over an hour. Every time they finished one story, a new one sprang to mind, just as funny, just as heartwarming.

They celebrated the end of the day with fish and chips and a sugar mouse each for dessert, which they sat and ate on one of the benches by the river. They could have spent a couple of hours, after shutting up shop, more productively, restocking the jars and making a list for the suppliers. But while Holly wanted to do as much as she could ASAP, she could sense that what Maud needed was a little distraction.

'I can't believe this is actually happening,' Holly said, as she reached the sugar-coated string tail of her sweet. 'Honestly, I can't. It doesn't seem real.'

'No it doesn't, does it?'

'Just One More.'

Unable to suppress the grin on her face, she watched a group of children squirt each other with water pistols. The March air had more than a nip to it and how they weren't shivering was beyond her. Still half watching, she thought back to her own childhood, when she and her parents would often do the same thig after a long bike ride, although not using water guns. They'd just scoop up handfuls of water and end up soaking themselves far more than each other.

'Oh bugger,' she said, as another thought crossed her mind.

'What is it?' Maud asked.

'I still have a job. I have to hand in my notice.'

* * *

For most of the walk back to the pub, Holly simply enjoyed the quiet, but as she approached The Seven Hounds, she pulled out her phone. No more messages from Dan today – that was something at least – but there were a couple from work colleagues, checking that she was okay. Guilt gnawed at her. There were also three missed calls from her mother. She would have to ring her soon, too. Wendy always got suspicious when she didn't contact her for a few days, even when there was nothing to be suspicious about.

Back in her little room, she checked the rest of her emails and found one from the broker. He had forwarded her message to one of his colleagues who dealt with commercial mortgages. This Jenny Smythe-Doyle was clearly a model of efficiency, having already replied, outlining all the information she would require to submit an application. Most of it seemed straight forward enough: type of business, address, valuation of the property, deposit amount and, of course, a copy of the accounts, which Maud's accountant had also just sent to her. It was difficult to make out all the numbers clearly on the small screen of her phone, but everything seemed to be in order, although the shop clearly wasn't doing as well as it used to. Despite this, she remained confident that she would be able to turn things around. So, with confidence and enthusiasm brimming, she forwarded all the relevant information to Ms Smythe-Doyle.

She then composed a second email. This one to her boss. She

explained as rationally as she could her abrupt decision to leave and hoped he would accept her resignation with immediate effect, using her accrued holiday – which was not insignificant given how frugal she and Dan had been with trips away – to cover her notice period. It all felt very final and it was with more than a little trepidation that she finally hit the send button.

Given that she had already eaten a mountain of fish and chips, she didn't need anything else but it was only just gone seven and it felt far too early to spend the rest of the evening in her pokey little room. She had just ordered herself a glass of Prosecco at the bar, when she heard a familiar voice.

'Holly *Verity* Berry, fancy seeing you here.'

There was only one person who ever said her name like that, emphasising her middle name. The hair on the back of her arms rose and a long shiver spider-walked down her spine as she clenched her fists by her side, pushed her cheeks up into a smile and turned around.

'Mum,' she said. 'What a lovely surprise. What are you doing here?'

6

Holly wondered if, even at twenty-nine years old, she would ever reach a point when she didn't feel the need to seek her mother's approval. It was silly. She paid her own bills, lived by her own schedule and was, to all intents and purposes, a fully functioning adult. And it wasn't as if her mother judged her for anything. Not really. Any interfering or meddling only ever came from a place of concern. Yet she still held a deep-rooted worry about letting her down, one that intensified as she saw her sitting there, in the wing-back chair by the window.

'What do you think I'm doing here, Holly Bear? I'm here to see you. Honestly, you travel all this way and you're staying in a pub? What's going on?'

'I'm sorry,' she replied, walking around the table to squeeze her mother in a tight hug. 'I promise, coming to see you and Dad was at the top of my to-do list. I just got a bit side-tracked, that's all.'

Her mother stroked down her hair, and brushed invisible lint from her top, like she was still five years old.

'Dan rang me,' she said, a look of pity creeping onto her face.

'He wanted to know where you were. Thought you might have headed to us. Said you'd had a bit of a disagreement.'

'Is that what he said?'

'He did.'

Her stomach knotted. It was one thing for him to mess her around, but getting her parents involved was just downright low.

'What else did he say?' she asked, despite her better judgement, though she dreaded to hear the answer.

'Well, he said you'd had a misunderstanding, and I asked exactly what the nature of that was, given that my daughter is an extremely intelligent young lady and that, in my opinion, most of the time when someone says *there's been a misunderstanding* it's because they've screwed something up and don't want to admit it.'

Holly laughed. 'What did he say to that?'

'Oh, I don't know. Something whiney. Then he asked me to contact him if I heard from you. Honestly.' She paused, the pity returning to her eyes. 'Do I want to know what he did?'

'Just the normal.' As Holly felt the tears building, she realised why she hadn't gone to her parents straight away. It had been one thing talking to Maud but this, talking to her mum, made it real and hurt in ways she really didn't think she could deal with. She felt her breath quicken. She didn't want to start blubbering here. Not in a public place, in the village where she had just bought a business. The shop. That single thought switched on a light inside her, pushing all memories of Dan to the back of her mind. The possibility of tears immediately disappeared and, instead, she found herself grinning.

'I bought the sweet shop,' she blurted out.

'Sorry?' Her mum's eyes widened.

'I bought it. I bought Just One More. Maud was going to sell it to developers. She couldn't run it any more. I just happened to bump into her. And I had all my deposit money from the house that Dan and I... you know. So I did it. I bought it. Well, I'm buying it. I obviously have to sort out some stuff and wait for the mortgage to come through, but other than that, it's mine. The shop is mine.'

'You are buying the sweet shop?' Her mother repeated. The look of pity now replaced by one of pure disbelief.

She nodded, her lips pinched together as she waited for her mother's further reaction. Wendy was not normally easily shocked, but the stunned expression on her face was showing no sign of fading.

'Well, say something,' Holly said, after seconds had passed and her mother still hadn't uttered another word.

'Good for you.'

'You mean that?'

'I think you've certainly got an adventure ahead of you,' she replied. 'But is this what you really want?'

The question didn't take any time to answer.

'It is. Honestly, I know it sounds crazy, but once I'd decided, it made sense – me coming back to Bourton like this – it all makes perfect sense.'

'Well then, this is going to be fun,' Wendy said with a smile. 'Now, go and get me a glass of that fizzy wine so we can celebrate.'

They talked like they hadn't spoken in months. Well, they hadn't in person. Sure, they'd video called, sometimes several times a week, but that wasn't the same as having her mum right there next to her, giggling and laughing as they gossiped about the future.

'So you are buying the whole thing? Not just the lease?' Wendy asked. 'The building and everything?'

'Every last brick and lollipop. I still don't quite believe it. I just hope I can do her and Agnes proud, you know.'

'Oh you will, my love, don't you worry about that. You've already done that, just by being you.'

They chatted on a little longer, until her mother noticed the time.

'Are you sure you don't want to stay with us while you sort the shop out? There's plenty of room, and it might be nice for you to have some company. We can help too, if you need us. I've always been good with numbers, you know that.'

'Thank you, Mum. I have another night already booked here, but I'll bring my stuff over tomorrow, if you are sure.'

'Of course I'm sure. It's your home too, you know. Your dad will be made up.'

'Well it'll just be until I sort out somewhere of my own.'

'As long as you need.'

It was only as Holly was walking her mother to the door, about to offer her a farewell squeeze, that a thought crossed her mind.

'How did you even know I was here?' she asked.

Wendy shook her head, before tapping the side of her nose, a gleam in her eyes. 'You're back in the Cotswolds now, darling. No secrets here.'

7

___

The following morning, when Holly arrived at the shop, she was surprised to find it closed. True, she was a little earlier than they had arranged to meet, but time went on and soon it was half past nine, thirty minutes after they had agreed and the only visitor to turn up had been the scruffy cat from two nights ago.

'What do you think?' she said, crouching down and rubbing the top of his head. 'Do you suppose she's just overslept? I wouldn't blame her. I could do with a bit more sleep too.' As Holly continued to stroke the cat, she pondered the situation. The last thing she wanted to do was go round to Maud's cottage and start pestering her about being late. But, then again, she thought, what if something had happened? What if she'd had a fall, with no way of contacting anyone? Besides, Maud never used to mind when people just showed up on her doorstep. If anything, she and Agnes liked it that way. After five minutes more loitering, she started the walk up Station Road to Maud and Agnes' cottage.

Set a little way off the main road, it was one of only a few left in the village that still boasted a thatched roof. Out front was a small courtyard garden with paved slabs, a dry-stone wall and a small gate. Back when Holly used to live in the village, large troughs filled with lavender and fresh herbs, mint and lemon balm had sat beneath the windows, filling the area with colour and life, not to mention scent. Now, the only plant life she could see was ivy, which had overgrown one of the windows almost entirely.

The gate wobbled on its hinges as she pushed it open and then rapped on the door.

'Just coming!' Maud's voice called from inside. A moment later, she appeared. 'Holly, my dear, I'm so glad you called round; I was just going to phone you. Come in. Come in.'

'Is everything okay?' She followed her in, unable to suppress the hint of nervousness running through her. At least Maud didn't look injured or ill. That was something. But as she stepped from the hallway into the kitchen, she noticed the suitcases, neatly stacked, as if ready to go. 'Are you off somewhere?'

'I've just put the kettle on,' Maud said. 'Will you have a cup?'

She nodded. A sense of numbness was creeping in. She had changed her mind, was the thought running through her head. Maud had changed her mind and decided she wanted to keep the shop. Shit, she'd handed in her notice. Maybe it wouldn't be too late, she thought, as her heart rate started to rise. She could explain; after all, they couldn't have filled her position already. It had only been a day.

'There's no need to look so worried.' Maud dropped teabags into a floral pot and poured on the water. 'Everything is fine with the shop. It's just that I've spoken to Eleanor – you know, Agnes' sister – and I'm going to get the train up to Scotland this afternoon.'

'Today?' She struggled to hide her surprise. 'But there is so much to sort out.'

'Nonsense, you know what to do. And what you don't know, you'll figure out. Besides, I'll only be on the other end of the phone, if you need me.' She sighed, before heading to the fridge for the milk. She took her time pouring it into the mugs before bringing Holly's across to the table and placing it down in front of her. 'I'll be honest with you. Now the decision has been made, I need to get away. You'll be keen to get in and get started too and I'm too tired and emotional to be part of that.' She took Holly's hand. 'I know we still need to finalise the sale, but the shop is yours now; paperwork is just paperwork. It's time for me to move over.'

Holly let out her breath in a long stream. Wow. That was it then. The nerves she'd been feeling earlier returned, along with a bucket load of sadness. She had thought she'd get a little more time with Maud. Time to catch up and make up for all those years she hadn't been there for her. But this was obviously want Maud needed, how she wanted to handle it.

'Of course, I understand.' She picked up her tea and blew the steam from the top. 'You don't need to worry about me. Or the shop. We are going to be just fine.'

A smile of relief rose on the old lady's face, lifting a fraction of the weight Holly had begun to feel.

'You should know I've put the cottage on the market, too,' she said. 'I spoke to the estate agent a few days ago. If I'm honest, I speak to him a lot. He probably thinks I'm barking. I must have been in there every six months since Agnes went, saying I want to sell up and leave but never have, obviously. I know the housing market's not what it was, but there aren't many places like this about any more so, hopefully, I'll get a good price.' She gazed out of the kitchen window, before turning back to Holly. 'Anyway, here are the keys to the shop,' she said, digging into her pocket. 'You might as well take them and make a start. The tourists will be upon you sooner than you think.'

'You'll come back and visit? Make sure I'm doing you both proud?'

'Try keeping me away. Besides, I'll have to return at some point to choose what I'm taking with me and dispose of the rest.'

'Well, I should leave you to your packing. I need to go and do some myself. I'm giving up my luxury suite at The Hounds and staying with Mum and Dad until I find a place to live, too. It's only ten miles away but...' She couldn't suppress the shudder that rippled through her. Going back at twenty-nine was hardly a blistering start to her new, independent life.

'Why don't you stay here until I sell the place?'

'Sorry?' she replied, still imagining the horror of having to tell people she'd moved back home.

'I said, why don't you say here?' She plucked another key from out of her pocket and pushed it into Holly's palm. 'I don't know how long it will be for, of course. Hopefully, the place will sell quick enough, but it should give you a few weeks or more to get yourself sorted. Probably months with today's market.'

'What? Don't be silly.'

'It's not silly. It makes perfect sense.'

Holly stared at the key in her hand. First the shop, now this. It was like she was stepping into Maud's life.

'Are you sure?'

'Of course I am. I'll straighten things up this morning so it'll be ready for you this evening. And I'll let the estate agent know that you're here, just in case he needs to show people around. It'll be perfect. Better having you here than leaving the place empty when people want to come and view it.'

'Are you sure?'

'I insist. You'd been doing me a favour. Another one.'

Holly found her eyes drifting down to her feet. What were you supposed to say to someone at this point, she wondered? At the moment when a door closes so firmly on the past of someone's life that you can almost hear it slamming?

'Do you want a lift to station later?' she finally managed, finding a way to break the silence. 'It wouldn't be any problem.'

'It's fine. There's a nice young lad over the road. I pay him a little to drive me about when I need it. You go back to the pub and get yourself sorted. It's going to get busy for you now.'

And then, because there was nothing more left for the pair to discuss, they hugged, said their goodbyes and parted company.

* * *

Walking down the narrow path that ran behind the back of the churchyard, it felt to Holly as if she was stuck in some bizarre, twilight world. As if she had somehow slipped out of her old life and was in a new, parallel one, in which she had never left Bourton. She now passed the primary school she had gone to, only to notice all the buildings had changed. The grey porta cabins in which she had received most of her primary education had been replaced with a sleek, wooden-framed building that looked more like an art gallery than an educational establishment. The secondary school, just a short way further along, had been rebuilt too, and even had a sports centre and swimming pool. She felt a pang of sadness at the absence of the rooms where she had spent so much of her childhood. Try as she might, she found it impossible to recall all the times she had come back to the village since moving away to university. There was Maud and Agnes' official wedding, and there was the funeral, of course. There must have been other occasions, too, but she was struggling to remember them. After her parents moved away from the village – not far away, but far enough – she'd rarely made the time to visit Bourton or the shop. Most of her childhood friends had also moved on, so there was very little reason to return. But now she was here and Just One More was going to get its first new owner in nearly forty years.

8

Her mother tried hard to hide her disappointment when Holly told her about Maud's offer of the cottage, and as usual Holly ended up feeling guilty. In a small attempt to appease her, she had gone to stay the night at her parents' in Northleach.

Her dad had shaken off his tiredness the moment he saw her and wrapped her in bear hug.

'I'm sorry about Dan, my love,' he said, when they finally broke apart. 'Your mother always did think he was a bit beige.'

'She's right. He was. And I'm not going to dwell on it,' she assured him. 'I've got far too many exciting things about to happen.'

'So I've heard.'

A rare and lovely family evening followed as they drank cocoa, ate biscuits and reminisced over family escapades of years gone by. Afterwards, while her parents settled down in front of the telly, she sat with her phone, going over her bank statements and cancelling direct debits for anything to do with her old house. Those were Dan's problem to figure out and she'd told him as much in a text. Right now, she had to make sure her own finances were in shape.

There was enough money in her current account to tide her

over, especially without any rent to pay, meaning she wouldn't have to touch her deposit money, tucked away in her savings account. She had also heard from her boss, who was *dreadfully* upset to lose her but wished her well for her future endeavours. She could still expect almost a full month's wages at the end of March.

As she switched off the bedside lamp, her body was alive with nervous excitement. Tomorrow morning was going to be the start of a whole new chapter in her life, although it was one that probably needed to begin with her washing some clothes.

* * *

Once again, the wooden gate wobbled on its hinges as Holly pushed it open and headed up the path to the little cottage. A *For Sale* sign had already appeared in the garden, although when on earth the estate agent had sorted it she had no idea. Hopefully, it wouldn't sell too soon. A couple of rent-free months would be a godsend.

With her duffle bag in one hand, and a plastic bag of bits and pieces from the supermarket in the other, she unlocked the door and stepped inside. The curtains weren't quite closed and motes of dust danced in the morning sun that bled through the gap. She dropped her bags and opened them up fully. A deep sadness struck home. Back in her teens, she had spent a significant amount of time there. After particularly busy days at the shop, the three of them would head back and sit out in the front garden, drinking exceptionally diluted Pimm's and laughing at the ridiculous things that customers had said to them that day. After both her GCSE and A Level results, Maud and Agnes had insisted on throwing celebratory, afternoon, tea parties, accompanied by Champagne and more chocolate than any one person should consume in a year. It had been a house filled with laughter, with jokes and kindness and the fondest of memories. Now there was just cobwebs and neglect. As she moved from the hallway and into the living room, she tried to ignore the mounting guilt.

'Oh Maud,' she said out loud. 'I'm so sorry.'

Like its owner, the house was now a shadow of its former self. Gone were the silver frames that used to line the mantelpiece and hang on walls. Gone were the brightly coloured rugs that Agnes had collected on her travels through India in the sixties. The bizarre artwork that her mother had always so admired was nowhere to be seen. The scented candles and thin, coloured, incense sticks that weaved their aromatic smoke into thin tendrils in the air had gone. The life. The laughter. All gone. No wonder Maud had looked so frail. She had packed up her life years ago. Only now did Holly realise how lonely the last few years without Agnes must have been for her. Would life be that difficult without Dan, she wondered? She dismissed the thought almost immediately. Of course it wouldn't. She and Dan had never shared what Maud and Agnes had, that much was certain.

Brushing aside her melancholy, she walked through to the kitchen, switched on the kettle and hunted out a mug. Only when she turned around did she notice the small pile of folded fabric on the kitchen table. A smile flickered on her lips.

It might be fifteen years ago, but she could still recall her first day as an official employee at Just One More as if it were yesterday.

* * *

She'd been told to be there Saturday morning by eight-thirty to help open up at nine, but having been so excited at the prospect of earning money and beginning her very own Willy-Wonka adventure, she was sat waiting by the river at just gone eight. She'd picked a bench on the other side of the road, opposite the shop, next to two sleeping mallards, and was keeping an eye out, not knowing which direction the women would arrive from. As it happened, they crept straight up behind her.

'A least we know punctuality won't be a problem,' Agnes had said, causing Holly to nearly jump out of her skin. 'Maybe we'll get a few lie-ins, if we can train you up well enough. Now, we just need to feed the ducks and we'll get inside.'

From out of a wicker basket, she'd pulled a large brown paper bag, which she opened up and offered to Holly. Sure enough, it was filled with stale bread.

'We pick it up from the bakery on the way here. We always like to start the morning like this, feeding the ducks. Puts you in a good mood. Until they start pecking each other, that is, but we try to ignore that.'

Still not exactly sure what was going on, she had pulled out a piece of dry bread, watching as the two women followed suit, before tearing off small pieces and throwing them into the river. The two, previously sleeping mallards were now wide awake and waiting expectantly. News spread fast, and almost immediately they were joined by nearly a dozen more. Despite the numbers, it was all very calm, no flapping or squawking, just the occasionally dash to get there first. When all the bread was gone, Agnes had tipped out the remaining crumbs into the water, at which point the birds had begun a frenzied flapping fest to get to the last of the food.

'Right,' she'd said, turning to face Holly, as she'd folded the paper bag and put it in her basket. 'Now that's done, we should get on with the day.'

Never in all her life could she remember feeling more nervous as she hurried behind them to the shop. Sweat was building on her palms when the bell above them jingled as Agnes opened the door. Maud was asking her questions, she couldn't recall what. All she could think about was being behind that counter and weighing out sweets on those enormous, metal scales.

'So, first day at work,' Agnes had said when they were all inside. She'd slipped the key back into the lock, turned it and made sure that the sign was still set to *Closed*. 'You must be excited. I'm glad to see you're in comfortable shoes. You'll be glad of those. You'll be on your feet almost all day. We've got a delivery coming at ten and the fudge and nougat boxes will need carrying upstairs.'

Nou-gar? Holly had thought to herself. She'd guessed she'd work out what that was soon enough.

'Your lunch break will be half an hour, the same as ours, and don't worry, one of us will always be here with you, but I'm afraid you'll have to be flexible with when you can take it. We can't very well let you go during the lunch rush. We just have to see how busy it is.'

'Don't worry though, we won't let you starve,' Maud had added from the other side of the shop, where she was straightening bows on fancy-looking boxes of chocolates. 'You can always help yourself to a stick of rock, if you need to.'

'Oh, I brought sandwiches,' Holly had said. 'I'll be fine.'

A look that Holly had read as either disgust or confusion flashed crossed her new employers' faces and had caused her pulse to spike.

'Sandwiches? Don't be silly. We won't have you bringing your own lunch. We need to support the other businesses. We have a rota. Today's Saturday, so that means... What does it mean, Maud? What do we eat on Saturdays?'

'Pasties and Pies,' Maud had replied, having now moved across to straighten the jars. 'And don't ever eat the rock. It's horrible stuff. It'll rot your teeth.'

'Pasties and Pies. That's right. From the bakery by the museum. Doesn't matter what time of year it is. We get all our food from the village. Helps us to catch up on local news on quiet days, and it doesn't hurt to have people to talk to, either.'

'Oh,' Holly had felt like she had missed a teacher's notice and had forgotten to revise for an important test. Not that this ever happened. 'I didn't bring any money to get lunch.'

'Of course you didn't. We didn't tell you to. We'll pay for that. Think of it as a perk, in addition to your salary.'

Her salary. It had been one of the first questions her friends at school had asked when she'd told them she had a job, at which point she'd realised that she didn't have a clue. Even now, as she was standing in the shop, ready to start work, she had no idea what she was going to get, other than some form of pie or pasty, by the sounds of it.

'Ah, yes.' Maud had moved away from the shelves and joined them at the counter. 'We forgot to talk about money, didn't we? So, we used to have a regular Saturday girl, who we paid three pounds an hour. That was last year, mind, but she did have experience. So we think it's only fair we stick to the same rate.'

'Plus a little bit for inflation,' Agnes had added. 'Don't forget that.'

'I hadn't,' Maud had insisted. 'Your pay will be three pounds twenty-five an hour and we'll expect eight-hour days from you. We'll start off with just Saturdays for now, while you learn the ropes then, during the holidays, it will likely be four days a week – Thursday to Sunday – and if you need a day off, we'll need at least a week's notice.'

'Unless it's an emergency, of course. We do understand emergencies.'

Four days, eight hours, Holly was trying to do the maths in her head, but the women weren't done yet. 'We won't pay you for your lunch break, as we're getting your lunch, but if things go well and you're still here at Christmas, then we'll look at moving you up to three-fifty. Obviously, we don't mind you eating the odd sweet here and there, just don't go mad, and you'll get a fifty percent discount on anything you buy. How does that all sound?'

They'd lost her at the lunch break, but she didn't care. She knew enough to realise that, for the first time in her life, she would be earning enough money to buy her own jeans and books and presents for her parents and maybe even start saving for when she was older, too.

'That all sounds fine,' she'd said, hoping they'd remind her of the details later.

'Fantastic,' Agnes had replied, and for a moment she'd found herself totally absorbed in the woman's smile. She thought of it frequently now. The way it stretched across her entire face, shrinking her eyes to almost nothing, yet at the same time making them shine, was something to behold.

'Good, now that that's sorted, I guess we'd better give you your uniform. Maud my love, if you would do the honours?'

With a smile that had matched her partner's, Maud had withdrawn a perfectly folded piece of fabric from behind the counter. Up until that moment in her life, uniform had meant only one thing to her: greyness. A grey school shirt and grey school skirt and a maroon tie that, even though it wasn't grey, she'd hated with a vengeance. This uniform, though, had been one she would be more than happy to wear.

'It's like something out of film,' she'd said, as Maud had handed it over. Holly had taken in the matching aprons the two older women were wearing. The design was simple: powder-blue cotton, slightly cinched at the waist, with a crinkled edges and the words Just One More stitched in deep green across the breast pocket. But, despite its delicate appearance, the material was thick and heavy.

'It will be your job to keep it clean,' Agnes had said, still not able to suppress the smile that Holly would learn was a permanent fixture. 'You might not believe it, but you can get quite messy in this job. And we will not be happy if you look untidy.'

'I'll make sure it's washed after every shift,' she had promised.

'Now, the shop opens at nine o'clock promptly and by five past nine we'll have customers waiting. So, let's get you started.' She'd picked up a plastic, gun-shaped item from the counter behind her. 'This is a pricing gun.'

Holly couldn't imagine how many boxes of chocolates she must have stuck labels on over the years. Thousands, probably, although she never forgot those on that first day. Nor did she forget her first attempt at using those massive, brass scales.

'When they ask for a quarter, they mean a quarter of a pound. Now we aren't allowed to use imperial measures any more, so you tell them that we weigh and charge per hundred grams and you need to make sure the pointer reaches here.' Agnes had pointed to a thick line on the scale reading. 'And if they want a half pound, you double up. We always go a little bit over then. It's important you also go slightly over. Don't try to get it dead on. Understand?'

'I think so?' she'd replied honestly.

Any time either of the two women had a spare moment, they'd shown her something new. They'd explained how some people said *nou-gar* while others said *nugget* and she wasn't to correct them, because how people pronounced things was nobody's business but their own. The most important thing, Agnes had told her was that the moment before they switched the sign on the door from *Closed* to *Open*, you always smiled.

'We're a sweet shop,' she'd said. 'No miserable faces. So if something's wrong, you don't let people see it. It's not what they want. You get over it upstairs, then wipe your face, come back down and get on with it. There are no bad days in here.'

* * *

Holly stood in Maud's dusty kitchen and held the freshly pressed apron to her chest. Her boyfriend had cheated on her and she'd quit her city job and moved to a tiny village to saddle herself with a rundown sweet shop. But she wasn't having a *bad* day. As she slipped the apron into her bag and headed off to the shop, she smiled. She was actually having the *first* day of the rest of her life.

9

Despite what Maud and said about opening the shop up later now, Holly was ready in her neatly ironed pinafore at 9 a.m. sharp, waiting for that morning rush and still trying to remember all the regulars from the old days. They were the best part of the job. The same customers would show up requesting the exact same things each time. Some of them had been coming there long before Holly had started work and she suspected had continued their visits long after she'd left. There was the woman who came in every Sunday morning to fill up her chocolate box, so that it was well-stocked for the week should she have any visitors and another who always carried a thermos flask under her arm and ordered a quarter of liquorice allsorts so that she could have an afternoon treat by the river. Then there was the man who brought his own tin he wanted filled with peppermint creams: chocolate-coated ones on the bottom, plain on the top, and was not best pleased if you ever put them in the wrong way around. Lastly, she recalled another, elderly gentleman who always wore his shirt buttoned up to the top and would buy three bags of sweets on a Friday afternoon, ready for when his grandchildren would arrive at the weekend.

Her cheeks ached with a smile as she remembered them all. Hopefully at least some of them were still around. Now she wished she'd made note of them, kept a record of all their names and favourites purchases, so that she could greet them and ask if they still remembered her and strike up a conversation about all the things they'd been doing over the last decade and a bit. But it wouldn't take long to get to know them all again, she told herself. After all, she was going to be standing behind this counter seven days a week for the foreseeable future.

At quarter past nine, the shop was still empty, and at half past she remembered how much she disliked standing in a quiet shop. She also remembered that even if there weren't any customers around, she still had many jobs on her to-do list. Like digitising the stock sheets that Maud still kept in a huge, old lever-arched file. Calling in a locksmith was also a high priority. All these jobs would have been far easier using the internet. However, given that reception in Bourton was comparable with living in a yurt in the Mongolian wilderness, she'd have to wait until she got back to the house where the signal was stronger. So, dusting, refilling the jars and rearranging the shelves it was then.

'At least I'll get fit doing this,' she said to herself, bringing down all the close-to-sell-by-date bags from the stock room, ready for her grand promotion. 'Maybe I'll be the first person to ever actually lose weight working in a sweet shop.'

The set up in the shop was almost exactly as it had been all those years ago, with three quarters of the shelf space filled with the large glass jars. They were visible from the window and from the moment you stepped inside, but now that she looked at it, she wondered if maybe things needed shuffling around a bit.

A whole shelf by the entrance was dedicated to sticks of rock, in the very same place it had always been, but in the busy, summer months, people reaching for the minty, sugary treats would end up blocking the way in for other potential customers.

On the furthest side of the shop from the door were the most expensive items: assorted white boxes dressed with red, velvet bows and filled with high-end chocolates, in sizes up to a kilogramme. These were what you bought someone when you really wanted to pull out all the stops for a special occasion or extravagant workplace gift. Although, even at fifty quid a box of pralines, they wouldn't be enough to get Dan back in her good books. That was done with.

Still, she couldn't help but feel that the most expensive items in the shop should be in a better location, somewhere more prominent. Maybe if the rock stand was at the back of the store instead, people might be tempted with all these other delicacies as they passed by them on their way to it.

She still wanted the selection of boxed fudges, with their attractive, Cotswold scenes on the front—hugely popular with the tourists—in the middle of the room, and the children's favourite sweets had to be in their line of sight. She also needed to get as much on the shelves as possible, without making them look cluttered. This was starting to feel like a giant jigsaw puzzle.

By eleven thirty, the whole floor was covered in stock. It wasn't great that she hadn't had a single customer but, then again, March wasn't exactly known to be the busiest time of the year and it had given her the opportunity to sort things out.

An hour later, everything was neatly back on the shelves, having been thoroughly dusted and sorted according to sell-by date too.

Stepping back, she surveyed her handiwork.

'Not bad, even if I say so myself.'

With a satisfied smile, she moved to the door to get an even better look, when a gaggle of voices arose outside.

'Can you believe she'd say that?'

'Seriously, she is like the biggest cow, ever.'

'Totes.'

Given the little world of her own she'd been in, it took her a moment to realise what was happening, and she wondered for a split second if she'd become invisible, or at least semi-transparent, as a wave of teenage girls pushed straight past her and into the shop. All dressed in the same: grey trousers, grey sweaters and maroon ties. Her heart leapt. At last, customers.

Like a great tide, they flooded inside the shop, spreading out and filling the space.

'What are these things?' one girl demanded, picking up the jar of cola cubes.

'Actually,' Holly tried to position herself so she could answer the question. 'They're cola cu—'

'Ain't you been in here before?' another girl said, snatching the jar of out of her friend's hand and dropping it on an entirely different shelf. 'They do all sorts of weird sweets. Old stuff, like.'

'Yeah, my nan loved it. She used to get all these odd, jelly ones. They were well gross.'

The girl in question had a jar of jazzies in her hand. The white chocolate discs, covered in hundreds and thousands were always popular among the young children and Holly was about to ask her if she wanted to put them on the counter or at least hand her the jar while she looked at other things, but the moment she moved towards her, the girl twisted away and walked to the other side of the shop, shoulder to shoulder with two of her friends.

'Look at these mice things. Do you think you can eat them?'

'This one here say's its mint cake? That sounds gross too.'

'Where are the Mars Bars? I just want a Mars Bar.'

Holly didn't know which way to turn first. A small group was standing directly in front of the till, but from what she could see, they didn't have anything they were ready to pay for and no one had asked her to weigh out any sweets at all.

'Does anyone need help?' Her voice was completely lost among the chatter. She tried a little louder. 'If anyone needs anything, just ask.' They continued to mill around, a murmuration of school children moving so quickly that she was having trouble following what each of them was looking at.

A second later and one of the girl's voices rose above the other.

'Let's get out of here. I want a can of coke. And we got to be in class soon. Let's go.'

'I wanted to get some of these.'

'Nah, they're way too expensive.'

'Yeah, there's nothing good here anyway.'

It was over in an instant. One second the shop was full, and a moment later every one of them had swept out of the door, leaving Holly standing in a stunned silence. What had just happened? What had she just witnessed? Half a dozen children and not a single sale. How was that even possible? And to make matters worse, the shop was now in a complete state. Head down, she moved to straighten up the shelf with the chocolate mice, when her eyes fell on the boxes of chocolates.

'You have to be joking.'

Had she not been rearranging the shelves for the past three hours, she wouldn't have noticed, or would at least have doubted herself. But one glance was all it took for her to realise that at least two of the largest boxes of chocolates had gone: the most expensive items in the shop. From outside, she heard a cackle of laugher.

'You little sods.'

She ran out the door and screamed down the High Street. The group of children were still well within earshot.

'Hey you! Come back! Come back here this minute!'

A couple of the girls looked back over their shoulders, their grins wide as they threw back their heads and laughed again. A second later they broke into a run. Holly flipped. There was no way they were getting away with it. No way. She may not have run since she got caught in a thunderstorm half a mile from home last June, but that wasn't stopping her now. Teeth gritted, she raced down the road, the ground speeding away beneath her feet.

In her normal frame of mind, she'd have had no problem recalling the exact layout of the village, including all the narrow pathways that tourists never found and the exact places where various roads stopped having pavements. But at that moment she was too angry to think straight about the maze of roads and footpaths. She was too angry to think straight about anything at all. Which was why, as she rushed along, she momentarily forgot that, only two shops further down, there was a rather large road, wide enough for traffic. She also forgot about the fact that it was quite a busy street and that lots of people used it to drive in and out of the village. She forgot too that it was lunchtime, meaning more cars on the road. She forgot about all of those things until, that was, she stepped out into the road and right into the path of a bicycle.

10

So focused was Holly on chasing down the school girls with her stolen chocolates that she'd left the pavement without even turning her head. Then, in her peripherals, she caught sight of it. The gleaming handlebars. The yellow safety helmet. So close, that the cyclist was almost on top of her, his eyes wide and mouth aghast, before she knew what was happening. Then everything seemed to go into slow motion, like a scene from a movie. She opened her mouth, about to scream as she prepared for impact. But, at the last moment, he yanked the bike to the side and pulled hard on the brakes. Frozen to the spot, she watched as first it began skidding and then both it and rider slid to the ground. As it went past her, the back wheel caught her outstretched foot, swiping it from under her. She just managed to maintain her balance, but there was a sudden spike of pain. She steadied herself and gingerly returned her foot to the tarmac.

'What the hell do you think you were doing?'

She'd barely had time to process what had happened before the man was on his feet, his long-sleeved shirt now torn at the elbows.

'You could have been killed. You could have got me killed. What if a car had been coming the other way? Or a small child?'

'I... I...' The shock was making coherent speech impossible. 'I'm sorry. I'm so sorry. I wasn't... I wasn't thinking.'

'That much is obvious.'

As her senses began to reassert themselves, she could see it wasn't just his shirt that was torn. All up one side of his trousers there was a rip and the light fabric was darkening with speckles of blood. Her hand went to her mouth.

'Are you hurt?'

'Hurt? Did you hear me? I said you were lucky you didn't kill someone. Children cycle down this road every day.'

'I... I...' She could feel the tears building.

'You're an absolute menace,' the man said, inspecting his tattered clothes.

'Is everything all right here?'

Holly turned to see a small crowd had gathered. Stepping forward from the group was a man in his twenties, with sandy-coloured hair and grey eyes that were currently glowering at the cyclist.

'Oh absolutely great.' The cyclist rolled his eyes, clearly unimpressed by the appearance of the man in front him. 'Just what I needed. Not that it's any of your business, Caverty, but what happened is this fool damn near got me killed. And she was bloody lucky she didn't get herself killed into the bargain.'

'Perhaps you should have been watching where you were going a little more closely. The lady is clearly upset. And it's not as if any real harm's been done.'

'Yes, God forbid we actually expect someone to know how roads work. Or take responsibility for their actions. Though something as logical as that is probably beyond your comprehension.'

'Really? I can't help feeling that you're overreacting. And, let's be honest, that wouldn't be unusual now, would it?'

Whilst Holly was undeniably confused by the turn of events, she was distracted by the man's bike, the handle bars of which were twisted the wrong way round and it appeared there was a long, fresh scratch on one side of the front fork.

'It was my fault,' she said to the grey-eyed man. 'I wasn't watching where I was going. I was trying to... trying to...' Shaking her head, she pulled herself together. Shock or not, she needed to put this right. 'It was totally my fault and I am so sorry. I will pay for the damage to your clothes and the bike. Just let me know how much it is.'

'It's not about the money,' the cyclist snapped. 'It's about safety. You're lucky I don't call the police.'

The police. At that moment, two thoughts struck simultaneously. First, she had seen the man before, standing outside the shop, accusing her of loitering. Second, the shop. She had left it wide open with the keys and her wallet and everything inside, ripe for the taking. Knowing her luck, the school kids had doubled back without her noticing and were cleaning the place out.

'Again, I am so sorry, but I have to get back,' she said, turning around. 'You can bill me. Is that okay? I'm at Just One More, up the road.'

She twisted around, ready to race back, only for her ankle to give out and send her tumbling forwards. A pair of arms swung in and caught her, just a few inches from the ground.

'I can't help but think you're in need of little assistance.'

It was quite possibly the most beautiful accent she'd ever heard, she now realised. Long round vowels and every single consonant perfectly enunciated.

'May I?'

Finding herself temporarily mute, although whether from the effect of the eyes, the accent or the pain in her ankle, she wasn't sure. She nodded and allowed herself to be hoisted back upright.

'Here, let me help too.' The cyclist dragged his bike out of the road and moved towards them, but her sandy-haired hero held out his hand and shook his head.

'Don't worry. We're just fine here. I'd hate for you to be late back to work.'

Damsel in distress was not a look she would ever choose, particularly when the rescuer looked like he had just stepped out of a Hallmark movie. But putting any weight on her ankle, without knowing yet how badly hurt it was, didn't seem like a sensible idea. Leaving the cyclist with his bent bike, she allowed herself be guided back down the High Street.

'I'm Giles, by the way,' the man said. 'Giles Caverty.'

'Holly. Holly Berry.'

His eyebrow arched.

'My parents have an interesting sense of humour.'

'Well, Holly Berry, not that I mind at all, but where exactly am I leading you to?'

'Just One More. Do you know it?'

'Ah yes, you did say. The sweet shop. Indeed, I know it very well. A special place. So much character.'

'I know, I have just taken it over.'

He stopped.

'Taken it over?'

'Yes, I just bought it. Well, I'm in the process of buying it. It's crazy, I know. Probably the only spontaneous thing I've ever done in my life.'

Still wanting to get back to the shop as quickly as possible, she went to continue walking but Giles was taking much of her weight and seemed rooted to the spot. Fortunately, he got the hint and started moving again. After a few seconds of struggling almost on tiptoes, she gave up and let him practically carry her.

'I'm not sure that this is a good omen for my first day.' She gestured to her foot.

'Oh, don't worry about that. Just bad luck that you were caught in the path of the most infuriating man in the village. Don't give him a second's thought. I know I wouldn't.'

When they reached the shop, she was grateful to find the shoplifters hadn't returned while she'd been gone. Taking hold of the edge of the counter, she extracted herself from Giles' grip.

'I'll be fine now,' she said.

'Don't be silly. You need a chair. Do you have one?'

'Up in the storeroom,' she said, and before she could tell him not to worry, he was bounding up the stairs. A few moments later he was back down again.

'I'll put it behind the counter. There, is that okay? I'm guessing you don't want to be sitting out in the middle of the shop floor.'

'That's great,' she replied, balancing by the jars of coconut ice and strawberry pips, as she prepared to try and move round towards it. She had barely lifted her foot off the ground when he was back beside her. What the hell was going on?

'Wait for me,' he said. 'Here, put your arm around me.'

'Honestly, I'm fine.'

'Let's not risk anything.'

He wrapped his arm securely around her waist and guided her to the seat. Once she was down, she let out a sigh of relief.

'I saw a fridge upstairs. Does it have a freezer compartment? Have you got any ice?'

'Umm...' Holly thought back. It was unlikely the same fridge that Agnes and Maud had over a decade ago, but the one back then did have a tray of ice in the top. 'To be honest, I'm not sure,' she admitted.

'No problem, I'll just go and check.'

For a second time, he hurried up the stairs, leaving her to wonder if she'd slipped into yet another parallel universe. This time when he returned, it was with a blue and white tea towel balled up in his hand. Without waiting for her to object, he was on his knees beside her.

'Do you mind if I roll up your trouser leg?' he asked.

'You really don't have to do that.'

'It's fine. Honestly. As long as it's okay.' He smiled, now causing the arrival of a swarm of butterflies in her belly. She would have probably responded with a smile of her own, only, at that moment, he placed the ice pack on her ankle and a lightning bolt of cold pierced straight through her, far worse than any pain she'd experienced so far from the injury.

'Jesus!'

'You okay?'

'That's cold. Really, really cold.'

'Yes, ice does tend to have that characteristic.' He grinned. 'Do you mind if I have a feel? It doesn't look swollen.'

'Are you a doctor?'

That would be right. Being saved by a handsome, chivalrous doctor, who most likely had a supermodel wife back at home.

'God, no,' he laughed. 'But I've had enough sprains in my life. Falls from horses, rugby injuries, that type of thing. Although I can get you the doctor, if you want? He's just up the road.'

She shook her head. As she looked down, she noted a pale bruise blooming right across her instep. Fortunately, the pain didn't get any worse as she tentatively rotated her foot.

'I think it'll be all right. I'll just keep the ice on it for a bit.'

'As long as you're sure?'

She nodded.

In all honesty, she was struggling to keep her thoughts strictly on her ankle. But he was just being neighbourly, that was all. That's what people were like in a village. Excluding the cyclist, of course. But those eyes. Who knew grey was such an attractive colour?

'So why were you running out into the middle of the road?' Giles asked, shifting back onto his heels while he kept the ice pack pressed firmly against her ankle. 'Don't tell me you're running away from village life already?'

'No. Just a tough first day. Shoplifters,' she clarified. 'A whole gang of them. I thought they came in for sweets, but now I think they planned the whole thing. Obviously, I didn't catch them, and I haven't had a chance to see how much they took yet, but whatever it is, it's more than I could risk losing right now.'

His eyes narrowed on her as he pinched his lips.

'Let me guess, a group of teenagers, incessantly talking, who bamboozled you by somehow being in fifteen places at once.'

'You know them?'

He rolled in his eyes in a manner that implied he did.

'Most of the shops have a two-school-children-at-time policy. You can see the signs on the doors.'

'Really, you can you do that?'

'Of course you can. It's your shop. You'll want to get yourself CCTV too. That stops them in their tracks pretty quickly.'

Holly considered the suggestion. CCTV wouldn't be cheap, but if this was a regular thing, it was probably something she needed to think about. She was about to ask whether he could recommend anyone to install it, when his phone began ringing in his pocket.

'You get reception in here?' she asked, with more than a hint of jealously.

'Sorry,' he said, standing up and offering her the ice pack as he glanced at his phone. 'I just need to get this.'

'No problem. I'm fine now. You don't have to stay.'

'Are you kidding? I get the feeling there's something very special about you, Holly Berry.'

And then he smiled and waved goodbye as he left.

Dan who? she thought to herself.

11

Holly Berry did not have a crush. Crushes were not something she did. Particularly not when she was only days out of a relationship on which she had expended far too much of her energy. It was just flattering, that was all. Nice to been acknowledged, particularly by someone so attractive. And not just in the looks department. Clearly, he was some kind of a modern knight in designer chinos. Forcing herself to her feet, she shook the feeling away. He was well mannered and he was simply being polite. She'd likely never hear from him again.

Business picked up a little during the afternoon when two coach loads of tourists disembarked just outside her door. Even in March, the coaches came. Although it was nowhere near the number of visitors she remembered from her summer holidays, they still emptied the jars of caramel fudge and chocolate hedgehogs, creating another job for her and she was forced to look through Maud's files to find out exactly who the suppliers were.

Serving customers with a sore ankle posed a bit of a challenge and, more than once, she thought she was going to drop a jar of sweets as she reached up on tiptoes to grab one from a top shelf, but it always held out long enough for her to get back to the till and the antique weighing scales. A bruise, that was all. At worst, a slight sprain. Still, she was going to have to walk back to the cottage on it.

At 5 p.m., she turned the sign on the door to *Closed*, although she was a long way from being ready to go. She may have sorted out the shelves and sweets but layers of dust were caking the inside of the windows. There was a mop upstairs in the tiny toilet to the side of the storeroom, but she seriously doubted it had been used in a long while. There were so many other jobs needing attention too, so much to do. But it wasn't like she had any other calls on her time.

Mopping was surprisingly easy. Her ankle now only throbbed if she moved suddenly or put too much weight on in. A sense of guilt churned through her, though. She had apologised to the cyclist about his busted-up bike, but not mentioned all the cuts and grazes on his arms and legs. Maybe she would try to track him down to apologise. Giles seemed to know who he was. She could always ask him; that was, if she saw him again. That exact thought was running through her mind when the bell jingled.

'Sorry, we're closed,' she said, turning back towards the door.

'I should jolly well think so. It's gone six. You'll make the rest of us look terribly lazy if you're here working all hours, you know.'

It was ridiculous how happy she was at the sight of him. His sandy hair was tousled in a scruffy yet decidedly curated manner that looked undeniably good.

'Giles, I didn't expect to see you again so soon,' she said, honestly.

'No? Well, hopefully it's a pleasant surprise. I assume you've got friends in the village and most likely have plans tonight. However...'

'No,' she blurted out, far more eagerly than she'd intended.

'No?' He raised an eyebrow.

'I mean no, I don't. Have any friends, that is. Well, I do have friends, obviously. Just not in the village. I used to know people here, but you know what it's like. People get older, they get married, get jobs.'

Oh, good God, could somebody please stop me? she thought to herself. The rambling. She always did it when she was nervous, and she absolutely hated it. Why was it so difficult to simply stop talking? After a deep breath to regroup, she tried again. 'What I mean to say is that I don't have any plans for tonight.'

'Glad we've got that straight,' he said, with an ever-so-slightly crooked smile creeping onto his lips. 'And with that sorted, perhaps I can take you for dinner? You're clearly a very interesting person and I'd love to hear how you got old Maud to sell you her shop.'

An interesting person. She wasn't even sure it was a compliment, but she felt her cheeks turning fuchsia nonetheless.

'That sounds nice.'

'Fantastic. Do you want to grab your coat?'

'You mean now?'

'Of course I mean now. Only if you are hungry.'

That question needed little thought. Yes, she was definitely hungry. Having no one to cover her for lunch, and forgetting to bring anything with her, a bar of chocolate-covered marzipan was all she'd managed since breakfast. And so, one minute she was standing with an ancient mop in her hand, ready to hobble upstairs and flush the dirty water down the toilet, and the next she was desperately trying to see her reflection in the foxed mirror of the same toilet, wondering how the hell this was all happening. Having checked her teeth for stray sweet remains, she took a whiff of her armpits and grimaced. Well, there certainly wasn't going to be any chance of anything romantic happening that night, she thought. Not that that it would have been on the cards anyway, of course. It's not like this was a date. At least she didn't think it was.

After the best tidy up she could give herself in the circumstances, she headed back down to the shop, where Giles was, by some miracle, still waiting.

He had changed since earlier in the day and was now dressed in a salmon-pink shirt, unbuttoned at the top, with a knitted sweater thrown over his shoulders, just like a model in a magazine. Perhaps he was one, she thought. After all, she knew absolutely nothing about the man and he was certainly good looking enough.

'Ready?' he asked.

'As long as we're not going anywhere fancy,' she replied. 'I feel a complete mess.'

'Well, you look delicious. My car's just outside.'

Trying to suppress the colour she knew was rising in her cheeks, she felt around in her bag for her keys.

'I just need to lock up.'

Only when she inserted the key into the ancient door lock, did she recall that it was near the top of her to-do list. As she twisted it, the entire metal casing shifted to the point where she thought it was going to come away in her hand. Looking at it now, it was a miracle she'd been able to unlock the place that morning. She tried again to click the mechanism into place. It still wouldn't budge. Fighting the urge to use as much force as possible, she removed the key, took a deep breath and tried again. If she wasn't careful, she'd snap it off, knowing her luck. Then she'd have to cancel her not-a-date with Giles and wait for a locksmith to come out. Thankfully, on the second try and with a little jiggling, it gave a reassuring click.

'Well, that's the first day...' She stopped mid-sentence as she turned around and found herself lost for words. 'That's your car?' she asked.

'One of them,' he said, patting the roof of the dark-green, vintage, sports car. The crooked smile that had such inexplicable effects on her pulse, reappeared. 'Now, come on. Get in. I'm going to take you somewhere special.'

Climbing into a low-slung, sports car was far more difficult than celebrities and models made it look. Bending her knees as best she could, she held her balance just long enough to ensure that she was squarely above the seat, before dropping down and landing with a thump.

'Don't worry. You'll get used to it,' he commented, in a way that didn't sound as horrendously patronising as it could have done, although he followed it up by saying, 'You might want to tie your hair back though.'

'My hair?'

'It's up to you, of course.'

She watched as he undid a couple of buckles above the windscreen and then pushed the roof backwards. Once it was safely stowed away, he hopped into the driver's seat.

'You couldn't have done that before I had to contort myself to get in?'

'Now where would the fun have been in that?'

The minute they started moving, the wind whipping past blew her hair every which way. To start with, when they were driving through the village, it was just about bearable, but then they were out on the country roads and Giles really put his foot down. For mile after mile the car sped through narrow lanes, heading up and out of Bourton and then through other villages and towns that were dotted around. First Clapton, then towards Burford, with its large river, wildlife park and brilliant garden centre. Small, Cotswold-stone cottages were interspersed with grand, country houses, their dry-stone walls marking out the boundaries between one manor and the next. Had she looked, she suspected there might be the odd deer in a field, or babbling brook with a weeping willow cascading over it. However, there was no chance of seeing any of it as she concentrated on holding her hair against her head, trying to stop it from lashing at her face.

Hollywood had a lot to answer for. In the films, people would laugh and hold conversations and take it in turns to point out all the wonderful things they were passing on their romantic drive. The women would have their heads thrown back as their hair billowed in the wind. Turns out, being in a vintage sports car wasn't like that at all. And it wasn't just the hair. The thing was loud.

'Are you okay there?' Giles asked and not for the first time.

'I... urgh... I...'

There was no point attempting to reply. It was already taking all she could to hold back her hair, shield her face from the wind and try not to bounce all the way out of the seat every time they hit a pothole. But after about twenty minutes of this, she decided she at least needed to say something.

'Where are we going?' she shouted over the roar of the engine and rushing wind.

'Not much further,' he said. 'You all right to keep going a little longer?'

She nodded in response, with no idea whether he could actually see it or not.

In one way, the disaster with the hair was a good thing. It was certainly a good distraction from how utterly terrified she was. Somehow, she didn't think this car, with its flimsy seat belts and wooden steering wheel, was going to be fitted with the latest side-impact bars or airbags. Not to mention the lack of roof. This, in turn, took her mind off the hunger cramps she was getting.

Five minutes later, they slowed to a speed at which she could actually hear him speak.

'Sorry about that. I think it's something you just have to get used to. Hopefully, it will be worth it though. This place is pretty special.'

Only then did Holly finally take a moment to look around her and see where they were.

The first green buds of the year glinted on the branches and a small river ran alongside the road. It was nothing like the one in Bourton, with its perfectly precise, stone edges and pristine bridges. This was rustic and rough, and the water sprayed white as it bubbled over the rocky riverbed, a pair of swans nestling on the bank. Tiny cottages of sandy-coloured stone, covered in ivy and famous for their appearance in a thousand adverts for the area, formed neat rows tiered up the hills on either side. Bibury. The gem of the Cotswolds, although not somewhere she'd ever visited before. It was too far to walk or cycle from Bourton and the bus routes barely touched these places. She found herself lost in the picturesque view as the setting sun glimmered on the water.

Giles took a right turn onto a narrow track, and then another up a wide driveway with impressive open lawns. Now at a slow crawl, he guided the car into the parking area of one of the most impressive buildings she had ever seen.

'So,' he said, switching off the engine. 'Shall we?'

12

'I feel extremely underdressed,' Holly said, as the maître d' led them from the formal entrance and through the wide corridors of the building, where alcoves offered plush, velvet-cushioned armchairs and leather chaise lounges.

'Don't be silly. It's fine. Besides, we're eating in the library. It's far more relaxed in there than the main restaurant.'

Holly didn't dine out. She and Dan had avoided restaurants, mainly because of the cost, but there was also the added factor that she could cook pretty much any dish they might want. During the first couple of years of their relationship, she had tried to be adventurous: gnocchi with sun-dried tomato, freshly made raviolis, you name it. She'd enjoyed spending time learning new skills, but Dan had been more of a beans-on-toast type man, and she'd felt bad spending money on extravagant ingredients. Still, she didn't need to be a regular at her local Nando's to know that the library was definitely not relaxed.

Dark, wooden tables were covered with starched, white table-cloths, and each place setting included at least three pairs of knives and forks. There were two wine glasses per person, too, and a large jug of water, filled with lemon slices and mint leaves.

'Here will be perfect,' Giles said, moving to a table by the fire-place. 'We'll have to come back in the summer. They set up the tables on the patio. Croquet on the lawn. Great evenings.'

She could imagine, although thinking beyond the next weekend was currently a struggle. It didn't help that her mind had fixated on one particular burning question. Was this a date? The way he'd asked her, so out of the blue; was he being friendly, or was it some-thing more? It was definitely too soon after Dan for her to consider any type of relationship, but how did she say that without hurting his feelings?

'Is everything okay?' he asked, pulling out a chair for her. 'We can move to a table closer to the window, if you like?'

'Everything's fine.' Was it, though? Even if you overlooked the date issue, there was also the fact that she had just got in a car and driven to the middle of nowhere with a man she had only met that morning. Crap, she thought as she realised the ridicu-lousness of the situation. Almost thirty minutes in a car with a man she didn't know, to a place she had no idea how to get back from. And the fact that he had just swept her up in the moment meant she hadn't even messaged anyone to let them know where she was going. It was the stuff true-crime documentaries were made of.

'That's a lovely watch,' she said, attempting to distract herself from the concerns running around her head.

'Thank you.' He lifted his wrist and allowed the watch to drop down a fraction. To be honest, she thought, it was brash, bordering on vulgar, but she had needed something to say, and it was defi-nitely a talking point.

'It is a Rolex,' he said. 'I know, a cliché, but they are worth the expense. My parents bought it for my eighteenth. I was rather precious about it back then; now I wear it every day. That's the thing with quality items. They're made to be...'

'You're not a serial killer, are you?'

'Sorry?' He stopped mid-sentence. 'Am I what?'

'It's just, I don't actually know anything about you. I mean, I know your name, but you could have made that up. And you've driven me all the way out here...'

'Holly.' He placed his hand on top of hers, causing a tingle to run up her arm. 'I can assure you, I am not a serial killer.'

'To be fair, that's exactly what you'd say if you were.'

'You're right.' He grinned before pulling out his phone. 'Who do you want to speak to?'

'Pardon?'

'Who do you want to speak to? So you're not worried, that is? I can try and get my mum on the phone? She'd probably vouch for me, unless she's at some benefit dinner. My uncle should be available, if that would help? He'd probably be the best one. He's very well known around here. You can ask anyone.'

'I don't want to speak to your uncle,' she said. 'Or your mum.'

'Then what? Ah, I know.' Leaving his seat, he moved around the table, taking his phone with him. Then, crouching behind her, flicked on the camera. 'Smile!'

A moment later and a picture of a confused Holly, next to a frustratingly attractive Giles, appeared on his phone. 'Right now, are you on Facebook?'

'Barely.'

'But you have an account?' He tapped away on his screen. 'Wow, there are a surprising number of Holly Berrys. Ah ha, here you are.' He held the phone up to compare her to her profile picture. 'Giles Caverty is with Holly Berry at the Windrush Court hotel. There.' He put his phone back into his pocket. 'If you go missing, the police will immediately know it was my fault. Can you relax now?'

As her own phone beeped with the notification, she found herself too stunned to respond. It was a genius idea and made perfect sense. So not only was he charming and chivalrous but also appeared to be blessed with the rare attribute of great common sense. She could think of absolutely nothing to say to him in response. Fortunately, her saving grace came in the form of an exceptionally smart waiter.

'Good evening, Mr Caverty. It's been a while.'

When Holly had worked as a waitress, while at university, she had worn jeans and a black top. This guy looked like he had just stepped out of the pages of *The Great Gatsby*.

'Peter,' Giles said, offering him a warm smile. 'It's been far too long, hasn't it?'

'Everything well with your uncle, sir?'

'Very good, thank you. You know how he is. Working himself towards an early grave.'

'Let's hope not.'

Adjusting his focus momentarily to Holly, he offered her a polite, professional smile. 'Welcome, madam. This is your first time with us.' It was said as a statement rather than a question.

'Um, yes.' This all felt so unreal.

'May I suggest that sir and madam sample our tasting menu?'

'Yes please, Peter,' Giles said, jumping in to answer for them. 'You do eat meat, don't you?' he asked her.

'Sure.'

'Great. And we'll have the wine pairing to go with it, too.'

'Very well, sir.'

A moment later, the waiter was gone, and Holly found herself feeling even more conspicuous than ever. That was it? That was the food ordered? What about a menu? Starters? Mains? Did exceptionally rich people not deal with things like that? Maybe she should keep a change of clothes at the shop in future, she thought, in case something like this happened again. Not that she even had anything that would be suitable for a place like this.

'So, tell me about yourself,' she said, forcing herself to speak before panic engulfed her entirely. 'What work do you do? I'm guessing your hobbies include driving around the countryside in flashy sports cars and picking up random women to take for dinner.'

He smiled at her. 'I don't consider you random. After all, technically, we're neighbours.'

'We are?' She tried to consider how that was possible, given that she didn't even have a permanent place to live at the moment.

'The shop next door. The Willow Tree gift shop.'

'That's yours?'

'Well, my family owns it. I must confess I'm not terribly hands-on. I pop in occasionally to check on the lease holders. We rent out a few of the shops in the village.'

'So what do you do?'

His shoulders rose in a half shrug.

'To be honest, I'm a Jack of all trades. I help manage the family properties, and I do a fair bit of work with my uncle. He restores vintage cars and I sometimes I help out there, but mostly I organise sales for him.'

'Did you restore the one outside?'

'Oh no. I wish. He wouldn't let me near anything that expensive.'

It was a relaxed self-deprecation. Quite endearing.

'Now enough about me. Tell me about you? How did you end up here? You grew up in Bourton?'

'I did. Never thought I'd return, if I'm honest.'

'So why did you?'

Why indeed? Because she'd needed to get as far away from her cheating ex and everything about that life as possible. That was the first answer that sprang to mind. But that didn't feel like the type of information to give right now.

'I guess I just needed a break from the rat-race,' she said, instead. 'A slower pace of life after the city.'

'Ah, the classic, slower-paced life.'

As conversation moved on to her job in London, the first course was brought to the table—a tiny plate with a single scallop perched on green, mashed potato and accompanied by a large glass of white wine each.

'Cheers,' Giles said, lifting his, against which she obligingly clinked her own. 'To new friends.'

'To new friends.' Holly smiled as enthusiastically as she could, but inside her heart sank. One scallop. One, single scallop. Her stomach growled angrily. There was no denying it looked perfectly cooked; she had prepared them a couple of times herself, and she knew from the smell it was going to taste amazing. But if this was the starter, the main was probably going to be a similar-sized portion. It would be a drive to the twenty-four-hour Tesco after this, given she had nothing at all in Maud's fridge yet.

'Don't worry, you'll be stuffed by the end,' Giles said and she wondered if, as well as being obscenely handsome and charming, he could also read minds.

* * *

As the waiter removed her seventh plate, Holly rested her hands on her stomach. Giles had been right. While every course was barely more than a couple of mouthfuls, there had been so many of them. Poached pears on wilted spinach with smoky bacon, asparagus and leek soup with Chantilly cream and chestnuts, seared duck breast with dauphinoise potato. Those were the ones she could remember. And there was still dessert to go.

'I'm not sure I'm going to make it,' she said, when the waiter placed what she hoped would be the final plate down in front of her.

'Of course you can,' Giles responded. 'I have faith in you. You can do anything!'

'This is amazing,' she said, taking a minuscule spoonful of the chocolate-mousse topping, then following it immediately with a substantially larger one. 'What flavour did he say it was?'

'I've no idea.'

For no reason she could fathom, she erupted into full-blown laugher, at which point he promptly followed suit. Along with endless food courses, there had been plenty to drink. Whites, reds and now a sparkling wine. A different glass for every course. She hadn't felt this drunk since a hen-do two years ago and would never normally have considered drinking so much with someone she didn't know, but it had all felt so natural. Giles had an ineffable ease about him. She would hate to sound so clichéd as to say they had *clicked*, but it seemed they had. She felt so relaxed. So comfortable.

'So, she agreed to sell to you, just like that?' Conversation had returned to the shop.

'Yep.'

'That's insane. You know it hasn't made a profit for years, don't you?'

'It makes a small profit, although it's going to have to make more, and fast. The deposit is going to take all my savings.'

'Well, if it doesn't work, you can always sell it again.'

'I guess.'

A short silence fell between them and his eyes fixed on her.

'You really are rather remarkable, Holly Berry.' Whether because of the wine or the temperature of the room, she felt a sudden rush of heat to her cheeks.

'I don't know about that,' she replied.

Remarkable or not, she was determined to finish the dessert in front of her. The chocolate mousse, the gold leaf. It looked like it belonged in an art gallery instead of on a plate. It certainly put her flourless chocolate cake to shame.

'I don't think I've ever eaten a meal like this in my entire life,' she said, as she went for the next spoonful.

'No? Then we'll have to do it again.'

Dessert finally defeated, Giles reached into his pocket and pulled out a blister packet. 'You'll have to forgive me for this,' he said, as he popped one of the greenish tablets into his hand and then into his mouth. 'Nicotine gum. Trying my hardest to stop, but every now and again I struggle. To be honest, I don't know which habit I find more disgusting, smoking or chewing this damn stuff.'

'Smoking,' Holly commented. 'Definitely smoking.'

'Not a smoker then?'

'No. Not a smoker.'

'I'll make sure I keep the gum on hand, then.'

When their table had been cleared away, they moved onto one of the sofas.

'Shall we get a nightcap before we go?' he suggested, indicating his now empty glass. 'They have a decent range of scotch, if that's what you're into.'

She wasn't, but considering how her life had taken such a strange turn, she could be. Although before she said as much, another thought struck her.

'How are we going to get back?' she asked, momentarily sober. 'You can't drive. We've had far too much to drink.'

'It's fine,' he waved a hand. 'It's a hotel. We can get a room.'

Holly stiffened. So that was what this was all about. The sense of calm and ease she had been feeling all evening was replaced by pure anger, at herself as much as anything else.

'Oh, of course, you good-looking rich guys, you're all the same. I should—'

'I meant separate rooms,' he added hurriedly, reaching out and taking her hand. 'I promise I would never make... I didn't even consider...Oh God, you thought that I... No, not at all. If you'd rather, we can get a taxi. I can get Peter to order one for us.'

Amazed to see him looking flustered for the first time, a relieved and slightly embarrassed Holly sank back onto the sofa. Of course, he was a gentleman. He probably had a title to go with it too. Maybe he was a lord. Or a marquis? Was that a real thing? she tried to recall. In her drunken state, words didn't sound quite right.

'I not sure I should have any more,' she admitted. 'I don't even know what time it is.'

He flicked up his wrist to reveal the Rolex. 'Just before twelve.'

'What? Midnight?'

'You know what they say, time flies.'

It had. It really had. A whole evening and part of the night gone on food and wine. And on a weekday, too.

'Maybe we should grab that taxi,' she said, perturbed by how much her head was spinning and the number of jobs awaiting her in the morning. 'I don't want to be late for work tomorrow.'

'You're your own boss now,' he reminded her. 'You can turn up as late as you want. Heck, you could not go in all day. It's entirely up to you.'

It was true, she thought, and she really was having a great night, but pulling a sickie on day two was not the most responsible way of starting her new venture. 'I think a taxi is probably the best idea,' she replied.

'No problem,' he said, the same relaxed twinkle in his eye. 'I'll just get the bill.'

With a wave of his hand and a quick nod, he conveyed his desire to the waiter. A couple of minutes later and the young man appeared and placed a small silver tray with a folded paper on the coffee table in front of them, Giles immediately reached for it.

'We'll split it,' she said.

'No, I'll get this,' he replied.

'Don't be silly.' Holly placed her hand on the tray, her finger tips right next to his.

'Nonsense, it was my idea to bring you here.'

'And I've had a wonderful night. Honestly, if you hadn't taken me out, I'd be sitting in Maud's old cottage, probably eating tinned hotdogs and watching re-runs of *Love Island*.'

It was true. As nice as it was to have someone offer to pay for her – Dan was always the type to have the calculator on his phone ready before the bill even arrived – that was not the type of person she was, or wanted to be. She paid her way fair and square.

'Please, let's split this.'

'Well, if I've saved you from such a terrible night, it does only seem fair.'

That look, she thought, leaning forwards and wobbling a little from all the drink. How were his teeth that good? Maybe they were fake. That was the only way anyone could have a smile that perfect, surely. With his eyes locked on hers, she felt something visceral turning in her stomach. Maybe fate was real. Maybe this was all part of some greater plan. Perhaps the sweet shop wasn't going to be the only serendipitous thing that happened to her this week. It would definitely make a good story at the wedding, she thought, now letting herself get completely carried away. The story of how she ran into the road, nearly colliding with a bicycle only to be rescued by a charming stranger who happened to be fated to be with her.

'At least we know it's an even split,' Giles said, breaking her daydream.

'Sorry?'

'The bill. We both had the same.'

'Oh yes, of course.'

'Great, so we'll just go halves.'

With Giles finally letting go of the silver tray, Holly took the paper and glanced at the number at the bottom. Several moments of silent blinking followed, during which her throat grew incredibly dry and her head incredibly sober. She brought the thin slip of the paper even closer to her eyes, just to make sure she wasn't imagining extra zeros. Finally, when her body had flushed from hot to cold and back again, she lifted her gaze, looked at Giles, and forced herself to smile.

'I'll need to put this on my card,' she said.

13

Four hundred pounds! Four flipping, hundred pounds! In the cold light of morning, with a very strong instant coffee down her throat, it still didn't bear thinking about. Obviously, she had only paid for her half, but that was still two hundred pounds, more than her monthly shopping bill. More than her monthly shopping and clothes bills combined. For a moment, back at the restaurant, she assumed there'd been a mistake. After all, how could dinner for two come to that amount? But it had been there in black and white. Two tasting menus at one hundred pounds each, and two wine pairings at another hundred per person.

And the cost hadn't stopped there. In agreeing to split the bill, she'd felt obliged to do the same with the tip – which Giles said he gave as a standard ten percent – plus the taxi home, which was another fifty pounds. All in all, the night had cost her two hundred and forty-five pounds. And this after a one-hundred-and-twenty-pound bill for her stay at The Seven Hounds, only the day before.

On top of that, her fridge remained empty and her wardrobe not much better. At some point, she knew was going to have to think about what to do with all her belongings in London, but as her head was pounding with the mother of a hangover, that was one job that would have to wait. The shop, on the other hand, could not.

Given her thumping headache and the fact that she needed to give her ankle a rest – it was no longer hurting but the pain might be masked by the excessive number of painkillers she had taken because of the hangover– she drove down to the village that morning. It was lazy; she knew that – not to mention horrendous for the environment – but it wasn't going to be something she'd do regularly, as much because, most of the time, driving and parking in Bourton was far more hassle than it was worth. Fortunately today, luck was on her side as she pulled into a spot directly in front of the shop. Unfortunately, one glance at the front door and her feeling of optimism took a downward turn.

Again, it was a battle to even get the lock open. Next, there was the usual problem of trying to sort out anything in a place with no phone reception and no internet. Yes, there was the landline, but in order to source a locksmith, she had to go outside the shop to find a signal, to get on the internet, to find a number. And every time she went to do it, a customer appeared. Eventually, at just gone eleven and two hours after opening, she found a number and picked up the old phone to call it.

'Hello, is that the Cotswold Locksmiths?' she asked.

'Aye, it is. How can I help you?'

'I need a lock fixing. It's a shop door and I don't think it's been looked at in sometime. I'm worried the whole thing is going to break, to be honest.'

'So, it's an emergency call-out, is it?'

'Um.' She glanced at the door, where the metal handle was currently hanging at an unusual angle. 'Well, the sooner the better,' she said.

'I'm backed up this morning, but I should be able to get to you this afternoon. Does that work for you?'

'That's fine.' It wasn't like she was going to be going anywhere. She was just about to give him the address when she considered the contents of the till and last night's obscene dinner bill. 'You couldn't give me some idea of the cost, could you?'

The sound of smacking lips reverberated down the line.

'I'd have to have a look at it. A shop door, you say? Old one?'

'Yes, definitely.'

'Probably needs replacing then.'

Her optimism faded a little. He was right. 'I think so.'

'Probably needs a specialist fit, too, then. I'd say you'd be looking at a hundred and twenty for the lock and handle, then another sixty on top for the emergency call out.'

The maths took less than a second. 'A hundred and eighty pounds?'

'Sounds about right.'

'Sixty pounds for a call-out?'

'It's an emergency call-out.'

'Well, it's not an emergency if you're not coming 'til this afternoon, is it?'

'If it's not an emergency, then I'll fit you in after the weekend. Monday okay? Only a fifteen quid if you want to wait 'til then?'

With her heart rate on the rise, she had to do some quick thinking. Last night, she'd had to use her credit card for the first time in years. There were the security cameras she needed to get, as well. Not to mention new stock and the utility bills. The thought of these ever-rising expenses caused a tightening in her throat.

'Don't worry,' she said, at last. 'I'll sort it out.'

'You will, will you?' A snort rattled down the line. 'What you gonna do, watch a YouTube video and do it yourself?' He laughed.

'What I do is none of your business,' she replied, with a curtness she usually reserved for cold callers.

'Suit yourself. But just so you know, if you need an emergency call out after six or over the weekend, it goes up to a hundred quid. I'll be hearing from you.' His laughter was still echoing in her ear as she slammed down the phone.

She was livid, not only that someone could charge sixty pounds simply for turning up to do their job but because of the sheer condescension with which he had spoken to her. For all he knew, she could well have a first-class degree in mechanical engineering. She didn't, but that wasn't the point. After all, changing a lock wasn't exactly rocket science. She had just opened the door to head outside for phone reception to start searching YouTube videos when a customer appeared in the doorway.

Dressed in jeans and hair under a woollen, beanie hat, she was holding a large, cloth bag under her arm from which rose the smell of freshly baked bread.

'Sorry, are you closing?' she asked, noting Holly's apron.

'No, no,' she said. 'Come on in.'

'Fabulous. I promised some old folk I'd bring them sweets on my next visit. You know what they're like. Half of them can't remember my name, despite the fact I've seen them every week for the past three years, but they could tell you the exact time, date and colour of the top I was wearing when I promised to pick them up a quarter of rosy apples and a box of York Fruits.'

The woman appeared to be of a similar age to herself, and had a warm smile that Holly immediately felt herself reciprocating.

'Have you got any acid drops?' she asked, her eyes moving up and down the shelves.

'Should do. They're normally over here.' Holly scanned the bottles. 'There you are,' she said, grabbing the jar from one of the lower shelves and placing it by the scales, ready to weigh. 'Anything else you need?'

'Yes, loads. Now let me see, there's the York Fruits, some cherry lips, a bar of Kendal mint cake and some... fudge ice? I don't even know what that is.'

Holly grinned as she headed around to the front of the counter and pulled out a bar of mint cake, before finding the other jars of sweets.

'It's coconut ice, coated in fudge,' she said, showing her the pink, white and brown confectionery cut into perfect, sugary cubes.

'No wonder the old girl has no teeth left. Now, I also need some plain toffees and treacle toffees.'

A small chuckle left Holly's lips. This was exactly how she remembered it. This was what working in the sweet shop had been about. Yesterday had just been a little blip.

'Do you mind me asking who all these are for?' she said, as she started weighing them out, before tipping them into little paper bags.

'I do some volunteering,' the woman explained, fishing in her bag for her purse. 'At a nearby care home. They're a lively bunch. Still got plenty of spirit in them. To be honest, I buy these sweets for me as much as for them. I love all the stories they tell me when they start tucking into them. It's as if they unlock hidden memories for them.'

Holly rang up the final item on the till. 'Sweet memories,' she said, as much to herself as the woman. What a brilliant concept. Maybe that was what she needed. A proper marketing plan. Back when she was working there before, Agnes would always take charge of the A-frame blackboard that sat outside the window. She would write the latest offers on the front, or draw pictures of sweets and lollipops that children's grubby hands would inevitably have decimated by the end of the day. But it got people's attention. She could see if it was still upstairs. Perhaps it would help draw attention to the shop again. 'That's sixteen pounds, fifty-eight pence,' she said, reading the total from the till. 'I hope they enjoy them.'

'Me too. See you again soon.'

And, for a reason she couldn't explain that had nothing to do with the profit element, she really hoped it would be true. But, for now, she had another job to be getting on with.

14

The minute the woman was out of the door, Holly flipped the sign on the door to *Closed* and raced upstairs to have a rummage. Fortunately, in a storeroom the size of Harry Potter's bedroom under the stairs, there weren't too many places for things to be hiding. After a minute on her hands and knees, she slid the wooden-framed blackboard out from underneath a cupboard. Cobwebs and dust bunnies tangled between her fingers, but all the grime in the world couldn't wipe the grin off her face. This was going to be fun.

With a damp cloth, she wiped the board clean and, finding some chalk in the drawer by the till, got to work. There was no denying, as jobs went, drawing pictures was far more fulfilling than typing numbers into a computer all day.

What hidden memories will you find inside? she wrote. Her calligraphy wasn't the best, but the letters were clear and evenly spaced. Even if it brought just one more customer in, it would have been worthwhile. Then she started drawing sweets. Had she been braver, she would have liked to have studied art at college, but there was too much risk attached to something like that. She had seen her dad made redundant, through no fault of his own, from jobs that he was more than qualified to do. Choosing a sensible, steady, corporate job had kept her secure all those years. Trying to earn a living as an artist would have been a life of constant worry. Much like her situation now. Oh. The thought made her swallow hard. However, doing this was proving somewhat therapeutic. And besides, the sweet shop had provided Maud and Agnes a steady income for half their lives. Why shouldn't it work the same for her?

After several attempts, she was satisfied enough with her handiwork to place the sign outside the window and, whether or not it was a coincidence, it didn't take long for the customers to start rolling in.

By mid-afternoon, she had served over a dozen people, including a dad with triplets in a huge pushchair and a woman who didn't get off her phone or even acknowledge her as she placed half a dozen jars on the counter followed by a twenty-pound note. It wasn't exactly polite, but Holly didn't care. At this stage in the game, she couldn't afford to be choosey.

Besides, she was on a roll now. Not only had she served customers, but had also found Maud's list of suppliers and started putting together a proper stock list. She did admit to herself, at this point, that she missed her computer a little bit. Maybe, when things picked up, she could get a little laptop for the shop. She even discovered a corner of the shop, next to one of the windows, where she could get enough phone reception to download YouTube videos. Yay! She was just about to watch the first one on how to change a door handle and lock when two young children came running in.

'I want sugar mice.'

'I want cola bottles.'

'*I wants* don't get,' quickly followed, in an adult voice.

'Chocolate mice, too. Granny said we had to get her chocolate mice.'

'No, she didn't. She said sugar mice.'

'No, she wants chocolate mice. She doesn't like the sugar ones. She said the string is too chewy.'

'You don't eat the string, you idiot.'

'Oi, watch your manners, the pair of you. Let me worry about your grandmother and you two can choose some sweets.'

The mother dragged herself into the shop, two heavy bags of shopping weighing down each arm. Strapped to her chest was a third child, currently fast asleep.

'And don't you go messing up those shelves either,' she warned. 'Touch something, that's it. That's what you're having.'

A small smile bloomed on Holly's face. Earlier that morning she'd had to stop a small boy from seeing if he could fit the large end of a lollipop into his ear, while his parents were talking, totally oblivious. It was good to see they weren't all like that.

Already liking the customer, she waited for her to approach the counter.

'Hi, do you still have chocolate... Oh my God! I know that face. Holly? Holly Berry?'

Holly started. 'Sorry, do I know you?'

'It's me. Caroline.'

Holly's eyes widened. 'No! Caroline Stubbs?'

'Technically not Stubbs any more but, yes. Wow! How have you been? What are you doing here? Timothy, if you pick those up, then I am going to make you eat every last one of them. And you know what happened the last time you stole one of your grandad's liquorice torpedoes.'

The child, who didn't bat an eye at his mother's ability to see out the back of her head, moved his hand away and turned to the much more child-friendly sweets.

'So, tell me everything,' Caroline continued, like she hadn't just shown superhuman powers. 'How? When? Why? I never thought I'd see you back here.'

'Oh, it's a long story,' she replied, surprised by the sudden elation she felt at the sight of her old school friend. 'What about you? I thought you'd moved away, too?'

'I did, I did, and then I came back. I guess we just can't stay away. Seriously though, how long has it been?'

Letting out a long whistle, Holly thought back to those last few weeks before she'd left for university. Back then she'd not planned on returning to Bourton, ever, and it had very much been a summer of goodbyes.

'I know,' she said, the memory springing to mind. 'There was that party, over in one of the barns towards Stow. Do you remember? That weird guy from the year above us threw it. Now what was his name? Michael, Mick...'

'Michael Danton,' Caroline answered.

'Of course, that's it. Michael Danton. He had a lazy eye and it made him look really creepy. I wonder what happened to him.'

'Actually, I married him.'

'Oh, no. Oh, I'm so sorry. Not that you married him, of course. I didn't mean that. I'm sure he wasn't nearly as creepy as he came across.' Holly felt a rush of heat flooding her cheeks. 'I'm sure he's really great.'

'Yeah, he's okay. Far less creepy since he had that lazy eye fixed. I mean, see for yourself.' She indicated the children. 'I'm sure he'd love to catch up, too. You should come around for dinner. Are you living in the village?'

'I am at the minute.'

'Fantastic. Then let's arrange a date. When's good for you? Do you have a husband? Or a boyfriend? Or a girlfriend?'

An involuntary cough rattled in Holly's throat. 'Let's say that, until recently, I was unknowingly in a polyamorous relationship with my boyfriend.'

A furrow formed between Caroline's brows. 'Oh no. That's awful. But don't worry. We've all been there.' Then once again adopting her stern mother voice and without looking around, 'Jessica Danton, you are far too good at maths to think that all that lot is only going to cost me two pounds. Now put something back.' With a shake of the head and a shrug, she carried on the conversation. 'But seriously, this is fantastic. Look, give me your number, type it in my phone now. I've got to be honest: since these guys came along, it feels like I've lost the last seven years of my life to mum groups, where all we talk about is how little sleep we've had and compete to see which of our children has had the longest bout of constipation.'

'That sounds horrendous.'

'It is. Well, not the having children part. That's okay. Just the talking about it all the time bit. Do you have any?'

'No,' she replied, with a drawn-out vowel sound.

'Great, that means we could have wine. Please, please can we get wine?'

'That sounds perfect.'

'Tonight then?'

Between the pleading look in her eyes and the way it really did feel amazing to bump into her after all these years, Holly knew there was no way she could say no.

'Tell me your number and I'll text you the address,' she said.

Caroline grinned.

'Brilliant.'

* * *

She felt like a cheapskate. But having scoured the aisles of the local Co-op for the best wine deals, even splashing out four pounds seventy-five felt over indulgent, given her splurge the night before, and using her credit card was supposed to be for emergencies only. She also grabbed a couple of bags of veg from the reduced section.

After the richness of the meal with Giles and the sweets she had been picking at all day, a hearty vegetable soup felt like exactly what she needed and, while she left it to simmer on the hob, she got on with other jobs before Caroline turned up, including signing up for internet for the shop and watching as many YouTube videos on how to change a door handle and lock as she could find.

The more she watched, the more she felt like the locksmith had definitely be trying to pull a fast one. He probably thought she sounded young on the phone. Young and naïve, not to mention female, so had tried to rip her off with such a ridiculous call-out fee. Well, not on her watch. From all the things she'd seen, it was going to be fairly straightforward. There were a few things to watch out for, like making sure she got the right size barrel and ensuring that you fitted the handle on both sides before testing the lock, but only a fool wouldn't do that. She would go to the hardware store first thing and, all things being equal, would have a new lock fitted by lunchtime.

* * *

'I just can't believe you're here. It's been so long.'

Caroline had arrived armed with a bottle of wine and a large bag of kettle chips, both of which sat open on the coffee table in front of them, in Maud's little living room. 'Honestly, I never thought you'd come back.'

'It definitely wasn't planned.'

'I can tell. And what about this place? How long do you get to stay here?'

'I don't know. Maud says it's on the market, but things aren't moving at the minute. Still, I know I should probably start looking for somewhere else straight away, just in case.'

Lifting her wine glass, Caroline scrunched up her nose and shrugged. 'These things take ages to go through. Last time we sold a place, it was six months before we actually moved out of it.'

'That's good to know,' she replied.

Words flowed with an ease she wouldn't have expected after so many years apart. The conversation – following a brief dissection of Holly's disastrous love life – was centred mainly around what they had been up to in the last decade. Caroline, she learned, had spent two years working as a chalet girl and ski instructor, before reconnecting with Michael over Facebook and eventually getting married. They had been living in Bourton ever since and, by all accounts, loved it.

'The thing is, all the stuff that used to drive us mad as teenagers – you know, being so far from the cities, nothing but countryside all around – that's what we like about it now. There's no need to rush. Life happens at its own pace. It's such a great environment for the kids, too. Not that you need to worry about that,' she added, hurriedly.

'Not for a long while, I suspect,' Holly added.

For the first time all evening, the slightest tension flickered between them, but thankfully Caroline barely let it settle.

'So, what about the shop? Have you got any exciting plans for the place?'

And though the comment was said more in passing than anything else, Holly felt a tingle of excitement at the prospect of what was to come.

'You know what? Yes, I have.'

15

Holly Berry was prepared. She was ready. She was, dare she say it, excited. In fact, she was genuinely buzzing. Even a crappy message from Dan couldn't ruin the mood.

Rent is due next week

Her phone had pinged with the message at seven-fifteen in the morning. Next had come:

I don't have your half

She fired straight back:

That's because I don't live there any more

It didn't take long to receive a reply.

So, what am I supposed to do about money?

Several replies ran through her head before she found one she thought was at least borderline polite.

Try asking the lodger that was using my bed. Or sell your guitars.

She pressed send and dropped her phone into her bag. She didn't need any of that. She didn't need him in her head on what was going to be a positive day. If he messaged again or tried to call, she would block him altogether. After all, it was no less than he deserved.

Outside, grey clouds and drizzle were attempting to dampen her spirits too, but she actually thought this could work out in her favour. If the weather stayed this way for a couple of hours, she should be able to get the door sorted without having to worry about dealing with customers at the same time.

First stop was the sweet shop. Having parked up in her usual spot on the opposite side of the road to Just One More, she took out her phone and a measuring tape she'd found in Maud's bathroom cabinet. After several minutes of wiggling the key, the door finally unlocked and she began to inspect what she was going to be dealing with.

Rust. That seemed to be the main issue. Lots and lots of red-brown rust. Yet, despite that, she found herself smiling. Having watched a dozen videos on removing and installing door locks – or mortice locks, as she now knew they were called – she had come to the decision that she was going to swap out like for like. One mortice lock and metal handles for the same thing again. That was it. In less than five minutes, with measurements taken and half a dozen numbers jotted on her phone, she headed back into the drizzle.

The hardware store in Bourton was the same place it had always been, smack bang in the middle of the High Street, between the supermarket and a gift shop. It didn't just sell hardware, though. It sold everything from Black & Decker drills to Bourton-on-the-Water rock. It seemed everywhere in the village sold rock, she thought, as she pushed open the door. Surely something like that should be a sweet shop's prerogative? After all, you didn't see her selling wall plugs just because she could. With little time to spare, she went straight to the counter where a woman was sitting on a small stool, her nose buried in a paper.

'Good morning. Could you tell me where your door handles and locks are, please?' she asked, smiling broadly. Not that the woman noticed. Without so much as lifting her gaze from her paper, she pointed to the back of the shop.

'Down there. Next to the fuses,' she muttered.

'Great,' she said, trying to maintain her upbeat manner, despite the lack of encouragement. 'And screwdrivers?'

The shopkeeper waved her hand, to indicate the next aisle over.

'Fantastic.' Holly forced herself to remain smiling, even as she hurried away from the counter to the back of the shop.

The store was at least three times bigger than Just One More and an absolute treasure trove, with each shelf stacked to the brim. Despite the appalling lack of customer service, it took her only a couple of minutes to locate what she was looking for. Given the aesthetics of Just One More, there was really only one suitable option among the array of handles that she could choose: cast iron with nice curves. With that sorted, she checked the notes she'd made on her phone and picked out two locks, almost identical to the untrained eye. Satisfied with her choice, she promptly took them and a screwdriver to the counter.

'Excuse me,' she said, after standing at there for longer than seemed reasonable and receiving no acknowledgement at all from the woman. She ploughed on regardless. 'I read on the internet that most sash locks are either sixty-four or seventy-four millimetres. Is that right?'

'Sounds 'bout right,' the woman grunted.

'Great. Obviously, I only need one, but I won't know which until I've removed the old one. I'm replacing the lock on my shop... Just One More? I'm in the process of buying it, actually.'

Given that they were practically neighbours, she expected something more than another grunt, and yet that was all the woman offered as she slipped the items into a bag.

'Fantastic. That will be £67.97,' she said.

'Great,' she said again, holding out her debit card, only to withdraw it before the woman could take it. 'I just need to check your returns policy,' she said, with the forced smile. 'Like I said, I only need one lock, but I won't know which until I've taken out the old one. I mean, I think I'll need the sixty-four-millimetre version, but there's not really any way I can tell yet. So, I'll bring back whichever one I don't need this afternoon. Or tomorrow, if you're closed. Unopened, of course.'

With a sniff that could clear the most congested of sinuses, the woman pointed to the handwritten note stuck on the front of the till.

No Returns

Holly cocked her head to the side. Below said sign was another which read,

You break it, you pay for it

and yet a third, typed on yellowed paper:

The customer is not always right. I am.

It was certainly an interesting approach to customer service, she thought. Realising this would not be quite as simple as she'd hoped, she tried again.

'Right, I see that. A pretty standard policy for independent shops like ours, right? I have exactly the same one, not that I would expect people to return sweets, obviously, but the thing is, I'm only four doors down. And I'm not even going to open the lock I don't need.'

'Sign says no returns.'

A click reverberated through Holly's jaw. 'I can see that, yes. And I get why you'd need that. People buy a hammer and return it once they've done that little job.' She was definitely going to have to keep that screwdriver now. 'But I won't open both of them. One will stay in the packet, completely untouched. In fact, I won't even get it out of the bag.'

'No returns.'

Wondering if the woman was some form of android, or if this was what she was going to turn into should she spend too long behind a counter of an empty shop, she considered her options. There was already no chance of returning the screwdriver, but even buying two locks, it was far cheaper than using the locksmith was going to be. But what would she do with the extra one? Sell it on eBay for half what it had cost her? That would be too much effort.

'Okay, give me a minute.'

She weighed it up in her mind. From what she had seen, almost all locks were sixty-four millimetres. She could buy that one, go back to the shop, unscrew the old one and check. If it was the right size, great. If it wasn't, she'd have to bite the bullet and come back for the other one. But, to do that, she'd have to put the old one back and close the door securely. With the amount of rust on it, the whole thing would probably disintegrate in her hand, and where would that leave her?

It was a fifty-fifty chance, and she was going to take it.

'Fine, I'll buy the sixty-four-millimetre one,' she said and handed over her card.

The woman looked up. 'So, you don't want this other one after all.'

The disgusted look which accompanied her comment would, in Holly's opinion, have been more appropriate for someone who had dumped an unwanted kitten at the roadside, as opposed to simply changing their mind about a purchase in a hardware store. How the hell the place had stayed in business so long was a miracle, she thought. Still, they were neighbours, and she kept her smile in place as she punched her PIN number into the card machine and picked up her shopping. Now it was time for the fun part.

The awning offered a good amount of protection from the rain, which had grown heavier during the time spent with the obnoxious shopkeeper. The bad weather was still proving useful, keeping customers at bay. Holly really wanted to get the job done before it cleared up.

'Okay, Hols, let's see how much you paid attention in D.T. class.' She gave herself the mini pep-talk as she propped open the door with a wedge. 'Nice and easy does it. There's no rush.'

All the videos she'd watched showed them removing the door handle with an electric screwdriver, whilst assuring her that a normal one would do the job just fine. One minute in and she was starting to realise that *fine* was code for *twenty times longer*. But that was okay. Better that than she snap something off. Besides, going slowly gave her the chance to really appreciate what she was dealing with. It was safe to say that she had never given the door more than a cursory glance. Being so close now, she could see all the beautiful intricacies of the woodwork. And the glass had an incredible patina, a fluidity you just didn't see these days. After several minutes of concerted effort and delicate handling of the rusting contraption, the screws were loose enough to remove. Double checking the wedge was still firmly in place, she pulled them out and wiggled both handles free.

'First part done,' she said to herself, quite pleased. Now she needed to remove the lock, which would reveal if she had been right in her decision to go for the sixty-four-millimetre version, or whether she was going to have to head back to the hardware store and that awful woman and shell out another thirty pounds. As she eased it out, her heart leapt. Even without measuring, she could see. She'd got it right! All she had to do was get the new bits in place and screwed in tightly, before any customers turned up. After slipping the new lock into position, she got the handles ready to attach.

'Ms Berry?'

She paused and looked up. Standing over her was a man, shielding himself from the rain with an umbrella.

'Yes, can I...' Her heart sank with the realisation of who it was. There were no scuffs on his trousers and no cycle helmet on his head. Even so, it was a face that was hard to forget, particularly after how much he had shouted at her before. 'Oh, it's you.'

'Yes, it's me.'

Her heart was now at basement level. It wasn't that she had forgotten about what had happened. Only, the dinner with Giles and then bumping into Caroline and catching up with her had made it completely slip her mind. And now he'd had to hunt her down, like she had deliberately been trying to avoid him. Not only was she going to be even more out of pocket, but she was looking like a terrible person into the bargain.

'I am so sorry. I honestly meant to trace you to give you money for your damaged bike. I've just been up to my eyes with taking over the shop, that's all. I really am sorry. Would you mind holding on a couple of minutes while I finish fixing this?' She motioned to the handle that she was currently holding in place. 'Or maybe you could come back later?'

The man stared at the door through narrowed eyes, although whatever issue he had with it, she wasn't in the mood to ask.

The screwdriver head slipped. She cursed internally. Why the hell was he just standing there watching her? Could he not see that now wasn't the right time for a conversation, let alone one that required a modicum of attention? A breeze gusted past her, through to the shop. She must have left the window open upstairs. So much for March; it felt more like December right now. She tried again to get rid of the man, so that she could focus on the task at hand.

'If you'd like to leave your name and a number, I can ring you?'

Finally, his attention turned back to her. 'I was simply passing, that was all,' he said. 'I wanted to check you were all right. The bike is fixed. Nothing a little bit of elbow grease and a spanner couldn't put right.'

'Oh,' she said, strangely taken aback. 'Thank you. Are you sure? What about your torn clothes, then?'

'Don't worry. I'll leave you to it. Unless, of course, you'd like some help?'

It sounded like the most insincere offer of help she'd ever heard. A bit like someone saying they'd be happy to stay and clear up after a party. She'd been there enough times, volunteering herself because it was the polite thing to do, even though she'd hoped to be turned down.

'It's fine,' she said, desperate to get back the lock. 'And thanks, about the bike, that is. If you discover any further damage that does need paying for, do let me know.'

'Like I said, it's all sorted.'

He hesitated, lines creasing his forehead. Then he was gone and she was finally left in peace to finish the job.

Thankfully, the distraction hadn't caused her to lose track of what she was doing. After making sure the handles and lock were securely in place and confident in what she'd achieved, she removed the wedge. It took a few moments longer to check everything lined up properly and worked, but at nine forty-five and with the rain now pelting down around her, Holly Berry stepped back, a new accomplishment under her belt. Not only was she a shop owner but well on her way to becoming – in her opinion, at least – a first-class handyman.

'Take that, Mr Locksmith,' she said to herself.

Grey clouds continued to roll overhead, thick and foreboding. She didn't hold out much hope of the weather clearing up by lunchtime, but it didn't matter. Still beaming and holding the hardware store bag over her head in a vain attempt to fend off the rain, she stepped towards the road to admire her handiwork from further back. Brilliant! But, as she returned to the door again, she saw a figure looming across the road in the reflection of the glass as it opened.

16

With her high-vis jacket and ticket printer in hand, there was no mistaking who – or rather what – the person was standing behind Holly's car. All the years that she had lived in London, she had never once got a ticket. There was no chance she was going to get one now. Not when she knew full well that she was definitely parked legally.

'Wait!' she yelled, racing across to where the officer was now checking her watch and then the number plate. 'What are you doing? This is a parking bay.'

The woman's sigh was audible even above the wind and rain.

'Parking here is limited to thirty minutes only,' she said.

'What? No, that can't be right. I parked here yesterday,' she said, shielding her eyes from the rain.

'Thirty minutes only, Friday to Sunday.'

The parking attendant pointed to a sign, partially hidden in flapping foliage. There, beneath the ivy, in tiny lettering, was the proof that she was right. A new level of panic rose in Holly.

'I'm so sorry. I didn't know. It was a genuine mistake. I'm here now. I'll move it. I just need to lock up my shop. I'll be one minute.'

She looked across. The door was swaying ever so slightly with the wind. 'That's all I need. Less than a minute. Half a minute.'

'Too late, I'm afraid. It's already in the system.'

Without so much as blink, the woman looked down at the device in her hand, before lifting the stylus from the edge. Steeling herself against the gusts of air, Holly clenched her fist.

'How can it already be in the system? You only just came to the car.'

The attendant's eyes locked on hers.

'I'm sorry. Are you saying I'm lying?'

'No, no, I'm just... Like I said, it was an honest mistake. And I really can't have been here much longer than thirty minutes,' she lied. 'Is there not some way to remove it? Surely there must be? I mean, you must make mistakes, now and again?'

'And now you're saying that I'm not capable of doing my job properly?'

Holly could sense the hole she was digging herself into. A hole she had no idea how to get out of. What she should do now was stop talking. Definitely, stop talking. And yet she could feel her mouth starting to move again.

'All I'm saying is that you are human, just like I'm human. And I made a mistake by not reading that sign properly and perhaps you could maybe consider that we're all human and make mistakes sometimes...'

There was little doubt that this gibbering was unlikely to succeed in rescuing her from the parking ticket. But as the stream of words made its way from her mouth, another gust of wind came, this one so fierce that the branches on the trees behind them creaked and lashed around and her words were blown away. Rubbish fluttered out from a nearby bin, and the parking attendant clutched at her hat to save it from flying off. And across the road, under the threadbare awning, the door to Just One More juddered momentarily before slamming shut with such tremendous force that the antique panes shattered into a thousand shards.

* * *

'It's a disaster, Mum. It's a complete nightmare. I don't know what I was thinking.'

'You weren't thinking, my love. You were living. You were following your heart.'

'I was being irrational. I was clearly unstable. Why on earth did you not talk me out of it? I've not even managed a week.'

As Sod's Law would have it, the wind had dropped shortly after her entire shop door had exploded, and a glorious, blue sky brought a flood of tourists out for the afternoon. Not that Holly got to serve a single one of them. Instead, she had had to wait around, not only for a glazier to turn out but also for the bloody locksmith, as the new lock had also bust, when the door slammed shut. The silver lining – if it could be considered that – was that the glass had now been replaced with the modern, safety variety, without the nice swirling patina but at least shatterproof. So at least it shouldn't happen again.

When that was all sorted, rather than heading back to the cottage, she had hopped in the car and gone to her mum and dad's.

'Maybe I should forget the whole thing and just call up Maud,' she mulled, breaking off another forkful of cake. 'I'm sure she'd understand.'

Already on her second cup of tea, she was sinking further into a well of self-pity.

'Firstly,' Wendy said, flicking the kettle back on in preparation for number three, 'I couldn't talk you out of it, because you didn't actually tell me you were going to do it, remember? You just did it.'

Holly grunted.

'And secondly, you are only one week in. Did you think it was going to be easy? Do you think it was for Maud and Agnes? Or did you expect it to be the same as it was when you were fourteen years old and had no actual responsibilities?'

'This feels remarkably like an attack,' Holly grumbled, in a voice that sounded ridiculously teenage-like.

'It's not an attack, my love. I would never do that.' Abandoning the kettle, she shifted over to the chair next to Holly's. 'Listen, I get it. It's not the fairy tale you imagined it would be, but nothing in life ever is. Remember, the grass isn't greener on the other side. It's greener where you decide to water it.'

'Maybe.'

'There's nothing maybe about it. Think about it this way. When you told me about buying the sweet shop, how did you feel?'

'How did I feel?'

'Yes. Surely you remember. We were sitting there in the pub, and you told me about Dan and you were about to feel sorry for yourself, when you remembered the shop.'

'I did? I did,' she recalled, however hazily. How could a week feel so very long?

'And when you mentioned what you'd done, your whole face just lit up.'

'It did?'

'Yes, my darling, it did. Which is why I knew that, whatever the outcome, you'd made the right choice at that given moment. You made the decision you needed to make, because nothing that makes you smile that insanely could possibly be a bad idea.'

Not for the first time that day, Holly could feel the sting of tears in her eyes, yet for once they weren't from frustration or anger.

'Now I'm not going to tell you that you should keep the shop. That's not up to me. But do you really want to give it up, just like that? You took it on for a reason. Several, probably. Don't you owe it to yourself to give it more of a go? Getting a job, earning money, there are a hundred ways you can do that. But following your heart? That opportunity doesn't present itself every day.'

Holly put down her fork and picked at the cake crumbs with her fingers. Her mum was right. If she gave up now, developers would turn it into a soulless franchise.

'Mum, you have no idea how much this is going to cost. Not just buying the shop, but all the other costs.' The air of defeat was still there in her voice. 'I've just signed up for internet connection and I need to get CCTV cameras, not to mention replacing the stock.'

'Get a bigger mortgage.'

Holly shuddered. 'That's hardly the best start. Besides, I don't even know if I could get a bigger mortgage. There is a little bit that I held back from putting up as the deposit, which I was hoping to keep by for a rainy day. I suppose I could dig into that.'

Wendy stood up and took the plate and mug to the sink. Her mum always had wise words of advice at the ready, but she was now being completely and utterly silent. It didn't sit well.

Finally, with the things rinsed, she came back and sat with her daughter again.

'Holly darling, there's nothing wrong with taking a risk. If you want to do this, you're going to have to be able to let go a bit. You're going to have to trust other people. And you need to learn to trust yourself, too, if it helps you keep your dream alive. Now, are you staying the night? It's just that Fridays are choir practice and I can't spend the whole evening giving you a pep talk.'

'Choir? Mum, you can't sing.'

'No, but they always head to the pub afterwards for a glass of wine, and I can drink. So, do you want to stay? It won't take me a minute to make up your bed.'

As nice an offer as it was, two hours later, Holly was tucked up in bed back at Maud's cottage, laptop open, taking yet another look at her finances. With everything now on spreadsheets, it was far easier to make sense of all the numbers. And while they weren't great, they were still doable. She could still make this work for Maud and Agnes. She *would* still make it work for them. Besides, tomorrow was Saturday, and the shop always used to be at its busiest at weekends.

_____

17

Following the close call with the traffic warden the previous day –
the woman turned out not to be an ogre and, while Holly had stood
there in tears over her smashed door, she had somehow managed
to cancel the entry on her pad after all – Holly decided to walk to
the shop. Given the unpredictable weather, she had searched out an
umbrella at the cottage, just in case there was a downpour.
However, she needn't have worried. Saturday morning proved to be
the most perfect day, in terms of weather at least, since arriving in
Bourton. The cerulean sky added to the sense of optimism she had
been feeling since she woke up.

When she'd arrived back at the cottage the night before, she'd
found three carrier bags of clothes on the doorstep, with a note
from Caroline saying that she had been going to send them to the
charity shop but did Holly want to take a look first? A quick sift
through and she'd discovered almost everything was in her size.
Style had never been too much of an issue with her as long as
things weren't too garish, which they weren't. Also, after that, a
quick search online turned up a CCTV camera that would link to

her mobile phone for only thirty pounds, and better still, it was on a two-for-one deal.

When she opened up, she could already see the car parking spaces filling and, by 10 a.m., she had taken more money than the rest of the week combined.

'Do you have any more sherbet lemons?' a man called over to her from the door.

'I'm afraid we've run out. If you come back Monday afternoon, I should have, though.'

'Are these pink shrimps gluten-free?' someone else asked.

'I'm not sure about that.' Holly was trying to concentrate on weighing out the items in front of her, whilst fielding the questions.

'Actually, I'll take two hundred grams of those strawberry millions. No, let's make that three.'

With her shoulders starting to ache, she tipped more and more sweets into the big, brass scales.

'Busy day?' asked the next lady in the queue.

'Really busy. But I'm not complaining.'

'Well, it's a lovely little place you've got here.'

'Thank you.'

'You know I came here for my honeymoon. Thirty-three years ago, it was. It's like stepping back it time.'

Holly grinned. This was what running a sweet shop was meant to be like.

As the lady who had honeymooned in Bourton took her purchases and moved away from the till, another customer stepped forwards, this time with sticks of rock and a jar of white mice for her to weigh a helping. The person after that had toffee slabs with hammers, marzipan animals and a fizzy sours selection that she wanted a massive half kilo of. Holly was weighing with one hand, typing in the till with the other and could have done with an extra three to pack the bags, take the money and hand back the change. Everything was flying off the shelves. How the hell Maud had managed this at her age, she had no idea. She'd already worked up more of a sweat than she'd ever managed on one of her power walks. And just as she'd think there was a lull, another new rush started.

It was nearly lunchtime and Holly was half way through weighing out a bag of fruit jellies for a man in a checked lumber-jack shirt, when something caught her eye. The shop was still busy, with people craning up to see what delights were stocked on the top shelves, but not so busy that they didn't all have enough space, which had happened earlier. Behind a woman with a pushchair, and yet another with a massive wicker basket, she spotted a lone girl in ripped black jeans with a cap pulled low over her eyes. That was suspicious enough, but then there was the massive bag slung over her shoulder. She may not have been in uniform, but it didn't take Holly two seconds to recognise the bag. The same, dull grey with maroon emblem hadn't changed since her time at the school. As she was sizing her up, the girl's hand reached for the zip.

'Not this time you don't,' she muttered, before turning her atten-tion back to the man with his fruit jellies. 'Sorry sir, would you excuse me for a moment?'

'What about my jellies?'

'I won't be long.'

It was a squeeze, getting out from behind the counter. The woman with the pushchair was blocking her route, and while tipping small children out onto the ground wasn't her style, Holly was determined that not a single chocolate hedgehog was going to be stolen on her watch again. Not when she was so close to getting the bloody CCTV cameras.

'Sorry, do you mind if I squeeze past? Can I... If I could just...' Another half dozen people had filed in from the street and had somehow managed to find a space.

'Can I pay now, please?' the man with the fruit jellies called across from the counter. 'I've got a bus to catch.'

'Just one second, sir. I'll only be a second.'

Her heart was racing. There was no chance they would get away with it this time. Not with so many people in the shop. This time she had witnesses. And people who could block the door for her. Shuffling half a step at a time, she continued to offer her apologies until she was only an arm's length away from the girl. The grey bag was now open and, to make matters worse, she was heading for the back stairs. Maybe she knew that was where the stock was kept. Could she really be so brazen?

Someone blocked her route yet again, but that didn't matter. In a split-second, she stretched her arm out between the two women in front of her and snatched the girl's bag off her shoulder.

'Ha!' she yelled, lifting it up into the air, over the girl's head. Karma was about to get a payday, she thought.

'Hey!' The girl span to face her, glaring furiously between thick layers of black eyeliner. 'What the hell are you doing?'

'Me?' Holly laughed bitterly. 'Your time is up.'

'What?'

'You and your friends. I know your game. Well, you might have got away with it before, but not this time. Just you wait. If I find single sugar mouse in here.' She shook the bag for emphasis. 'I'm calling the police.'

The shop had fallen silent, apart from the child in the pushchair, who had started to whine. Even Fruit Jelly Man at the counter had nothing to say. All eyes were on Holly and the girl and the grey bag.

'Give me back my bag.'

'Not until I've called the police.'

'For what?'

'For stealing.'

'I ain't stolen nothing.'

'Yeah? We'll see about that.'

'You're crazy. I'll have you up for harassment.'

Holly snorted. The girl wasn't one of the ones from earlier in the week, but even with the heavy eye makeup and generous application of dark-red lipstick, she couldn't have been over sixteen. Her hair was dyed black, with bright pink streaks down the front and she was chewing gum like she was out of some American, high-school movie.

'You were going towards the staircase,' Holly said.

'Of course I was.'

'So, you admit it. You were going to steal.'

'What?' Shaking her head, the girl frowned. 'I'm sorry, but who the hell are you?'

'Who am I?' Holly fought back the urge to grab the girl by the collar and throw her straight out of the shop. She'd been under no illusion that teenagers were becoming more and more brazen, but this was ridiculous.

'Who am I?' she repeated, taking another step towards the girl. 'I'm the owner. This is my shop. And it's my sweets you were planning on stealing.'

The girl's expression changed. The furious anger she'd been displaying up until that point was replaced by confusion, then outright astonishment. Her jaw dropped. Good, Holly thought. Now you know you're busted.

'You mean she was serious? No way! I thought she was joking.' The girl staggered a little before resting her hand against the wooden banister of the staircase, as if she needed it to keep herself upright. 'Maud wasn't joking? I know she rang me and everything, but she's done that before. I just thought. I just thought...'

The girl was shaking her head, and several of the customers –

who were looking as confused as Holly was now – were whispering amongst themselves.

'Whilst I'm sure that many of us would be intrigued to know the outcome of these theatrics, could you please resolve this matter a little more swiftly?' It was the man at the counter again. 'As I mentioned before, I have a bus to catch.'

'Just one second, sir,' Holly said, in a voice that barely reached a whisper. Feeling like she was missing a massive part of a very small puzzle, she looked at the girl and then at the bag in her hand. Of course it was possible she knew Maud's name. All the locals would know her. She was an institution.

'What about your bag?'

'What about it?'

'You were opening your bag. You were planning on putting something in it.'

'No, I was planning on getting something out of it,' the girl said, unflinching.

'What?' she demanded. 'What were you going to get out of it?'

'Why don't you look for yourself?'

'Hmph!' Fruit Jelly Man huffed. 'This is ridiculous. I will not be coming back here.'

Even with her desperate need for repeat customers, Holly didn't bother trying to make him stay. She and the rest of the shop, remained perfectly motionless, waiting to see what trick the girl had up her sleeve. It was a trick. It had to be.

'Go on,' the girl said, gesturing to the bag in Holly's hand. 'Have a look. Help yourself.'

Swallowing the lump which had lodged itself in her throat, she pulled open the bag to reveal the contents. There wasn't much in there. In fact, to start with, she couldn't see anything at all, until she shifted her head slightly and noticed something folded neatly at the bottom.

'Take it out,' the girl said. 'But don't you dare crease it. Maud was always very particular about neatness.'

Her hand now trembling slightly, she reached inside until her fingers touched fabric. It was enough for her to know what it was. That high thread count that helped it keep its shape, even when you'd been running and up and down the stairs all day. Yet she waited until she'd pulled it all the way out to reveal the embroidery that was stitched across the pocket, to be certain.

Just One More, it read.

'You work here?'

18

'I'm really sorry,' Holly said, for what must have been the sixtieth time. Five o'clock had come around in the blink of an eye and they were upstairs in the storeroom, finally off their feet. Not for a single minute had there been any respite from the flood of customers. Fortunately, Andrea – or Drey, as she liked to be called – was more than capable. And as much as Holly had wanted to reject her offer to stay and help – pretty generous in the circumstances – she was glad she hadn't, particularly as she knew where everything was.

'I still can't believe Maud didn't say anything,' Holly continued. 'I mean, that's exactly the type of thing you'd tell someone if they were taking on your business, don't you think? That it has employees. I think they *have* to tell you that, actually.'

Drey shrugged. 'To be honest, these last few months, she'd been getting worse and worse. I'd try to do as much as I could on the weekends, restocking, writing orders, that type of thing, but she seemed to have stopped caring. To be honest, I don't think she's ever cared that much about it.'

A sadness tugged in Holly's chest.

'The shop was always Agnes' baby,' she said, flicking on the kettle. 'I just don't think she knew how to run it without her. Her heart wasn't in it.'

'Yeah, that's what I've heard people say. She used to talk about her a lot too, you know, Agnes. I would have liked to have met her.'

'She was a very special lady. Very special.'

A cascade of memories ran through her mind. The way Agnes would always give out free sweets when someone said it was their birthday, whatever their age. The way she would dress up in some outrageous costume in the middle of January, because she thought that was when people needed cheering up the most.

'I need to be honest,' Holly said, feeling the weight of responsibility on her. 'The financial situation here isn't ideal. To tell you the truth, I'm not sure how I'm going to pay myself at the minute, let alone someone else. There wasn't anything about paying anyone either, in anything I've seen.'

Drey nodded, like she knew this was coming.

'Well, I suppose, as we're being honest, I should let you know, I'm not technically an employee any more. Maud hasn't paid me for a while now.'

'What?' Holly put the kettle back down with a bump, spilling hot water all over the worktop. 'What do you mean, she hasn't paid you?'

The girl shrugged and looked down. This appeared to be one of her default responses, Holly realised, along with shrugging and avoiding eye-contact, although she'd seen nothing of that in front of the customers. With them she had been quick on her feet, smiley and charming. Now she was timid and reticent, not unlike herself at that age.

'It's not like I mind. To be fair, I'd rather be here than anywhere else. It's like a hobby. People don't normally get paid for their hobbies.'

'How long is a while?' Holly asked, slowly.

Another shrug followed. 'I guess when she first went to sell the place last year, around October. She spoke to solicitors and stuff and realised that with the books looking the way they did, she really couldn't justify keeping me on. Her accountant told her to fire me immediately, actually. So, she cut down my hours a lot. And then she stopped paying me on the day we agreed I'd finish.'

'But you kept coming, anyway?'

This time her question was met by silence.

'I don't mean to sound pathetic or anything,' she eventually replied, 'but it's not like there's much else to do around here, you know, in the village. I've no interest in sitting outside the chippy smoking all weekend, or getting the bus into town to buy some over-priced, crappy T-shirt that's made in a sweatshop in India. I don't do sports either. I do like music, but I'm too young to go to the pub and they only have those folk singers in, anyway. So, I just carried on coming in. I mean I didn't come in every weekend. Like, not if I've got plans or anything. But Maud, well, she's good company, you know?'

'I do.'

'I'm gonna miss her. Where's she gone? Up to Agnes' sister?'

Holly nodded. For some reason, she was feeling almost maternal towards this girl. It could have been her, fifteen years ago, she thought. What would she have done then if Maud and Agnes had said they couldn't afford to keep her on? She'd have been able to get another job somewhere in the village, having got that all-important experience, but would she have wanted to? No, most likely she'd have pressed on, helping out for free when she could, hoping that eventually the tide would turn and they'd have enough to pay her again. In fact, she'd have done exactly the same as Drey had. But for how long? If this girl was planning on going to university soon, then she'd need every penny she could get.

Leaving the kettle and one half-filled mug where they were, she stood up and marched to the top of the stairs.

'Come with me,' she said.

Without waiting for Drey, she strode down the stairs, past the counter, to the cupboard beneath the till, where she had just put the day's takings. It had been the best day of the entire week, and probably her first day of real profit... until now.

'What did she pay you?' she asked, opening the cash box, Drey having now caught up and looking extremely puzzled.

'Sorry?'

'What did Maud pay you, when she did pay you, that is? What was your hourly wage?'

The girl's eyebrows rose to her hairline. 'Umm, well, it was five pounds an hour. I mean, that was what she paid me at the end.'

Holly remained as impassive as she could as she considered the numbers. Twenty years ago, she had been on half that amount. Was that a good rate or a bad one? She didn't know.

'Okay, and you've been coming in for the last six months? Saturdays and Sundays, or just Saturdays?'

'Well, normally both, but not always.'

It was Holly's turn to raise her eyebrows.

'Okay yes, both.'

'So, I guess you've been doing about six hours a day, twice a week, for the last six months? That would make it, with a little rounding off, about fifty hours a month. That's about three hundred hours in total. Three hundred hours at five pounds an hour means the business owes you fifteen hundred pounds.'

The figure nearly made her eyes water. Still, she knew she couldn't live with herself if she didn't put this right. Besides, by the sound of things, Drey had been the one who'd kept the place going as long as it had. And her knowledge could be invaluable.

Holly counted out some notes from the cashbox and put them on the counter.

'This is thirty pounds for today,' she said.

Then, counting out a larger amount, put that down next to the first pile.

'And this a hundred pounds. The first instalment of your back pay.'

'You're joking, right?' Drey didn't move to touch any of it. She seemed rooted to the spot but was unable to take her eyes off the money. 'You can't be serious?'

'Of course, I am. I can't have you working all that time for free.'

'But... But I chose to.'

'Okay, and I'm choosing to reimburse you.'

Knowing it wasn't going to be enough to convince her, Holly shook her head and sighed.

'Look, this place is already crumbling around me. I can see that. I can also see that I can't get it up and running again properly on my own. Today's shown me that. I know I need help. You know the shop. You know the suppliers and the regulars. And you love the shop, just like I do. I think there are going to be some tough times ahead of us. I might have to cut your hours back, here and there. But I need to know that when I finally make this place work, and believe me I will, I did it the right way.'

Still, Drey didn't take the money.

'Please. I need to start this business on the right footing. This is a fresh start for me, and I need it to be exactly that. It won't feel right if this isn't sorted.'

Drey sighed. 'I won't deny, it would help for uni.'

'Great, then put it away in the bank and don't think about it again.'

With the money tucked away in her bag, Drey headed to the door.

'So I'm coming in tomorrow?' she asked, hesitantly.

'I hope so,' Holly replied. 'I don't know how I'd manage another day like this without you. Although you need to lose the gum,' she said, unlocking the door for her to leave.

'Sorry. Bad habit, I know.' She paused, hovering in the door way. 'Thank you,' she said, before finally turning to leave, although she didn't get that far.

'Hey, Humbug,' she said, crouching down as a familiar-looking, black-and-white cat strolled in. He purred as he rubbed his head against her legs, before moving past her into the shop. 'How are you? Shall we see if I've got some treats for you? Let's see what I've got.'

As Drey's hand slipped into the side pocket of her bag, Holly's stomach lurched with surprise.

'You don't feed it in here, do you? Not in the shop?'

Drey looked up from the floor. 'No, of course not. Well, not really. I'm not feeding him exactly. I just give him the occasional cat treat.' She pulled out her hand with a couple of dry-looking biscuits in them. The cat finished his lap of the shop, before returning to Drey, where he gobbled up the treats from her outstretched hand.

For a second, Holly was stunned to silence. 'We can't have a cat in the shop, Drey,' she said when she finally found her voice. 'Environmental Health would have a field day.'

'He never stays that long. Normally he waits outside for me, don't you?'

The cat looked up, obviously hoping there were more biscuits on the way.

'He only ever comes in when it's empty.'

'It can't come in at all. And you can't be feeding it by the front door. It needs to be well away from the building.'

She moved around the counter, ready to shoo him out, when Drey picked it up.

'Sorry,' she said, looking slightly crestfallen as she carried the creature out through the door. 'I think Maud was a little lax when it came to these things. I guess I picked up a bad habit. You hear that, Humbug? Outside only from now on.'

Still in her arms, the cat responded with a noise that was somewhere between a squeak and a purr. There was no denying it was a pretty cat, even though it was somewhat scruffy, but pretty or not, Holly did not want to see it in her shop again. Safely out on the pavement and knowing that Drey understood the new rule, Holly reached out a hand to pet it. Again, the squeaking noise in response.

'So, Humbug?' she said, looking up at Drey.

'You know because he is black and—'

'Black and white, yes I get it. Well as long as Humbug stays outside the shop, we won't have a problem, okay?'

Drey and the cat left. Holly turned back, smiling to herself, feeling brighter than she had all week. With summer just a few weeks away, it wouldn't take long to get the place turning a decent profit again. She was halfway up the stairs, when she heard shop bell jingle and stopped in her tracks, cursing herself for forgetting to lock up again.

'We're closed, I'm afraid,' she called out.

'Good, that means you're free to play.'

The smooth accent was unmistakable and a small fluttering started deep in her belly. As nonchalantly as possible, she turned around and came back down.

'I wondered what had happened to you,' she said, placing a hand on her hip. 'I assumed you'd ghosted me.'

'Please, I'm far too much of a gentleman to do that. And you, Holly Berry, are far too interesting to ever be ghosted. Now, tell me, what are your plans? I'm pretty sure I remember you offering to cook me dinner?'

She scoffed. 'Really? That doesn't sound like me at all.'

'No, I'm fairly certain you did.'

What on earth are you doing, Holly? she asked herself, as she continued to glare mockingly into those deep, grey eyes. He was trouble. A player. And the last thing she needed was another complication in her life. But then, they were such beautiful eyes.

'Fine,' she said, with only the slightest hint of a smile. 'I guess I could whip up something.'

19

'I'll be honest. I'm impressed.'

If she'd had a little more time, Holly would have planned a proper meal. Maybe not three courses, but at least two, carefully considered to complement each other. Instead, it had been a store-cupboard job. Spaghetti with a garlic butter sauce. Not in the slightest bit tricky, or anywhere close to a show stopper, but it tasted good, and that was what counted.

'It's nothing. I'm happy to teach you,' she replied, with a grin.

'Maybe I'll take you up on that.'

They were sitting at Maud's battered, kitchen table. If tables could talk, Holly would love to hear this one's tales. Maud and Agnes were never short of dinner dates, and always happy to tell people about their travels around the world and how they'd ended up in this little corner of the English countryside. If only she'd stayed in closer contact after she moved away, she thought, memories of Agnes' laughter playing in her mind. If only she'd had a few more meals with them here.

'So, you've lasted a whole week then?' Giles said, as he twisted another forkful of spaghetti around on his plate.

'One week, is that really all it's been?'

'Not thinking of throwing the towel in, are you?'

'Not just yet.'

For a second, he let the fork hover above his plate.

'You look tired,' he said.

'Yeah, well, it's been pretty full on.'

'I get it. That's what it's like running your own business. Always something cropping up. I've always loved it. You know, the uncertainty. That risk of whether what you're doing is going to pay off. It's a lot harder than the security of a nine-to-five, knowing that you're getting a steady wage at the end of the month. Particularly when you factor in things like pensions, or buying your own home. Not to mention starting a family. Running a shop is hell if you want that.'

The comments weren't said in a critical way, yet they took far deeper root than Holly would have liked. Did she want a family? That had always been the plan. She had daydreamed about it for years when she'd been with Dan. Two kids. She didn't mind whether they were boys or girls, but ideally no more than three years apart. The houses they'd been looking at had been based on the best school districts, too. God, she had been an idiot. And now here she was, twenty-nine and nowhere near ready to get into another relationship. Had the chance gone forever? The way Giles made running a shop sound, it felt like it wouldn't be possible, even if she did meet the right person. No, it wasn't something she could think about right now. One challenge at a time.

She scooped up her final mouthful of pasta, before putting her cutlery down.

'You know what, it's gonna take a lot more than one tough week to put me off. Me and this shop, we're fated to be together.'

'Is that so?' He grinned. 'Well, I admire your resilience.'

From the kitchen table, they moved to the living room, where they polished off the wine left over from her evening with Caroline. She needed to message her again, she reminded herself. She'd thanked her for the clothes but had not yet replied to her texts asking when they could meet up again. If she didn't respond soon, she might end up losing her only friend in the village, besides Giles, that was, although she wasn't entirely sure she could call him that. To be honest, she had no idea what he was. A distraction from the havoc of running the shop and the daily messages from Dan, probably

At nine o'clock, when her yawning had reached an uncontrollable level, Giles finished his drink and stood up.

'This has been great, Holly Berry,' he said, lifting his coat from the arm of his chair. 'You're quite good fun to talk to, you know that?'

'I have been told,' she said, also standing.

'We should do it again. And no more paying for dinners out either. Not now I know how well you cook.'

'Is that right?'

As he moved in towards her, she felt her heart skip a beat. Was he going to kiss her? And did she even want that? And why had he turned up like this again, after she'd just finished a full day's work, with no chance to have a shower or even retouch her makeup? He moved closer still. Her heart was speeding up, notch by notch. What was she going to do? Should she kiss him back? She had deliberately spent the whole evening in an opposite armchair so as not to give him the wrong impression. But now he was only inches away, leaning in. What was she to do? Tell him she wasn't ready for this? That she wasn't ready to move on so fast? With all these thoughts whirring around her head, she closed her eyes as his face approached. He knew about Dan. He knew she wasn't ready for a relationship, didn't he? Her knees trembled as she smelt his aftershave. Felt his breath on her skin. And then, just as she readied herself for what she thought was to come next, she felt the brush of his lips against her cheek in a quick, swift peck. A moment later and he was standing in the doorway, his coat slung across his arm.

'See you soon, Holly Berry,' he said.

Well, that made the decision easy, she thought.

* * *

The entire next week, almost all of Holly's non-shop-related thoughts were pre-occupied with where she stood regarding Giles Caverty. Was he really that much of a gentleman that he wouldn't even try to kiss her too soon? Or did he really just want to be friends? She'd had plenty of platonic male friends before, but not like this. Guys she'd got to know through work, or through Dan. Not ones that swept her away in their sports car. There was also the distinct possibility that she'd told him far too much about her history with Dan, after the wine-tasting dinner. Maybe that had put him off seeing her as girlfriend material. Maybe he just didn't do relationships, full stop.

'Earth to Holly?' Drey said, balancing precariously in the window display.

In what felt like a minor miracle, Holly had reached another Friday afternoon – and the end of her second week running Just One More – with no major mishaps. It had, dare she say it, gone relatively smoothly. There had been a steady stream of customers, both tourists and regulars, some of the latter seeming to have accepted that she was now a permeant feature there, as opposed to Maud. Some, however, still looked less than ecstatic. She'd win them round. The internet had been installed, too, and her laptop was now upstairs, meaning she could actually email suppliers and keep track of the accounts.

'Hello? Are you going to pass me those or what?'

This time, Drey's attempt to attract Holly's attention worked, as she snapped out of her daydream about Giles and what exactly he was doing when he wasn't belting around the countryside in ludicrously expensive sports cars.

'Sorry, I was just wondering whether I should have got those lollies or not,' she lied, with no intention of mentioning him to anyone at all, particularly her weekend shop assistant. 'Do you think they look out of place? Are they a bit cheap for here?'

'Nah, they look fine. Cheap's not always bad. People come in for a bargain and then leave with a whole bag full. Right, pass me that next jar.'

While Friday afternoons weren't technically one of Drey's days, Holly had done a mad, early-morning dash to the cash and carry to prepare for the weekend; the regular suppliers wouldn't be delivering until the following week. Having got there in time for opening at seven-thirty, she'd raced around the store at breakneck speed, paid and got back in time to open up the shop just an hour later than the normal nine-thirty. Unfortunately, with the constant need to be behind the till, it had been impossible to sort anything out during business hours and she couldn't face trying to do it all by herself anyway, so she'd called Drey and asked if she could swing by after college.

'We've got room for one more in here,' Drey said, now reaching up on tiptoes.

Grabbing a small jar from behind her, she passed it across. Tomorrow would be her eleventh day working without a break. Not that she hadn't done that before, in other jobs, but at least then she'd known there would be a weekend or a holiday around the corner. At this rate, her next day off would be Christmas Day, nine months away. She moved back towards the counter and stopped.

'Everything all right?' Drey asked.

Holly frowned. 'The scales, they look like they're jammed.'

Rather than pointing to zero, as the large, brass indicator should do when there was nothing in the pan, it was pointing to the left, a good ten degrees off centre. Abandoning the window, Drey came and stood beside her.

'They do that sometimes. You just need to give them a bit of a whack here.' With a closed fist, Drey thumped the side of the machine and the pointer quickly sprang back to the centre. 'See, no problem.'

Holly wasn't convinced.

'How long have they been doing that?'

'Oh, ages. They just have occasional sticky moments, that's all.'

Holly was uneasy, and sad. 'We'll need to get new ones,' she said, finally.

'What? Why? They still work just fine.'

She shook her head. 'No, we can't keep them.'

'They're a traditional part of this place. They've got to be as old as Maud.'

There was no disagreeing with that. They were as much of a feature as the jars on the shelves and their pale-blue aprons. But that wasn't the point.

'We can't have faulty scales. The whole business hinges on them. If Trading Standards come for a spot check when they're having one of their dodgy moments, they'll hit us with a hefty fine, at best.'

Drey crinkled her nose. 'It was okay last time. They just gave Maud a small fine and told her to get them sorted.'

'What?' Holly spluttered, nearly choking. 'She had a Trading Standards warning and didn't replace them?'

'Honestly, the way she talked about it, it didn't seem that big a deal. Just a slap on the wrist.'

Holly's jaws were starting to ache from being open so wide and her heart was racing. There's no way it would be just a fine if they were caught selling incorrectly a second time. Most probably they'd be shut down.

'New scales it is, then.'

20

___

Holly threw off her duvet with a sinking feeling. How was it only Tuesday? How was it possible that she was just one day into the week? Not that it should really make any difference to someone to whom weekends meant only more work. Groaning, she rolled over, only to find her muscles more than a little reluctant to move. Sure, since taking on the shop she had done more physical exercise than she had during her and Dan's ill-fated, get-fit pledge two years previously, but she was young in the grand scheme of things. Women twice her age – and more – were running marathons. It was not a comforting thought. The day felt grey already.

Cancelling the snooze button on her alarm, she crawled out of bed and into the shower. While the cottage may have been picture perfect from outside, this relic had the water pressure of a leaky garden hose and the hot-water tank was so small she was lucky to get even a decent hair wash out of it. After shivering her way into her clothes – memories of her childhood surfacing – she drew back the curtains and peered outside.

Given her current state of mind, she was expecting to see dark clouds shrouding the sky and the splatter of rain on the window.

Maybe even the odd bolt of lightning, too. But, instead, she saw a clear-blue sky and sunlight shining down on the crisp, green grass.

Maybe today would be all right after all.

Upon arriving at the shop, she was greeted by loud meowing.

'Good morning, Humbug,' she said, as she knelt down to give him a stroke. 'I'm afraid I don't have any...' She stopped short. 'Oh no, that's disgusting!' she groaned, only just stopping herself from retching.

Looking as proud as punch, he sat back and, using a front paw, pushed a dead mouse towards her.

'I do not want that!' she cried, jumping back as Humbug gave it another nudge, while looking up at her expectantly. 'That is not a nice present to give anyone.'

After fishing around in her handbag, she found a crumpled tissue which she used to gingerly pick up the tiny, limp creature by its tail. The cat looked on as she carried it over to the nearest bin and dropped it in. As she walked back to shut the door, he continued to look pleased with himself.

'No more treats for you, if you do that again,' said in a stern voice and shooed him away. 'Bad cat. You understand. Bad cat.'

* * *

After the rather unpleasant start to the day, things soon improved and it appeared every single person within a fifty-mile radius had decided to take advantage of the beautiful weather and head to the Cotswolds.

'And a quarter of the fruit pips, too,' the man said, as Holly rushed to grab another jar from the shelves. 'And do you sell sugar-free wine gums?'

She forced herself to take a steady breath.

'Not at the minute, I'm afraid.'

'I guess I'll just have to take the normal ones, then.'

It was hard to complain. Non-stop customers and not just buying one or two items but five or more. She also sold three of the boxes of chocolate pralines, over a dozen boxes of fudge, and was all out of chocolate hedgehogs. The difference was, on the weekends, she had Drey to help but today she had back-to-back lectures, and Holly was run ragged by herself. She was also on edge about the *sticky* scales.

'Oh, and just grab me one more of those peanut brittle bars will you, love?' the man said, just as she had taken hold of the wine gum jar.

Finally, she had everything rung up on the till.

'That's £18.24,' she said, packing his purchases away into one of their paper, carrier bags.

'That should keep me going for a bit then, shouldn't it?' he said, taking it from her and disappearing outside.

'Who's next please?' she called, as she replaced the fruit pips and wine gums on the shelf, before turning back to the counter.

'I guess asking if you've got time for a quick afternoon coffee would be a bit pointless?'

The baby that was strapped to her chest was currently facing forward, with two, bare, chubby legs poking out from either side of the harness, and while his mother's hands were once again laden with shopping she did, this time, appear to be managing only the one child.

'Caroline, oh I am so sorry.' The guilt of all the unanswered messages hit her squarely in the chest. 'I promise I kept meaning to message you back. It's just been so hectic.'

Simultaneously smiling and wiping something green from the corner of her baby's mouth, Caroline waved away her apology.

'Don't worry, I can see that. And I don't want to get in your way now, so I'll go. But just text me, okay? Any time you want. It can't be easy running this place on your own.'

'Thank you.' There was a relief that came from having someone understand that sometimes life got in the way, even when you didn't want it to.

'Tonight, tomorrow, whenever you want to talk is good for me. I'm just the other end of the phone if you need me.'

'Thank you.'

With Caroline slipping out of the queue, Holly smiled in anticipation at the next customer. Upon seeing nothing in his hands, her heart sank a little. When they brought the jars to the counter, it helped speed things up a little.

'Sorry about the wait, sir. How can I help you?'

One thing that you got used to, working in a sweet shop, was seeing all the happy faces and smiling back at them in return. This had been Agnes' number one rule, after all. She felt that, whether they realised it or not, it was almost impossible to feel miserable surrounded by such of kaleidoscope of sweets and chocolate. Almost impossible not to feel a sense of awe and joy at the endless array of colours and aromas that teased their senses. Unfortunately, the man currently standing directly in front of her was living proof that it was only *almost* impossible.

His tie was a skinny, red, polyester number and, to her mind, only served to accentuate his long, thin, reddish nose. His face was sallow, with patchy stubble, and as he cleared his throat, she wondered how it was possible that someone, who was clearly not much older than her, could look so very tired and worn.

'Are you the proprietor?' he asked.

'Well, I'm in charge of the shop,' she replied, suddenly a little confused how her unusual agreement with Maud defined her current role. 'How can I help you?'

The man inhaled through his nose, causing his nostrils to flatten. She kept her smile in place.

'I'm from the HSE,' he said, as if that were an explanation.

The expression on her face clearly showed the acronym meant nothing to her.

'I'm a health inspector,' he said, enunciating every syllable. 'And I'm here to check the premises.'

21

Had Holly inadvertently offended some petty village god? It could be the only explanation for the run of recent events that seemed to be plaguing her. The man with the long nose and cheap tie was staring straight at her, waiting for a response.

'You're a health inspector?' she finally said.

'Yes.' He opened his wallet and pulled out a small card but she was feeling far too disorientated to read what it said. Still, the bold-type letters that took up half the space were difficult to ignore: HSE. 'I am from the Health and Safety Executive.'

'Excuse me, can we get a move on?' The request came from the back of the queue. Several children were squirming to get out of their parent's grasp, already having stood still for an impressively long time as they waited to get their hands on their chocolate jazzies and milk bottles. There must have been at least half a dozen customers waiting.

She looked at the Inspector questioningly. 'Well?' she asked.

With what was less a nod and more a simple dip of the chin, he stepped to the side to make room for the customer behind him.

'We will start the inspection once you have finished seeing to these people.'

The transactions went without event. Bags were packed, money handed over and, before she knew it, the entire queue was quickly served and out of the door. The Inspector had changed the sign to *Closed* to ensure no one else entered. Now they were alone, she could see he'd brought with him a large briefcase. With the door locked, he placed said briefcase on the counter and out of it pulled a pair of rubber gloves.

'You have recently purchased this shop.' The words were said as a statement, not a question, although Holly felt the need to reply.

'Well sort of. I am in the process of buying it.'

'But you are currently in charge of the business?'

'Yes, I suppose so. I just didn't realise... is this something I should have prepared for?'

Whether or not he heard her, Mr Health Inspector chose not to answer as he performed a slow lap of the shop floor. Given that it was hardly vast, it shouldn't have taken that long, and yet every footstep was ponderous. Having completed one entire circuit, he stopped, sniffed and picked up a bag of fudge. Even from a distance, she could see that he had selected the handmade, lemon-drizzle flavour. With oodles of lemon zest and double cream, it was one of her favourites, although she suspected he had no intention of actually trying it. He wiped his gloved hand over the top and the bottom of the bag, before finally turning and looking at her.

'Did you make this on the premises?' he asked, holding it up.

'No.' She shook her head. 'Why? Is something wrong?'

'I don't know yet.'

With the fudge still in his hand, he moved along to the jars and stopped in front of the toffees. He was looking at the soft, chewy ones in paper wrappers. The dark, treacle-flavoured pieces had always been rather bitter for Holly's tastes. Although it was probably the perfect confectionary for her current company.

'What about this? Do you make this on the property?'

'No. I don't make any sweets myself.'

'Is that so?'

Wordlessly, he moved back to his briefcase, where he dropped the fudge inside, before handing her the jar of toffees.

'I will need a sample of these. For further inspection, you understand.'

She didn't understand. She didn't understand anything at all, expect the fact that health inspectors had the power to close places down. Realising he was still waiting, she hurriedly grabbed the jar and tipped some into a paper bag. How many treacle toffees did one inspector need, she wondered? One? Two? A hundred?

'Upstairs.' He pointed. 'What do you do up there?'

'It's the storeroom,' she replied, 'where we keep the spare stock.'

'Lead the way.'

The space, which doubled as the world's tiniest staffroom, had always felt somewhat claustrophobic but, at that precise moment, with the Health Inspector's long nose peering into everything, Holly was finding it so stuffy and hot she was worried she might pass out.

'This...' he said, indicating the yellow bucket that Maud had placed to catch the drips from the roof, 'is a trip hazard.'

'Sorry,' she said, grabbing it and moving it to the sink. 'I was doing some cleaning earlier; I must have forgotten to pop it away.'

He huffed before moving on.

'These sweets,' he said, jabbing one of the large, three-kilogram bags with his finger. 'These are what you put in the jars downstairs?'

'Yes, that's right.'

'And what do you use to transfer them?'

'Erm, we just kind of tip them in,'

The heavy sigh that reverberated from his lungs indicated that he wasn't happy.

'I mean we use gloves, obviously, and scoops too. We never actually touch any of the sweets.' From off a shelf, she pulled down a pack of disposable gloves and a scoop. 'We throw them away after each use. The gloves, that is, not the scoops. The scoops we wash. I know it's terrible for the environment. The gloves, I mean. I'd much prefer it if we had some sort of reusable option, but...' Holly stopped before she inadvertently dug herself in any deeper. Damn her over-talking under stress.

Offering the gloves and scoop little more than a cursory glance, the Inspector walked away.

'What about washing hands? There are no signs saying to wash your hands. You have other staff besides yourself, I assume?'

Holly could feel her heart rate increasing. 'Just the one. Part time.'

'You need signs. Signs to make sure they wash their hands.'

'Yes, I can see that now. I'll get on it straight away.'

After more peering and probing, he headed back downstairs and, for a moment, Holly thought this unexpected nightmare might be about to end. That was when the swabbing started, at which point she thought she might go into full cardiac arrest.

From out of his briefcase, he produced a series of extra-long cotton buds. First, he swiped the weighing scales. Then under them. Then he moved to the shelves where he took yet more samples: on, beneath, and inside whichever jars he picked. After each swabbing, he placed the cotton bud in an individual cellophane bag, which he dropped into his briefcase. And it didn't stop at the jars.

How it was possible for him to need to test so many places was a mystery to Holly, and the longer it went on, the more concerned she grew.

'Do you not need to label the bags to say where the swabs came from?' she asked.

He had taken them from both the counter and the doorknob too, now and, from what she could see, he'd placed the bags in his briefcase without so much as a number on them. Perhaps there were health inspector rules. Perhaps they always took them in a certain order. Or perhaps there were tiny labels on the cotton buds that she couldn't see. He offered her zero eye contact as he dropped yet another into an unmarked plastic bag.

'I don't tell you how to do your job. I'd appreciate it if you'd extend me the same courtesy.'

From that point on, she remained silent and just watched as he continued to make his way around. When this was finished, he lifted various items off the shelves and took photos with his phone, then ordered her to provide him with samples of a dozen other sweets, from mint imperials to sour worms, all of which went into his briefcase with the swabs. Outside, she could see buses arriving to take away the hordes of tourists, many of whom had not had the chance to set foot inside Just One More.

Finally, over an hour after he had first stepped foot on the premises and with a large selection of sweets and over fifty swabs in his possession, the Inspector clipped his briefcase shut and lifted it from the counter.

'I will be in touch,' he said.

22

By the time the Health Inspector left, Holly was in no mood to serve any customers. The whole experience had left her both exhausted and deflated. Besides, it was only ten minutes until closing time anyway, so she kept the door sign on *Closed* and set about straightening the shelves that he had left irritatingly untidy. She replaced the yellow bucket in its spot upstairs and then picked up her phone and ordered a new set of weighing scales with forty-eight-hour express delivery, in case some other official was lined up to pay her a visit. Next, she fired off a message to Caroline, to see if the offer of joining her for a drink that evening was still open. In less than a minute, the reply pinged back.

I'll be there at 6. That way I get out of bath time too.

At exactly 6 p.m. and only minutes after getting back to the cottage herself, Holly heard a knock on the door. This time, Caroline had arrived with a bottle of gin and a selection of flavoured tonics.

'I don't know how you're still standing,' she said, after Holly had recited everything that had happened since their last meeting.

She offered a short chuckle in response. 'To be fair, neither do I. I really don't mean to whine. The shop's doing okay, all things considered, but I haven't heard from the mortgage company yet. I really thought they'd have gotten back to me by now.'

'These things always take time and I imagine it takes longer with a business. And remember, no news is good news.'

'Maybe. I'm sure you're right. If they were going to say no, I'm sure they would have done it by now.'

'Exactly.'

'The Health Inspector dropping in like that was crap, though.'

Despite having announced when she'd first arrived that she wouldn't be having more than one drink, Caroline topped them both up with a second, extra-large measure.

'I'll be honest, I didn't think you made any sweets on the property. I thought you bought them all in.'

'We do. As far as I'm aware, there's never been anything made on the premises.'

'What about ice cream? Do you sell that in the summer?'

Holly stopped to sniff her newly poured drink and, judging it almost 100 per cent gin, topped it up with more tonic.

'The summer? I've only just made it through three weeks, remember?' she said, before actually answering Caroline's question. 'But no, we don't sell ice cream. Agnes always wanted to, but Maud thought it would be too stressful. Why do you ask?'

'It's probably nothing, but Michael used to work for the Council. He had friends at the HSE and I'm sure I remember one of them saying that shops like yours don't have Health and Safety inspections. Not unless they make food on the premises or they sold ice cream, because that counts as food. I'm sure that's what he said, because then we ended up in this daft conversation about how long could you live on Sherbet Dib Dabs. Or was it strawberry laces? I can't remember the details, but I'm sure that was the gist of it.'

Happier with her substantially diluted G&T, Holly pulled her knees up under her as she considered Caroline's comment. It was becoming apparent that she didn't know half as much about running a sweet shop as she thought she did.

'Maybe they changed the rules,' she said with a groan. 'They're always doing that, aren't they?'

'You're probably right,' Caroline replied, although Holly couldn't help but notice a slight look of uncertainty as she spoke.

Given how much she wanted to stop talking about yet-another disastrous day, she decided to broach a subject she'd been considering mentioning all evening. With her feet now firmly squashed beneath her, she shifted just a fraction.

'Caroline,' she said, trying to sound as casual as possible. 'Do you know anyone by the name of Giles Caverty?'

The twinkle in her friend's eyes was immediate. 'Giles Caverty? Everyone knows him.'

'They do? Why?'

'Charmingly suave, devilishly good-looking, wouldn't trust him as far as you could throw him? The question is, how do you know him?'

Given that it wasn't the most enamouring description of the man, she was reluctant to mention their previous semi-dates. 'He's just someone who's come into the shop a couple of times, that's all,' she said.

'Do people who come into the shop regularly give you their full name?' Caroline asked with a smirk.

'Fine, forget I asked. It was just out of genuine, adult curiosity, that's all. I can't have you as my only friend in the village, you know.'

'Trust me, Giles Caverty is only ever out for himself. Besides, why can't I be your only friend? I'm marvellous company.'

'You're right. I had completely forgotten that.'

Caroline's grin split wide across her face, causing a warmth that Holly considered only partially caused by the gin. After such a terrible day, she hadn't expected such a pleasant end to it.

'Let's drink to that then, shall we?' Caroline said, raising her glass ready to clink it against Holly's. 'To bloody good company.'

'To bloody good company.'

* * *

'Why the hell is the water bill so high? Have these people even seen how small this sink is? This is insane.'

Talking to herself had become part and parcel of her life alone in the shop. After Tuesday's perfect weather, the rest of the week had been bitterly disappointing, with a great, grey drizzle settling in and unwilling to budge. Customers had been slow coming, and even those that did head into the shop seemed reluctant to part with their money. Many walked out, grumbling over her prices (which were extremely reasonable, she thought) and most of her sales were limited to just one or two sticks of rock. Once again, the financial situation was at the forefront of her mind. If she could just get a good run up to Easter, and with a decent range of seasonal stock in place, then she should be fine.

Pile them high and watch them fly. That was what Agnes used to say, and she hoped she was right. Putting her personal credit card to work again, she now had extra jars filled with chocolate mini-eggs, chocolate praline eggs, Easter nests, chocolate bunnies and more. You name it, she had it. But you still needed customers to sell them to. So much for running your own business and financial freedom.

By Friday, the drizzle had turned to full-on rain and was so bad that even with her umbrella, her jeans were soaked to the knees by the time she reached the shop that morning. Fortunately, for the first time all week, the village was busy, and the rain was doing a good job of driving people into the shop. A bit too good a job.

'Can you please leave your umbrellas outside?' Holly had to shout, above the drumming of the rain against the window. 'There's an umbrella stand just by the door.

'Sir, if you could just put that down.

'I'm sorry, the dog can't come in.

'No madam, we do not have anywhere you can hang your coat to dry.'

'Excuse me, would you please stop your children using the sticks of rock for sword fights?'

It had been the same for nearly two hours.

'Need some help?' Amid the sea of the faces, she saw Drey, her black eyeliner just visible beneath her dark hood.

'Don't you have lectures?' Holly asked, breathless at the thought of a moment's respite.

'Not 'til later. I can spare half an hour,' she replied.

'You're an angel.'

Thankfully, the new scales were making life a lot easier.

'I didn't think I'd like them,' Drey admitted, measuring a hundred grams of chocolate eclairs in the shiny, new, metal pan, before typing the price onto the screen. 'But they make this so much quicker.'

'I know,' Holly agreed. 'And I don't think they look that bad. Honestly, it's just a relief to know they aren't going to get me in trouble like the last ones might have done. Besides, we have lots more room on the counter top now.'

Between them, they were soon able to get through the queue and still had time to spare before the half hour was up.

'Do you mind manning the fort for another five minutes, so I can grab a bite to eat?' Holly asked, unable to ignore her growling stomach. 'I've got some sandwiches upstairs. I just need to run up and get them.'

'It's fine. Put your feet up. I don't need to leave for a few minutes yet.'

'You're amazing. You know that if this place ever earns a decent profit again, you are definitely getting a pay rise. Although,' her eyes narrowed, 'are you chewing gum again?'

'Sorry. Forgot,' Drew replied, and hastily spat it out into the bin. 'Last time. I promise.'

Upstairs in the storeroom, she flicked on the kettle and grabbed her sandwiches from her bag. Five minutes. That was definitely too little time for a nap, though she desperately felt like she needed one. Closing the fridge door, she put the milk bottle next to her mug, when something cold and wet struck her on the back of the neck. Brushing it away, another droplet hit her hand.

'That doesn't feel good,' she said. She glanced at the container on the floor. 'Wow.' The little bucket, that usually had less than a centimetre in it at worst, was now three-quarters full. With all the rain they'd been having, it wasn't surprising. It had probably been filling up, bit by bit, all week. Carefully picking it up, she poured the water down the sink then returned it to its position on the floor.

By the time she'd made her tea and closed the fridge again, the bottom of the bucket was already covered.

Leaving her drink to cool, she watched as the water dripped rapidly into the bucket. Large, round droplets were splashing down. With all thoughts of lunch now abandoned, she stood on tiptoes and studied the ceiling. There was no sign of a hole, but there was a considerable wet patch and more than just a little bit of water coming through. If it kept raining like this overnight, she'd need a bathtub underneath it. Maybe she could find a way of blocking it off. Then she'd be fine. After all, today was meant to be the worst of the weather before it bucked up for the weekend.

Recalling a roll of gaffer tape in one of the drawers, she found it, dragged a chair over to the middle of the room and moved the bucket out of the way. She hesitated for a second, considering calling Drey up to help her. No, it was hardly a big job. Just a bit of tape over the region where the water seemed to be coming from. Besides, she could hear Drey talking to a customer downstairs, and the last thing she wanted to do was interrupt her in the middle of serving someone.

Climbing up onto the chair, she took the tape in one hand and stretched a length across the area where the droplets were budding. It wouldn't stick. This was hardly surprising, she thought to her herself, given how damp it was. She just needed to use a little more force, that was all. Reaching up on tiptoes, she pressed her palm up with as much strength as she could manage and then some. It was certainly lessening the flow, she thought, as the water now ran down her arm. She added a few more strips of tape alongside the first and then a few across at right angles, for good measure.

The water stopped. She stepped down from the chair to admire her handiwork and dry her wet arms. But, as she looked back up, she could see the tape beginning to bulge, just a little at first but then more and more. Almost holding her breath, she climbed back onto the chair and pushed her hand against the tape again. Oh dear. She could feel water sloshing behind it now. Then, with a sickening crack, the makeshift patch and a good chunk of the ceiling came straight down on top of her.

23

'DREY!'

A deluge of rainwater filled her nostrils as Holly screamed at the top of her voice.

'What the hell...?' Drey had appeared almost instantly at the top of the stairs, her jaw now dropping as she looked on, speechless.

In a futile and desperate effort, Holly was holding her hands against the hole in the ceiling, trying to stop the water that was now soaking her through to the skin.

'What happened?' Drey asked.

'I... I...'

'What should I do?'

'Quick, move out the way. I've got this.' It was a man's voice.

As two, strong hands helped her down from the chair, Holly realised Drey wasn't the only person who had raced upstairs. Currently taking her place on the chair and stripping off his jacket was none other than the bicycle man. Bunching it into a ball, he wedged his coat into the hole, although not in time to stop his blue, cotton shirt turning translucent with the water that was running down his arms and plastering his hair to his face as he held the makeshift plug in place. If the situation hadn't been so desperate, she probably would have given more thought to how well he would have fitted into a Jane Austin TV adaptation. But there was no time for that.

'Get my phone out my pocket,' he snapped at her. 'Ring Jamie.'

'Your phone?'

'In my trouser pocket. Hurry up, will you?'

She hesitated. Groping in a strange man's trouser pocket didn't feel like something you should do, even if they'd told you to.

'Hurry up!'

Not wanting to argue with him, as he was currently holding her livelihood together, she stuck her hand in and pulled it out.

'Is it working?' he asked.

She shook it and wiped off some surface water. 'Looks like it.'

'Good. The access code is 1234. Go to recent calls and find Jamie's number. It should be near the top.'

Thinking better of advising him at that moment that he really should use a more secure pass number, she found the name and tapped it.

'It's ringing,' she said.

'Good, hold it against my ear,' he said, leaning down as far as he could in the circumstances.

Whatever was said, whatever conversation took place, Holly wasn't aware. Everything was spinning like a whirlpool in front of her. Literally. The floor was soaked, with great puddles starting to form. The bags of sweets were drenched. Were there electrics in the floor? she wondered. Fixing a roof like this, what would that cost? Hundreds? Thousands? The *ifs* and *buts* swirled around in her head.

'I think the rain's stopped,' Drey said, her voice bringing Holly back to the present. She shuffled past the man, whose hands and jacket were still enclosed in ceiling plaster, and peered out of the window. 'Yes, it has. It's stopped. It looks pretty clear, in fact. I don't think it's going to start again any time soon.'

Despite the relief that should have come from this bit of news, Holly's attention was still on the man, whose shirt was now entirely see-through and clinging to his body. He now carefully lowered his jacket and then stepped down from the chair. Holly stared up. Beyond the damaged ceiling, she could just make out a small gap in the roof, where sunlight was now shining through. She was confused as to how such a small hole could cause so much destruction, but that was of little comfort at that precise moment.

'You need to close the shop,' he said.

'Really? I hadn't thought of that,' she replied, sarcastically.

Ignoring her comment, he turned his attention to her assistant.

'Drew. It is Drew, isn't it?'

'Drey.'

'Sorry, Drey. Do you have any spare towels or mops?'

She retrieved Maud's ancient mop and held it up. 'No towels, I'm afraid.'

'Okay, can you head over to the bank for me, please?'

'The bank?' asked Holly in surprise. 'Why on earth the bank?'

Ignoring her, he continued to speak to Drey.

'Just tell them Ben sent you. Ask for a couple of mops and a few packets of paper towels.'

'Sorry, I still don't understand. Who are you? And why exactly are you ordering my staff about?' she persisted.

'Why?' he said, finally turning to her. Water continued to drip off strands of dark hair that were plastered across his brow. 'I'm sorry, would you rather we leave it until all this soaks through to the electrics? Or do you have a better suggestion?'

Drey shifted uncomfortably between the pair.

'Should I...?'

'Yes, go to the bank,' Holly said, defeated.

With Drey gone, the pair were left in an awkward silence, broken only by the drip-drip of water that continued to invade her storeroom.

She should probably say thank you, she thought. After all, it might have been a lot worse, if he hadn't come up to help. Still, the words appeared to get stuck in her throat. As they stood there in their saturated states, the pause stretched out even longer, before finally he cleared his throat.

'Jamie should be here soon.'

Holly nodded, although she had no idea who Jamie was.

'I'm sorry,' Holly began. 'And thank you.'

'I'm Ben,' he stretched out his hand, only to notice his wrinkled skin and quickly withdraw it. 'Ben Thornbury.'

'Holly... Holly Berry.'

* * *

Jamie, it turned out, was a slightly built, vaguely familiar woman, similar in age to Holly, dressed in dungarees and a hard hat, who barely paused for a breath before pitching a ladder on the side of the shop and starting work on the roof.

Drey returned, armed with two mops, an extra bucket and half a dozen packets of paper towels.

Ben Thornbury now took his leave, with barely a farewell or a, 'Good luck'.

'Why don't you go home? I've got this,' Holly said to Drey, as she began the task of mopping up the water. 'There's not much more you can do here.' Another thought struck her. 'Oh crap! You had a lecture. Are you going to get into trouble? I'm so sorry. I can to write your teacher a note or something, if that would help?'

'A note? Not sure if those are still used any more, Grandma.'

Drey folded a strip of chewing gum into her mouth. Holly resisted the urge to shudder.

'Don't worry. It'll be fine.'

'Are you sure?'

'Honestly. They usually just go over the same old stuff because people didn't bother listening properly the first time around. I'll help you do this.'

Cleaning up was not an easy task. Fortunately, for the most part, the damage seemed superficial. By some miracle, the water had managed to miss all the plug sockets and had puddled mainly in the middle of the floor or on the sealed, plastic bags of sweets. In fact, the only stock that was ruined was a cardboard box of liquorice root. Given that she'd barely sold three pieces of the stuff since taking over, it didn't seem like a massive loss.

While Holly and Drey spent an hour ringing out mops and dabbing with paper towels, Jamie was hammering away on the roof above them, hopefully fixing the leak. She finally climbed down, an impressive tool belt laden with gadgets, Holly noticed.

'All done,' she announced, cheerily.

'Thank you, so much. I don't know what I would have done without you,' Holly said. 'I don't suppose you'd know anything about fitting CCTV would you?' The cameras had arrived a few days ago.

'Shoplifters?' Jamie asked.

'Just the once. They haven't been cheeky enough to try again, but I don't want to risk it.'

'Sensible thinking. Particularly when it comes to summer. Now where do you want me to put them?'

Where indeed?

They decided to position the first one in plain sight as you entered the shop, as an obvious deterrent, and angled it towards the display by the door, from where the expensive chocolates had been stolen. The second one had a wide-angle lens and she asked Jamie to fix it in the far corner on a wooden beam, where it would take in most of the shelves and the counter area. She could have placed it so that it pointed to the stairs. That way she'd see if anyone tried to gain access to the stock room. But she'd likely spot someone doing that, so discounted the idea. Within minutes she had a live feed relaying the camera pictures straight to her phone.

'Apparently it records everything and saves it to a cloud,' she said, quite impressed with her purchase.

By the time they were finished, all the other the shops had closed. The last of the cars was reversing out of its parking space and the rows of street lights that ran parallel to the river had started to flicker on, emitting their hazy, orange glow.

'Time for me to head home,' Drey said, after a brief gander at the video. 'I'll see you tomorrow, for more adventures?'

'Let's hope not.'

Jamie laughed. 'I take it this place has been a bit of a handful.'

With a long sigh, Holly closed down the video app on her phone and rubbed her eyes.

'Just feels like it's one thing after another,' she said. She waited until Drey was outside and out of earshot before she continued. 'This is just the latest in a long list of disasters. You might as well hit me with it. How much do I owe you?'

There was no point beating around the bush. It wasn't going to be cheap, particularly when you considered that the door repairs had come in at over three hundred pounds

'Well, it's not great. But it's not terrible. I checked the whole roof. There were half a dozen tiles that needed replacing, all told, or you'd have a swimming pool rather than a sweet shop by the time next winter comes, but the rest should hold out okay. Look, I don't know about you, but I'm parched. Why don't we look at the numbers over a drink in the pub? I promise it won't be that bad.

Also, you can tell me how you got Ben so enamoured with you. It normally takes him months to even speak to someone new, let alone a woman. And here he is, calling in the cavalry for you.'

'Ben Thornbury?' Holly needed to check they were talking about the same person. 'I don't think I've done anything to impress him at all. In fact, ever since I caused him to crash his bicycle, I'm pretty sure he thinks I'm the absolute worst.'

'That was you?' Jamie's eyes widened as her smile grew. 'He was fuming for days after that.'

'I can imagine. I tried to pay for his repairs but...'

Jamie shook her head. 'That's not Ben's style. He's got plenty of people in the village who owe him favours for this, that and the other when it comes to the bank. Wouldn't surprise me if the cycle shop fixed it up for free.'

'The bank?'

'He's the manager there.'

'Ah, I see,' she said.

'Now, how about you and I head to the pub to get that drink? Then I can answer every question you have about the state of the roof... and the village's number-one bachelor.'

And for reasons Holly couldn't quite fathom, she felt herself blushing.

24

'The Catherine Wheel okay?' Jamie asked, nodding her head towards a pub on the other side of the river.

'Sounds great,' Holly replied.

Bourton had always boasted a good selection of watering holes when Holly was growing up there, but now it felt like there'd been an explosion of them. There were bistros and bars, cafes and coffee shops, not to mention a good-old greasy spoon. Judging by its sleek décor and low-hung lightbulbs, this place was clearly new and, going by the number of people there, very popular. Jamie managed to spot a small, unoccupied table tucked away in a corner.

'You go and grab it,' she said. 'I'll get the drinks.'

'Are you sure?'

'Of course. You've had enough of a day as it is. Besides, while you had to shut up shop for the afternoon, I had an unexpectedly lucrative day.'

There was no arguing with that one, although the thought of what she must owe caused a knot to corkscrew in her stomach. Even if the cost of the roof wasn't as bad as she feared, it was still going to be another chunk of money from her deposit. Fingers crossed, the mortgage broker would come back to her sooner rather than later.

Once she had secured the table, she instinctively reached for her phone. What had people done when they were forced to wait by themselves in the pre-mobile days, she wondered? It was hard to remember now. Would she have read a book? Maybe, if she'd had one handy. Perhaps she'd have just people watched. Not that it mattered. She had her phone and, she noticed, several messages.

At the top of the screen, was one from Dan. Still messaging, although whether it was a grovelling apology or an angry expletive, she didn't even care any more.

'Delete,' she said, swiping her finger across it. And then his next one and the one after that. However, the following one she opened to read.

Fancy a drink? I can come to you.

Giles. It had been a while, but this was clearly his MO, sweeping in and out whenever he fancied it. To be fair, she had been way too busy to even think about seeing him, but the message made her smile, despite Caroline's warning. Maybe he was a player, and maybe he was only after one thing, but it wasn't like he was getting that from her. Besides, it was nice to get a little attention now and then.

At the Catherine Wheel. Horrible day. Come join us.

She had just pressed send when Jamie returned to the table, rather expertly carrying two glasses and a full, open bottle of wine.

'I think we're both in need of this.'

'You are amazing.' Holly reached up and took the glasses.

'So, I'm guessing from today's little escapade that the sweet shop's not been the most lucrative of investments?'

'It's had its ups and downs,' she replied. She didn't want to be cagey, but as nice as Jamie seemed, she wasn't going to start divulging details of her financial situation to all and sundry. So, instead, she changed the topic of conversation.

'Did you grow up in the village?' she asked. 'I feel we should probably have known each other from school, although I think almost everyone I grew up with here has upped and moved on.'

'Well, there's not that much work in the villages, is there? Not that I can complain; I get by just fine. All the new houses they're building. A shame, though. Soon all the countryside will be gone. Half a dozen walking trails have disappeared since I moved here, and that was less than ten years ago.'

Holly nodded sadly. She hadn't been on single walk or bike ride since she'd come back to the Cotswolds. Perhaps the favourite routes she used to know, the ones her parents would take her on every sunny, Sunday afternoon, had disappeared to make way for new estates. It was something she needed to look into.

'So how did you get into the whole roofing business?' she asked, after a sip of her drink. 'It doesn't seem like a natural career for, well...'

'A woman?'

'Turns out I'm the world's worst shopkeeper and the world's worst feminist.'

Jamie laughed.

'Don't worry, I won't hold it against you. I'm from the Lake District, originally,' she told her. 'Loved mountaineering, hiking, you name it. I've been climbing since I was born, strapped to my father. I dropped out of uni to follow a boy down here when I was nineteen and there was an apprenticeship going. It just seemed like the right thing to do. I was never really suited to academia; sitting and listening to people lecture on about things, it's just not my style. But I do other things besides roofing. You know what it's like in the current climate. It's important to have your fingers in a few pies.'

'It is?' With her previous, steady job, it had never really occurred to her, but now with a far less reliable wage, she could see how useful it might be. 'So, what other things do you do?'

Jamie paused to top up their glasses, even though Holly's was still quite full.

'Oh, I've got a few things on the go. I run children's art classes on the weekends. That's fun and brings in a bit of cash too. And I do painting. Indoor, paint-your-kitchen type painting, but also more artistic stuff, like murals, too.'

'That sounds cool.'

'Yeah, it keeps my creative side alive. I've also been known to run the occasional Ann Summers party as well, selling "massagers" to some of the more senior ladies in the village.'

Wine spurted from Holly's nose as she coughed in surprise. 'Sorry? You're not serious?'

'Course I am. They're the perfect clients. They've got the money to spend and they've reached that age when you don't care what anyone thinks. Besides, the parties are always a hoot. I tried doing makeup ones for a while, you know, like Avon and Body Shop, but I just couldn't be bothered testing out all the stuff and doing myself up beforehand. It's just not me.'

'But selling vibrators to old women is?'

'I like being around old folks. They say what they mean. It's refreshing.'

At the mention of that, it all suddenly clicked into place.

'You came into the shop before, when I first opened. You were buying all those sweets for the people in some home or other. Is that another of your jobs?'

While offering her a napkin for the wine Holly hadn't noticed she'd spat everywhere, Jamie shook her head. 'No, that's just because I enjoy it. I volunteer at the home once or twice a week. Whenever I get time, really. Like I said, I find them refreshing.'

Wow, Holly thought to herself. When she'd been living in the city, she'd had time for just two things: work and Dan. Now she'd moved, she was down to just work. Maybe she needed to look at how she was spending her time. Perhaps she could find out what other hobbies Giles had, besides old sports cars and turning up out of nowhere.

'So, the guy you moved here to be with,' she asked. 'What happened to him? Are you still together?'

Once again, Jamie laughed.

'God no. I was nineteen. And deluded. I think he moved to Brighton, or somewhere like that. I've no idea what he's up to these days.'

'Are you seeing anyone now?'

She was just about to answer, when the pub door opened and she stood up and waved her arms. 'Ben,' she called. 'Over here.'

When he arrived at their table, she wrapped her arms around him in a hug. 'You came. Great. You sit down, and I'll get you a pint. Cider?'

'Just a coke will be fine,' he replied, giving Holly the slightest of nods.

'Don't be silly. I'll get you cider. Holly, do you think we ought to get another bottle?'

'No. Definitely not,' she replied. Less than one glass in and she was already starting to feel light headed. That's what happened when you didn't have time for lunch and lived on a staple diet of sherbet lemons and strawberry laces.

'Maybe in a bit, then. Okay guys, I won't be a second. Don't get up to anything while I'm gone.'

As Jamie disappeared back to the bar, Holly couldn't help but feel an overwhelming urge to call her back. No matter how casual Ben was attempting to look, with no tie and his collar unbuttoned, she couldn't help but notice how her pulse started to rise as he took the seat opposite her. Obviously, he had to be a bank manager. The disapproving looks. The air of condescension.

'So...' she said, aware that the silence had now become embarrassing, 'did you do anything exciting today?'

25

Silence was something Holly was not good at. Generally, she'd waffle to fill the void, try to talk away the awkwardness. But at that precise moment, her throat was dry and her mind was blank. And by the looks of things, she wasn't the only one who was feeling that way. So far, Ben's eyes had gone from the bar and Jamie, to the ceiling, the table and back again. Basically, anywhere rather than looking at her. Neither of them said anything. They just sat there. In silence. It was up to her. If someone didn't say something soon, this could go on until last orders. She took a deep breath.

'Jamie did a great job.'

'Did Jamie manage to fix everything?'

Their questions came out simultaneously.

'Yes,' she said. 'At least I think so. I guess we'll see when we get the next storm.'

She'd meant the comment to be funny, but by the look on his face, it would appear that Mr Ben Thornbury, bank manager, wasn't much into jokes.

'Jamie's a very good person. She takes her job extremely seriously. Not to mention she does a lot of good work in the community.'

'Yes, she told me.'

A sudden realisation dawned on her: firstly as to why the whole thing felt so awkward and secondly, as to the reason he'd looked so surprised to see her there. Inadvertently, she'd become a third wheel.

'I didn't realise,' she said.

'Didn't realise what?'

'That you and Jamie are a couple.'

There was a spluttering sound more than an actual laugh, but when he removed his hand from his mouth, she was amazed to see him actually smiling.

'You two look like you're having a good time,' Jamie said, reappearing with Ben's cider. 'What's so funny?'

He arched an eyebrow. 'Holly was wondering if we were, well actually she assumed we were, you know... an item.'

Within an instant, the same spluttering laugh burst from Jamie's lips as she squeezed in behind him and took the seat in the corner.

'Ben and I would not be a good match. Don't get me wrong, I love him to bits, but he's... how do I put this?'

'I have standards?' he offered, at which point she thumped him playfully on the arm.

'Ben irons his socks,' she said by way of an explanation, 'and his hoodies. And his other underwear.'

'I think she gets the idea,' he cut in.

'I would find that a little intense,' she added, wrinkling her nose.

'Perhaps if you ironed any item of clothing now and again, you might find there is genuine pleasure to be found in wearing clothes that don't look like they've come straight out of the washing basket.'

'You could be right, but I have much more enjoyable things to be doing with my life. Wearing matching socks is good enough for me. Now, let's stop talking about us. We're dull. Well at least you are. Holly, tell me everything. Where have you come from? Why did you decide to move here?'

She took her time, telling them about her teenage years spent working in the shop, followed by a decision to move away from the village. When it came to why she'd moved back, she excluded the details of Dan and his cheating.

'So, you just decided to buy the shop? No business plan? No review of the accounts or viability analysis?' He looked incredulous.

'I guess,' Holly said, weakly.

'Well, I think it's fantastically impulsive,' Jamie said. 'Well done, Holly.'

'I know it sounds crazy, but in my heart, I know it's the right thing to do.'

'Cheers to that. Here's to following your heart,' Jamie said, raising her glass.

They clinked, even if Ben did accompany the action with a roll of his eyes.

'Talking of your heart, is there someone special back in the big smoke? Pining for your return maybe?'

'Well...' Holly was still reluctant to discuss this, but was starting to feel a little cornered.

'For goodness' sake, Jamie,' Ben butted in. 'Why do people feel compelled to ask that question straight away? How is someone's relationship status of any relevance? There are far more interesting things, like what their favourite holiday destination is. Or what sports they do. Have they broken any world records.'

'You've broken a world record?' Jamie's asked him, with a wicked glint in her eye.

'No, of course I haven't. I just mean there are so many inter-esting things about people. Like you: you do lots of interesting things. Your perpetual singleness is the least interesting thing about you. We already know that Holly is clearly crazy, buying that ridiculous shop, but I'm sure she has many, many more interesting aspects to her than whether she has a boyfriend.' Ben paused for a moment. 'Or girlfriend. Or whatever...'

Now it was his turn to stumble over his words, and Holly's turn to save him.

'Thanks, I think.'

'You're welcome,' he replied. 'I mean no one ever bothers to ask me about my passion for cooking. I'm actually pretty good.'

Holly took a moment to digest this outburst. For the longest time, the first thing she would usually divulge about herself was her relationship with Dan. Proud as punch, she would say how they had met at the end of university and had been together for four, five, six years.

'I am single. I might as well tell you that now,' she said eventually. 'But Ben is right. Dan – that's my ex – he wasn't the most interesting thing about me. This me – this me with the sweet shop – is so much more interesting.'

The confusion on Jamie's face now lifted and was replaced with a wide grin. 'Well cheers again,' she said, and lifted her glass once more. 'To being interesting enough as we are.'

This time, Ben's eyes locked on Holly's as he clicked his pint against the rim of her wine glass.

'To being interesting enough as we are,' he said.

Holly's attention was still firmly on him as she tried to read whatever was swirling around behind his deep-brown eyes, when a throat cleared next to her.

'Sorry it took me so long to get here. I got stuck behind a bloody tractor. Although I see you have company.'

He was standing there in the full country get up. Wax jacket, green Hunter wellies and a flat cap that should have made him look old, or at least old fashioned, but on Giles it somehow elevated the hat to a whole new level. And when she saw him, Holly felt her spirits lifted even further. Not because she was thinking of him as anything more than a friend, but because of the situation. Whether by accident or not, right now, at that precise moment in time, she had a group of people around her. Not yet a month into life back in Bourton and she was starting to feel that, maybe, if the shop would give her just a little break, there was actually a life for her here. A life for someone like her who was young and still wanted adventure and new friends, regardless as to whether she was single or not. She was just enjoying the moment, when Jamie spoke.

'What the hell are you doing here?'

26

Tension rippled through the air, although why Holly couldn't quite figure. Maybe she was mistaken. Maybe it wasn't tension at all. But then there was a glint in Jamie's eye. Was it anger?

'Giles, what I think Jamie meant to say was, that we don't see you down this way much these days.' Ben's voice broke the spell and in an instant the tension had gone, leaving Holly to wonder if she had imagined it in the first place.

Stepping forwards, Giles grinned.

'No, I don't know when I was last here. Not one of my usual haunts any more. But Hols messaged me, and I didn't know when I'd next be free, so I didn't want to miss out.'

Hols? Holly felt her skin prickle a fraction. It wasn't that she minded the name particularly. Dan had always called her that and so did most of her friends in London. But she'd never heard Giles say it before and something about it felt wrong. Forced. Besides, he was the one who'd messaged her.

'You made it,' she said, realising they were all looking at her and she hadn't actually said a word. 'What do you want to drink? We could grab another glass if you fancy wine?' While she spoke in what she thought was an upbeat manner, considering the day she'd had, it was hard not to notice Giles grimace. 'Is everything all right?' she added.

With a small, sigh, he removed his cap and proceeded to scratch his head.

'Well, this is a bit embarrassing. I'm really sorry. I didn't know we were going to have company.'

'Oh, sorry.' She suddenly felt about two inches tall.

'No, no. It's fine. Only, I know it was a little presumptuous of me, but as I thought it was just you and me, I ordered us Chinese take-away. I assumed you wouldn't have had dinner yet, and I was ravenous so thought I might as well save some time and order before I came to meet you. But you stay here. I can put the extra in the fridge at mine and I'll have it as leftovers tomorrow. The last thing I want to do is break this up.'

His lips lifted in a slanted smile although, for the briefest second, his eyes slipped beyond Holly to the others sitting at the table. Her gaze followed his. Truth be told, having only just settled in for the evening, she wasn't really ready to leave. She didn't know much about Jamie, but what little she did, she liked and wanted to learn more about. Not to mention there was still half a bottle of wine to get though.

'Oh, don't worry about this,' Jamie said, tapping the bottle as if reading her mind. 'Ben can help me finish it off. And I invited another friend to join us here, too. I thought you might like to meet a few more people.'

'That's so lovely of you,' Holly said, quite genuinely. 'Maybe we can eat the takeaway fast, then come back?'

Jamie brushed away her apology with a wave of a hand. 'Seriously, chill. It is not a big deal. How about dinner next week? I'll pop into the shop and we can arrange a time that's good for you.'

'Are you sure?'

'Of course.'

Standing up and leaning across the table, Holly offered Jamie a quick hug of thanks. When she broke away, she found herself looking directly at Ben.

'Thank you, for today,' she said. 'I'm not sure what I'd have done if you hadn't turned up.'

'Don't mention it,' he replied, although the way he said it made it sound more like a threat, than a pleasantry.

For a brief moment, all the other sounds of the pub faded away and all that remained was her and this little table.

'Well then,' Giles said, looping his arm into hers and bringing her back to the present. 'Shall we?'

As they squeezed through the pub door and out into the cool evening air, Giles's arm remained through hers. This was how friends walked, she told herself, aware of the fact that they were closer than they'd ever been before. She wouldn't think twice about walking like his with one of her female friends. So why should it be any different with a man? Giles was a friend. A good-looking one, but a friend nonetheless.

When they reached the river, she gazed across at the dark outline of Just One More. At this distance, all she could see were the shadows of the sweet jars standing behind the glass and not a hint of the destruction that had taken place that afternoon. It all looked so peaceful. So calm. How deceiving looks could be.

'So, I thought you didn't have any friends in the village?' Giles interrupted her musings. 'Have to admit, I'm surprised to find you cosying up to the local bank manager. Maybe you're a shrewder businesswoman than I gave you credit for.'

'You know Ben?' she asked. 'Is that through work?'

He lifted his shoulder in a half shrug. 'When you do as much business as I do, it's hard not to make friends, or enemies, with a few of the local bank managers.'

'So, which one is Ben? Friend or enemy?'

She felt the comment would illicit an interesting response, and even in the dusky evening half-light, she could see his eyes twinkle.

'Oh, our dear Mr Thornbury is far too strait-laced for us to be friends. Still, enough about me. I want to know how you made their acquaintance.'

'That's a long story. Although I guess you could say I first met Ben with the whole bicycle thing.'

A hearty laugh shook Holly's arm.

'Of course, that was him. How could I have forgotten? Brilliant. So, what happened today then?'

How did she start? she wondered.

'Did I tell you I had a small leak in the shop – up in the stockroom?' she asked, trying to sound casual about it.

'No, I don't think so. Why? Did it get worse?'

'Honestly, it was a miracle the whole ceiling didn't cave in. If it hadn't been for Ben turning up, it would have probably flooded the entire shop. Talk about the right place and the right time.'

'That does sound fortunate.'

'Well, once he'd blocked the hole, he called Jamie to come and sort it out.'

'Good old Ben to the rescue.'

For the second time that evening, she felt slightly uncomfortable. Was there an edge to his voice? It was difficult to tell. She didn't think so, but something about his mood had changed a little. As he removed his arm from hers, she felt certain that something was wrong and was about to say as much when she noticed that they were now standing right outside the takeaway.

'I'll go and fetch the food,' he said, striding towards the door. 'You wait here.'

'It's fine, I'll come in with you,' she replied.

'Trust me, it's so small and hot in there, it's really not pleasant. And I'm only going to be a couple of minutes.'

Without waiting for her to object, he disappeared into the shop.

Left outside on her own, her instinct was to feel for her phone, but something made her stop and, instead, she cast her gaze upwards at the sky.

'Wow.'

The word left her lips as a happy sigh. After spending so much time in the city, she'd forgotten how many stars you could see at night, out in the countryside. They always made of her think of her father. With her mother, everything was an event with noise, colour, and effervescent energy. Her father was so placid by comparison. A constant point in her life, like a lighthouse. When she was young, she would often find him outside, long after dusk had settled, just sitting on his gardening stool, his eyes lost amongst the constellations. Even now, when she would go home for special events, like a birthday or Christmas, they would always find an excuse to slip outside into the quiet, cup of tea in hand, and quietly watch the wonders of the universe unfolding from a million light-years away. Maybe she would go over there tomorrow night, she thought to herself, a surge of homesickness sweeping over her. It was daft being this close and hardly ever seeing them.

'You're not gonna believe it, but they've misplaced our order.' Giles's voice cut in. 'I'm so sorry. I mean, I was in there just minutes ago. They're cooking it now, but we've got to wait another fifteen minutes. Obviously, I've given them a piece of my mind. Can you believe it?'

Holly wasn't sure whether the question was rhetorical or not, but when she didn't answer immediately, she was surprised to see a look of concern in his eyes.

'Is everything all right?' he asked.

'With what?'

'With you? You seem very quiet.'

'Do I? I'm okay. Just tired, that's all.'

His frown remained and she felt the need to keep talking. 'It'll be fine. I'll be fine,' she said. 'The shop's okay, at least we think it is. Jamie said she'd have another look tomorrow when everything's dried out, just to make sure. And then it's only two weeks until Easter and it's always busy then, so that will be good. Drey said, last year, she was working nine-hour shifts and extra days, apparently. I think I'll be on seven-day weeks, too. Then it'll be a case of getting through to the summer. Of course, that's as long as the mortgage is approved.'

She was nodding as she spoke, trying to convince herself as much as anything, she supposed, that the shop wasn't a terrible money pit. Yet as she was speaking, she felt the weight of the day's disaster bearing down on her again. Surely, running an idyllic, little sweet shop wasn't meant to be this hard. Not when she didn't even own the place yet.

A car zoomed past them, going far too fast for a village road, although she didn't have long to dwell on the matter. The moment she turned back to him, Giles wrapped his arms around her.

'Look, maybe it isn't my place to say anything, after all I realise I haven't known you for that long, but we've got something, right? There is something between us?'

'There is?' It was only a half question.

'I think so. I feel like I know you, understand you. So, I have to ask, is this really what you want? To spend your life like this, constantly worrying about money and the building and everything else?'

'All businesses have their ups and downs,' she replied, pointedly.

'Maybe occasionally, but not like this they don't. At least, they shouldn't. I'm only saying this because I care, Hols. You know that. I just worry you'll always be fighting an uphill battle with that place. That first night we went for dinner, you were so full of life, so full of energy. It feels like some of that sparkle's gone already and you haven't even bought it yet. Maybe letting it go would be the best thing all round.'

Anger. That was the first emotion that rose through her when he finished speaking. How dare he? How dare he tell her what she looked like, or how she was feeling or whether or not she should run the sweet shop? But then, as she opened her mouth to say as much, she realised the truth: he was right. She was tired. Beyond tired. She was exhausted, and there was no let-up in sight. A day off meant closing the shop and there was just no way she could do that. Jamie had very generously fixed up the place at mates' rates, but how long would it be until the next disaster and then the next? All that romanticising about those happy, teenage days. Was she being realistic?

'I'll be fine,' she said, forcing a smile. 'I just need some food, that's all.'

Back at the cottage, they polished off the meal, accompanied by a glass of wine and generally amiable conversation. When they'd finished, she carried the plates through to the kitchen, unable to stifle the yawns that had been building up throughout dinner.

'Here, let me wash up. You go and sit down,' Giles said, coming up behind her.

'It'll only take me a minute,' she replied, turning on the taps. She was about to reach for the washing-up liquid, when she felt his hands on her shoulders, his thumbs moving in a circular motion over the top of her spine as he gently massaged her.

'You need to start taking care of yourself,' he said softly, his mouth next to her ear.

She felt the tension in her neck and back starting to lift a little, as the warmth of his hands began to ease the knots that were definitely there. She leaned into him, a moan of pleasure escaping her lips.

'You need to get your priorities right. I can feel the tension. It's not good for you,' he said. 'I've got a lot of work to do here.'

She hadn't realised how much she'd missed this, she thought, closing her eyes. In all their time together, Dan had never given her a massage, and yet here was Giles, buying her takeaway, offering to wash up and trying to ease the stress that had been building these last-few weeks. But what was she doing with him? That was the question. He was clearly charming enough to sweep half the women in the Cotswolds off their feet. Maybe that was how he occupied the rest of his time. But when he was with her... he just had this way about him. A way of making her feel like she was the only person in the world he wanted to be with.

His hands moved to the front of her shoulders now, massaging just above her collar bones. Why would he be here if he didn't want to be with her? she thought. He wouldn't. And he'd plainly been upset in the pub at the thought of having to share her for the evening. Maybe having a quiet night in and this massage was his way of making a move, of giving her a way in without being pushy. Butterflies swarmed in her stomach. She was just so out of practice at this.

Deciding it was now or never, she took a deep breath, turned around and planted her lips on his.

For the briefest moment, his body seemed to relax into hers and the butterflies erupted. She lifted a hand, but before it could reach his face, he broke away.

'I'm really sorry,' he said, his cheeks flushing red. 'But I think I should go.'

27

Idiot. Idiot. Idiot. Why the hell had she done that? Why hadn't she just accepted a nice, comforting shoulder massage in the spirit in which it had been intended, which was obviously not leading up to a snog? What a *stupid* thing to do, she cursed herself again. It had to be the tiredness, that and the wine, that had caused her to completely misread the situation.

Never had she seen the expression *making a bolt for it* so clearly demonstrated as when Giles had broken away from their kiss – no, *her* kiss. She was the one stupid enough to overthink what had just been a friendly gesture. She paced around the lounge, her minding flitting back and forth, trying to work out how she had got it so badly wrong. But had she? Why wouldn't she suppose he wanted more? It had been the obvious conclusion to jump to. Single man, single woman, late night drinks. And all that stuff about *I really understand you. I really care about you.* ARGH!!!

An hour later, a text came through, apologising for leaving in such a rush. She didn't reply. As she switched off her bedside light and curled up under the duvet, she told herself she would work out what to say in the morning.

As it happened, she felt exactly as awful about the whole thing when she woke up as she had done the night before. His message remained unanswered and she intended on leaving it that way, at least for the time being.

Given the mood she was in, a slice of toast or bowl of porridge simply wasn't going to hit the spot. So, leaving the house a few minutes earlier than normal, she headed straight out for a fresh cinnamon roll. Early morning queues at the bakery by the bridge were always impressively long. As such, when Holly finally arrived at her own shop, to open up, she wasn't surprised to find a figure standing in front of the door.

Leaning heavily on his walking stick, she could tell exactly who it was, even from behind: the gentleman who had been coming at least once a week, ever since she'd taken over.

'You're late this morning, Holly,' he said, as she tried to get her keys out of her bag, without getting icing from the cinnamon roll all over her coat.

'Sorry, I'll just be one minute. Two bags of sherbet lemons and a quarter of aniseed balls?'

'You catch on quick.'

'You make it easy for me.'

It wasn't until she was behind the counter, weighing out the third bag of confectionary, that she realised he'd referred to her by name. Somehow, amongst all the chaos, it had happened. She wasn't just an anonymous, new person in the shop any more. She was Holly. She felt a lightening of her spirit as she went to enter the last amount on the till, only to change her mind.

'Two pounds forty, please,' she said, holding out the bags to him.

He frowned. 'Are you sure? That sounds a bit cheap. Isn't it usually more than that? Three pounds seventy. That's what I normally pay.'

'Yes, well, the second bag of sherbet lemons is on me,' she replied. 'You know, for opening up a bit late and keeping you waiting.'

'You don't have to do that. I think I was probably early, actually.'

'Well, that's still no excuse. I should have been here sooner. But don't go arriving at seven-thirty every time now, will you, just to get free sweets?'

He grinned and it was infectious. She found her cheeks rising further in response. What an amazing start to the morning, she thought. Finally, some real affirmation that she was doing the right thing.

'Well, thank you. Thank you very much indeed.'

The man was still smiling to himself as he reached the door and paused to rearrange his cane and purchases for better balance. Maybe she could do this as a regular thing, she thought. Perhaps she could spring a little surprise on one of her regulars every week. She could even make it official, picking a name out of a hat.

'Excuse me,' she called out, racing around the counter as the old man stepped out onto the street. He stopped and turned to face her.

'Did I forget something?' he asked. 'Do you need me to pay the extra?'

'No. No, of course not,' she replied, a little saddened that he would even think that. 'I just realised that I don't know your name. I didn't ask you.'

'It's Bernard,' he said, with a small nod of the head and a definite twinkle of delight in his eyes. 'My name is Bernard.'

Today was going to be a fabulous day, Holly decided as she went back into the shop and got on with the business of opening up properly. Bernard's early arrival had meant she hadn't even had time to put money in the till, let along turn on all the lights or have a sweep around. Even the feeling of trepidation, as she climbed the stairs to check on the situation up there, couldn't dampen the feeling of happiness. This was it. This was what it was all about.

Despite her fears, as far as she could tell, the roof was holding fine. She had left the little yellow bucket in its usual place, just in case, and on brief inspection, it appeared bone dry. That was a first. Even the floorboards had dried out.

She didn't have to rely on her own, unprofessional opinion on the matter for long as, at nine-thirty, dressed in a short, denim skirt, woolly cardigan and Converse trainers, Jamie walked in the door. Guilt about the night before immediately resurfaced.

'I'm so sorry for walking out on you last night,' Holly began. 'I didn't realise that he was going to order food.'

'Oh don't be silly,' she said dismissively. 'Trust me, I'm a normal person. I don't get offended if people have an existence outside of me. Life's way too short for that. Although I didn't realise you knew Giles. Are you two old friends?'

'No, not at all.' She shook her head. 'I only met him when I moved back here. When I ran into Ben on his bicycle, actually. We've seen each other a couple of times since then.'

This felt like a complete cop-out, but was as close to the truth as she was willing to go.

'So, you know him then, Jamie,' she said, realising she might at last be able to get a little more info on the illusive Mr Caverty. 'What's he like?'

'Most of us around here know him, on one level or another. He's the type of person who likes to be known, let's put it that way. Anyway, I'm not here to talk about him. How's the roof? Everything okay?'

Not sure what to read into this comment about Giles, but also fairly certain that Jamie would tell her if there was something important to know, she didn't question her any more about him.

'I had a quick look first thing, and it seems to have dried out okay. Actually, it seems great, but I guess you're the expert on these things.'

'Do you mind if I go up and have a quick look? I'm afraid I'm a bit of a perfectionist. I always need to make sure I've done a good job. Particularly when I do work for friends. I won't be happy billing you until I'm satisfied.'

The word *friend* hovered in her mind after Jamie had finished speaking. There it was again. A little more confirmation that, maybe, despite all of the absolute chaos she had endured, moving here had been the right decision after all.

'Of course, I'll come with you,' she replied although, as she moved to close the front door, a young family entered, loudly discussing all the different things they wanted to buy.

'Don't worry,' Jamie said, reading the situation as she seemed to have an uncanny way of doing. 'It's not like I'll get lost or anything.'

'Thank you. Just call down if you need me,' she said, before quickly turning her attention to the customers. 'Good morning, how can I help you? Is there anything you're looking for in particular?'

As it turned out, the family were looking for quite a lot: sweets for party bags, chocolates for prizes and a whole range of other things for various relatives; each one of which they had a small anecdote about. She smiled throughout, listening with genuine interest as she weighed out one item after another. By the time she was done and the adults were ladened with two carrier bags of purchases, she was fairly certain she'd made one of the biggest sales ever. Positive that the day was only going to get better, she closed the till and looked up to smile at the person waiting behind them. That was when her heart sank.

28

With the same, skinny, red tie, accentuating that unusually florid nose, there was no way she would ever fail to recognise the Health Inspector. His image was now seared even more permanently into her mind, thanks to the orange anorak he was now sporting, and the unfortunate manner in which it clashed with both his tie and his nose.

'Miss Berry,' he intoned, his nasal inflection doing nothing to ease the queasiness which was now replacing her previous optimism.

'Good morning,' she said, trying to sound upbeat, even though she didn't feel it. 'Is everything okay? Are the results from the swabs back now?'

He sniffed, only to hack a bit back up and then swallow.

'Surprisingly, it does seem that everything is order, so far, in that department.'

'Fantastic news,' she said, feeling relieved.

'However, I have now been informed that there may be some other issues affecting the property, that might render it a possible health risk and even unfit for purpose.'

'Unfit for purpose?'

'Yes, I have it on good authority that this building is no longer structurally sound.'

She shook her head in disbelief. The queasiness had now ratchetted up to full-blown nausea. 'Not structurally sound? Why would I be standing here if it wasn't structurally sound?'

'So, is it not true, then, that you had someone carrying out work on your roof yesterday and without a permit?'

This further jump took Holly a second to catch up with.

'Permit? Since when do I need permission to fix my own roof?'

Tutting to himself, which caused a fine spray of spittle to fly from his mouth, he shook his head.

'This property is a listed building, Miss Berry. You can't just go changing things willy-nilly. It's the same for all the buildings in the High Street. To be frank, I'm not sure whether thinking such matters don't apply to you is a sign of ignorance or arrogance.'

What the hell! Gripping the underside of the counter, she peered briefly beyond him, to make sure that no one else had come in. Would it be a criminal offence to throw a bar of Kendal mint cake at him? Tempting as that was, she quickly changed her mind. The last thing she wanted to do was waste good stock on this jerk.

'I didn't change anything,' she said through gritted teeth. 'I fixed the roof because it was leaking and the ceiling nearly fell in on me.'

'So, it is structurally unsound then.'

'No it's not! Because I got it fixed!'

'So, you did carry out work on a listed building without a permit.'

'To fix the roof!'

She didn't know if she was about to laugh, cry, or – screw the stock – throw a whole box of chocolate hedgehogs at him, when another voice distracted her.

'Holly, is everything all right here?'

The Health Inspector's head snapped around to where Jamie was now standing.

'There's nothing to worry about, miss, but I'm afraid the shop is closed now, until we've undertaken a full inspection.'

'A full inspection of what?'

'As I said, miss, it's nothing for you to worry about. If you can simply pay for your purchases as quickly as possible and leave, that would be greatly appreciated.'

Much to his surprise, Jamie stayed exactly where she was.

'Sorry, I didn't quite catch who you were,' she said, instead.

Holly jumped in with the answer.

'This is the Health Inspector. He's come to inspect the roof. Says that he's received information about work on a listed building.'

A small crease formed between Jamie's eyebrows.

'You're a health inspector?' she questioned. 'Can I see your identification, please?'

He stiffened.

'I am afraid it's not pertinent for me to discuss issues with anyone other than the proprietor or manager which, I assume, you are neither.'

Whilst he had puffed out is chest, in what was most definitely at attempt at intimidation, Jamie remained entirely sanguine. She was so relaxed, in fact, that it set Holly even more on edge.

'Okay... the thing is, you still haven't shown me your identification. But, as I'm in a rather generous mood today, I'll tell you about me. You see, I have a T-level certification in building surveying – I assume you know what a T level is – and I happen to be the person who fixed this roof yesterday. I was just back to check over my work and, obviously, if I had found anything unsafe, I would have immediately closed the shop myself, in the exact same way I did yesterday, after I had reported the problem to the *correct* authorities. I can assure you that any issues with this building are entirely in hand.

'However, now that I have answered your question – in far more detail than you deserve, considering your absolute lack of manners or any modicum of professional standards – perhaps you could tell me exactly why somebody from the HSE would show up to do a job that is not part of his remit and, clearly, one that he is not qualified for. Unless you are spending your spare time moonlighting as a surveyor?'

When Jamie stopped speaking, you could have heard a pin drop. Then a strange, sucking noise seemed to come from the Health Inspector's lips. For once, it was impossible to distinguish the colour of his nose from the rest of his face, which had now turned the same colour puce. When he finally managed to speak, his voice came out a full octave higher than normal.

'You seem to have the situation under control, Miss Berry,' he said, dipping his head and turning, as if to leave. But Jamie was standing right there, blocking his way.

'You still haven't answered my question,' she said. 'And unless you do so in the next thirty seconds, I will be calling the police!'

His capacity for colour changing had now moved him on to a shade of green.

'What? This is ridiculous. I have my credentials right here, see.' He fumbled in his pocket to pull out the same HSE card that he had shown Holly on his previous visit.

'And Building Control is now covered by the HSE, is it?'

'A man can have more than one string to his bow,' he answered with huff. 'And needs to, for that matter, this day and age. The Council has us all covering a number of functions. Go on, ring them up. Ring them and see what they say. They'll tell you I'm legitimate. Go on. Here, take my phone. Take it.'

Having shoved his card back in his pocket, he was waving his mobile in Jamie's face. Holly was getting really worried now. HSE or not, the man was clearly unhinged. Jamie, however, wasn't even batting an eyelid. Instead, she simply peered down her nose at him, with undisguised contempt.

'I think you've wasted enough of Miss Berry's time now,' she said, 'don't you?'

Unwilling or unable to move, he stood there, quivering with anger.

'I shall be in touch,' he snarled at Holly, before finally pushing past Jamie and marching out of the door.

'No,' said Jamie, with complete certainty. 'He won't.'

Holly felt her knees go. Clutching the counter top, she gasped with relief. 'What just happened? What the hell was that?'

'Someone trying to pull a fast one on you.'

'You mean he's not a health inspector?' She felt queasy.

'Oh, I suspect he is legitimate all right. To some extent, anyway. He may well be a health inspector, but I don't think he was sent here by the HSE.'

'What? Then who? And why?'

Whether she'd heard her or not, Holly wasn't sure. Her attention was very much fixed outside, to where the man was now climbing into a battered Fiesta. After a minute, when the car drew away, Jamie turned back to face her, a series of worry lines, etched in her face.

'So, if I would have to make an educated guess, I'd say someone paid him to snoop around. Maybe one of the developers, scoping out whether or not they've still got an in, or even attempting to force the issue, unnerve you.'

'What? People would do that?'

'For prime real estate like this, they'd do a lot of dodgy things, including trying to worry you enough that you'd give up trying to buy the place.'

Still struggling to take this in, Holly tried to piece it all together.

'But surely it has to be legitimate? Otherwise, how did he know about the roof?'

'How would anyone know about it? I was up there for hours yesterday. Anybody passing could have seen me and guessed. Although...'

'What is it?' she asked, straightening herself up. Jamie might be a new friend, but she already recognised that she was someone who called a spade a spade. The fact that she was now hesitating gave her the distinct impression that she was holding something back. 'What are you thinking?'

'Okay... Please don't take this the wrong way, but how much to do you know about Giles Caverty?'

'Giles?' Whatever Holly had been expecting, it wasn't that. 'He's a friend, that's all. Why?'

Jamie's lips twisted. 'It could be nothing. It probably is nothing, but I know his uncle was one of the people trying to get Maud to sell to them.'

'His uncle?'

'He's a pretty big developer and he and Giles are close. Really close. He practically raised him. There's no chance Giles doesn't know about him wanting the shop.'

Holly was stunned. Giles had mentioned his uncle in passing but never that he'd been raised by him. Could he really be trying to sabotage her business?

'Look,' Jamie said, slightly worried now, 'see what you think. I could be completely off the mark here.'

'You're right,' Holly replied. 'I'm sure it's just a coincidence, that's all.'

But she wasn't convinced. She would definitely have to talk to him.

29

The day had gone downhill. Fast. From feeling she was becoming part of the village, to finding out that someone was quite possibly sending people to try and intimidate her, felt like a huge kick in the teeth. Add to that the fact that this someone might very well be Giles, who then had only spent time with her to get inside info on the shop. Was that really possible? As much as she didn't want to admit it, maybe it was. After all, only the night before, she had asked herself why he was content to spend evenings sat on Maud's threadbare sofa, eating takeaway with her when he obviously had more exciting ways of spending his time. It would explain the sporadic visits, too. Just enough to keep her interested, while keeping an ear to the ground. Was she really naïve enough to be taken in so easily?

'Excuse me, do you have any black and white humbugs?'

She blinked, taking a moment to register the fact that a customer was talking to her.

'Excuse me?'

'I could only find the black-and-yellow ones. I really wanted the black-and-white ones,' the lady said. 'I think they're called Murray Mints?'

Fixing a smile on her face, Holly hastened to help her. 'Of course, let me get those for you.'

Making her way back to the till with the jar, she turned quickly to Jamie, who had reappeared, having finished all her checks.

'Thank you for your help this morning, I don't know what I'd have done without you, yet again.'

'It's nothing, really, I'm just thankful you didn't have to deal with him on your own. Everything looks just fine up there. I'll let you get on, but I'll see you soon?'

'That would be nice.'

'And about that other thing. It could just be nothing, you know.'

'Yes,' she said, although she couldn't disguise the uncertainty in her voice.

The rest of the day went by in a daze. Customers came in waves. At some points, she could barely see through to the front door for all the bodies crammed inside, yet minutes later and the place was like a ghost town. And through it all, her mind was ever so slightly detached. Even Drey gave up trying to have any meaningful conversation with her.

She spent her lunch break checking emails. There was still no news from the mortgage company. Two to six weeks was what the broker had said and it hadn't yet been a full month. When her mind wasn't on when the approval would come through, she was struggling to keep it off the phoney health inspector.

Did people really stoop that low? she kept asking herself. What would be the point in sending in a bogus official, if he didn't have any real authority, anyway? Were they just hoping the hassle would put her off the whole enterprise and she'd just pack up and leave? Should she go to someone, the police maybe? And say what? What evidence did she have? If he worked for the HSE, he'd probably know people in high places. Had she inadvertently walked herself into an episode of *The Sopranos*? Something Caroline had said about health inspectors stirred in her thoughts, too; about them only visiting sweet shops if they sold ice cream, wasn't it? Throwing that into the mix, it really did look suspicious but didn't help her decide what to do about Giles.

At the end of the day, she knew she had two choices. Do nothing and continue to squirm endlessly, or confront him and ask him outright. Only the second of these options would give her an answer. Gritting her teeth, she picked up her phone and messaged him.

Any chance you're free for a quick drink?

Given how long it normally took him to get back to her, she wasn't holding out much hope of hearing back from him immediately. So she was more than a little surprised when a reply pinged back, only fifteen minutes later.

Busy tonight sorry.

She felt relieved and annoyed in equal measure, until she saw the three dots of an incoming message flickering on her phone.

Tomorrow?

It came through.
Tomorrow it was, then.

* * *

Pacing was her current default mode. She must have gone over the possible conversation a thousand times in her head already: what she would say, how she thought he would react. There was also the whole kiss thing that needed to be dealt with too, but maybe she wouldn't get as far as that. Her virtually accusing him of trying to sabotage her business would probably see him storming out before she even got the chance to explain. Not that she should have to do that. He was the one who'd put his hands on her, after all.

'How the hell do you get yourself into these situations, Holly?' she asked herself, finally taking a moment to stand still. She should have done some cooking. Baked some bread. Kneading would have helped relax her. Or tenderising some meat with a rolling pin. She had found both excellent forms of stress relief in the past.

Several times, she had almost reached for the open bottle of wine in the fridge but then refrained.

'You're both adults. Mature grown-ups.' She continued her pep talk. They would sit down together, have a drink, talk about their day a little bit, and then she would ask him straight out. But how could she make a question about possible sabotage not sound like an accusation? Oh God, she was going round in circles.

However certain she was that she was both adult and mature, it didn't stop her leaping half a foot into the air when the doorbell rang five minutes earlier than expected. Sucking in a deep breath, she then puffed out her cheeks, before letting out a long stream of air, then gave herself one, last, mental, pep talk.

Standing in the doorway, Giles was dressed that evening in horse-riding gear, with beige jodhpurs and dark-leather chaps strapped over his riding boots. If he had been soaking wet, he would have given Colin Firth's Mr Darcy a run for his money. Holly tried to think of what to say.

'Are you trying to sabotage my shop?' Is what her mouth decided, not as she had planned at all.

'Sorry?' He cocked his head to the side, quizzically, causing her stomach to perform multiple flip. She had started and there was no going back now. She'd nailed her colours to the mast.

'Are you trying to sabotage me? The shop. Just One More. Do you want it? Or does your uncle? Is he trying to ruin it? Trying to ruin me? I just need to know.'

'My uncle?' A whole host of previously unseen frown lines appeared on his forehead. 'Holly are you okay? Is this about the other night?'

'The other night?'

'When I was here, and you... you know. Kissed me. I know I responded badly. It was just... a surprise, that was all. Is that what this is all about?'

Confused by the sudden detour in the conversation, and worried to be discussing the kiss, when she had been hoping to ignore that subject entirely, she shook her head.

'No. Of course not. No... It's got nothing to do with that.'

In all the dozens of scenarios she'd envisaged, leading up to this meeting, never had she sounded quite such a mumbling wreck as she did right now. To make matters worse, she couldn't even remember what she'd already said, let alone what came next.

'Do you want to talk about this inside?' he suggested, looking even more confused than she was. 'I feel this isn't the type of thing to talk about on one's doorstep.'

At last, someone had said something that made sense.

In the kitchen, she headed straight for the cupboard to fetch two wine glasses although, before reaching the fridge, she had changed her mind and grabbed a large glass which she filled with water for herself instead. Water. That was what she needed. All of a sudden, the cottage seemed sweltering. She gulped it straight down and went back to the tap for a second, while Giles took the liberty of going to the fridge himself. He retrieved the bottle of wine and promptly filled the two glasses she had abandoned.

'Okay,' he said, after taking a substantial draw from his drink. 'Do you want to start again? Perhaps tell me where all this is coming from? You don't seem quite right. Has today been rough?'

'Today's been fine,' she said, the second glass of water now finished. 'Yesterday, on the other hand…'

'What happened yesterday?'

Good. This was where she could pick up the conversation where she had rehearsed it, in a rational, sensible manner.

'I had another visit from the Health Inspector.'

'Another one?'

'Exactly.' Her pulse had steadied a fraction, now she was back on track. 'And it turns out I didn't need one at all. I now have it on good authority that people around here – developers – are not past paying for "health inspectors" to visit, to try and intimidate shop owners.'

'Really?' He took a moment to contemplate the statement. 'I can see that happening. I think it's dirty, but it's not beyond the realms of possibility.'

So far, so good, she thought to herself. Everything was civil. Logical. But now she needed to get more personal.

'Is it true that your uncle tried to buy the shop from Maud?'

'My uncle? I don't know. Possibly. I know a lot of people were interested in it, and he already owns a few places in the village. I'd say it's quite likely he made an offer when he found out she was considering selling, but I don't know for certain. Why? Did the Health Inspector say something?'

Holly contemplated what to say next. So far, he hadn't denied or confirmed anything, which was the probable route to go down if you were either telling the truth or lying, which didn't help her in any way whatsoever.

'Turns out the Health Inspector hadn't come to do a health inspection; he wanted to check on the roof.'

'The roof?'

'Yup. He wanted to make sure it was structurally sound after the work that Jamie had done on it.'

'And was it? Was everything okay?'

'The thing is, health inspectors don't do that type of visit. Surveyors do.'

'Okay... So, you think someone paid him to, what? Spy on the place? What did he say? What did you do? Everything's still all right with the shop, isn't it?'

The earnestness in his voice caught her by surprise. In all her practices in front of the mirror, he had always been defensive, pleading his innocence. But there wasn't any of that. Not even a hint. So, either he was the best liar in the world, or he wasn't hiding anything at all. This thought caused all the tension to fly from her lungs in a loud sigh.

'Everything is fine,' she said, finally reaching for her glass of wine. 'Honestly, forget I said anything. Please, just another rough day.'

'But the thing with Inspector, how did it end up?'

'Well, it was horrid.' She took a gulp of her drink. 'Although at least that bloody cat hadn't left any dead mice outside the shop today.'

'Dead mice?'

'Oh, Maud and Drey have been feeding this stray cat and it decided to leave me a little present the other day. Anyway, he was asking all these questions about the roof and the building. Fortunately, Jamie arrived in the nick of time, and she knows her stuff. Sent him packing, in fact.'

'Ahh. Hmmm.'

Whatever response she had been expecting, it wasn't that. The frown lines had disappeared and been replaced with pinched cheeks and pursed lips.

'And let me guess,' he said. 'Jamie was the one who told you that people were sneaking about trying to stress you out and that there was a good chance it was my uncle. She suggested I would be the one to call the health inspectors on you?'

She hadn't planned on telling him about Jamie's involvement, but she couldn't backtrack now.

'She said he'd been interested in it, that he'd been asking about it, that's all.'

'He's interested in lots of properties. It doesn't mean he's going to start engaging in such underhand tactics. In fact, someone like him doesn't need to. He could buy every place in the village outright if he so wanted. Anyway, of course Jamie would point a finger at me. Bloody typical.'

The bitterness in his voice was something Holly wasn't used to hearing coming from him. In fact, she'd never heard anything close to it.

'Is there something I should know? Some kind of history between you two?'

His eyebrows lifted just a fraction. 'Let's just say not as much of a history as she'd maybe hoped for.'

'What does that mean?'

With a sigh, he lowered his head and scratched behind his ear.

'The thing is, she and I had a bit of a thing.'

'What type of a *thing*?' she asked, pointedly. Of course, Holly was fully aware what a *thing* meant, but *things* came in all different shapes and sizes. There was the type of *thing* that happened after one too many at an office party, versus the type of *thing* that had you wandering around a garden centre together, picking out patio furniture for a future home. *Thing* was rather a broad term when it came to relationships. However, given the differences between them, the fact that Giles and Jamie could be involved in a *thing* of any type, came as a surprise.

'It wasn't serious,' he said, reading her expression. 'To be honest, it was over before it even started. But, ever since then, she's been a bit, you know, edgy with me. Always jumping to conclusions. Always thinking the worst. Don't get me wrong, she's a great girl. Fantastic. Just not my type. You know how it is. You're just more attracted to some people than others.'

His eyes locked on hers, and while she was still considering how much Jamie would hate being referred to as a *great girl* in any context, particularly by a man she'd been in some sort of relationship with, it seemed a ridiculous thing for him to lie about.

Placing his wine glass down on the worktop, he slipped his hand into hers.

'I really like you, Holly. You know I do. You're so easy to spend time with. But I know how much you want things to work out now you're back here. Which is why, after seeing you with Jamie and Ben at the pub, the last thing I wanted to do was risk spoiling it for you. They are not exactly my biggest fans. They're nice people. A little dull at times, but nice enough. So, when you kissed me... I mean... if we started something, it would be bound to cause friction between you and them.'

Now it made complete sense why he'd bolted out the door. He'd been concerned he was going to get in the way of her new friendships. It was just about the most gentlemanly thing he could have done, other than tell her the truth there and then, of course.

'You know I think the world of you, Hols, and I want what's best for you, in every sense. I'd never do anything to hurt you or the shop. I just think that, right now, you and I would be better leaving things the way they are. At least until life is a little less complicated.'

As much as she didn't want to think about it, it was hard not to wistfully imagine a life that was *a little less complicated.*

30

That night, after Giles left, Holly had a long soak in the bath. Things could be a lot worse, she considered as she sank into the bubbles. Yes, she was exhausted, but that wasn't surprising, given that she hadn't had a single day off in over three weeks. Her feet were blistered in places she didn't know they could be, and it appeared someone was trying to intimidate her into abandoning the shop. But she had people around her. Good people. A few early nights was all she needed, she told herself.

However, ten hours' sleep later, she felt even more tired than before she'd closed her eyes. How was that possible? she thought, as she struggled to pull the duvet off her. It wasn't as though days at the shop were particularly long – she had certainly pulled longer stints when they'd had project deadlines at work – but now her whole head felt numb with exhaustion.

When she finally managed to drag herself out of bed, she dropped two, heaped teaspoons of coffee into a mug and downed it as soon as it was cool enough to drink. Did she feel better? she asked herself, waiting for the caffeine to hit. Maybe. Then again, maybe not. Perhaps some decent coffee would help. With the cottage's distinct lack of a Nespresso machine, her only option first thing in the morning was instant. Weak, bland, value, instant coffee.

Even when she'd finished dressing, she was still struggling to keep her eyes open. One step after another, she dragged her weary feet along the pavement, glaring up at the blue sky. Good weather meant a busy shop and, as much as she needed that, she wasn't sure she was going to cope. Only on a really quiet day could she justify closing up a little earlier. Perhaps she would today, anyway. One thing was certain though: tonight, she was going to be in bed by seven-thirty at the latest. Maybe she would head straight there after work, still in her apron and all.

Due to the distinct drowsiness clouding her thoughts, it was only when she arrived opposite the shop that she noticed people standing in front of it and not until she was practically on top of them, did she realise who they were.

'Good morning, sleepy head. We were wondering what time you were going to get here.'

Holly blinked, trying to make sense of what she was seeing. The whole scene felt very out of place. Jamie and Caroline were standing there. Together.

'You two know each other?' she said. It was silly that this fact surprised her, but having never seen the pair together before, the thought just hadn't crossed her mind.

'It's Bourton. Of course we do,' Jamie replied.

'Don't take this the wrong way, Hols,' Caroline joined in, 'but you look like you've not slept in weeks. And, trust me, I know what that feels like.' She bounced the baby carrier on her chest up and down to emphasise her point. 'Anyway, the other night at the pub, Jamie and I were talking about how you and I were at school together and about the shop, and then we got to thinking about the fact that it's been open every day since you took over. You've gone nearly a month without a single day off. Do you know how insane that is?'

From the tone of her voice, Holly wasn't sure if she was impressed or appalled.

'I'm working on it,' she replied, fishing in her bag for the keys.

'Really? Because we're both worried about you. This is not easy to do on your own without people to help.'

On other days she might have had a bit more patience, but it was early in the morning and the last thing she felt like doing was discussing all the shop's failings in the street. With the door unlocked, she turned and looked at her friends.

'Look, it's really nice of you to think about me, but I'll be fine. And the truth is, I'm barely earning enough to pay my Saturday girl, let alone myself. Unfortunately, anyone who has the knowledge, competency and legal age requirement to run the shop by themselves for even half a day is too expensive for me. Now, I don't mean to sound rude, but I really need to open up. Is there anything else you guys wanted?'

Whilst this had only been a minor rant, she was surprised at the effect it had on her two friends. Rather than offering words of comfort, or even looking slightly concerned, they were both grinning like mad women.

'It's funny you should say that, actually,' Caroline said.

'Because, yes, there is something we want,' Jamie jumped in. 'We want to run your shop for you.'

'What?'

'Not permanently or anything. We're not trying to usurp your position as Bourton's Queen of Confectionary.' Caroline grimaced at her own words. 'We just want to run the shop today.'

'I don't understand...' Holly said, stepping inside.

'You can't possibly keep going the way you are.' Jamie took over the reins. 'And we know it's not a long-term solution, but please, just take today off. We're here and we're both free. We've got this.'

There was no denying the look of sincerity on their faces and their clear eagerness to help. All the same, an ache of uncertainty swelled inside her. It was, quite possibly, the nicest thing that anyone had ever offered to do for her. But the logistics of it? It just didn't seem possible.

'You guys, it's a lovely idea b—'

Caroline cut her off. 'Don't say "but". Don't you dare say "but". We can do this. We are perfectly qualified to do this. In fact, we might even be over qualified.'

'I wouldn't go that far,' Jamie responded. 'But I'm quite capable of using a till and cashing up at the end of the day. And Caroline will make sure none of the kids picks their nose with a lolly stick or anything.'

The thought made Holly gag.

'Look, we know it's your business and your finances on the line here. And I know how I'd feel if someone was volunteering to take over my job, even for a day. But I also know that you're going to have to take a break at some point. You can't keep going the way you are. It doesn't have to be the whole day. Why not go for a morning bike ride? Check in on us at lunchtime and then decide about the afternoon. You must have a thousand other jobs that need doing. Besides, you need to be able to have some time to yourself. Otherwise, you're never going to keep the shop running, dodgy health inspectors or otherwise.'

As hard as it was to admit, it was true, but was it really that straight forward? Could she really just let them take over?

'Are you sure?' she asked, tentatively.

'Absolutely. We've got your number. And we've got your keys.' Jamie plucked them from her hand. 'Now go. Sleep, eat, shop.

Whatever it is you need to do. We promise the place will still be standing when you get back.'

Holly's eyes went from Jamie to Caroline, then around the shop floor.

'Maybe just for a couple of hours?' she said.

* * *

Jamie had been spot-on about her list of jobs and, given that she was already out, her first stop was the supermarket. Not being under any time constraints and knowing that her diet of white bread and beans wasn't exactly helping her situation, she filled her basket in the fruit and vegetable aisle. Back at home, she indulged herself in the kitchen. All this time in the house and she hadn't even baked a single cake, she thought, as she dished up a late breakfast. That was definitely something that needed to be rectified. Although maybe not that morning. Right now, she wanted to do something to help recharge her batteries. She just had no idea what that might be.

There was no denying she needed more sleep. Had her alarm not gone off, she could have probably slept until gone midday, but she'd never been the type of person who could go back to bed once she was up. Dan had been. He would think nothing of a mid-morning nap, or an afternoon one, for that matter.

It didn't take long for her mind to circle back to the shop. After all, did they really know what they were doing? Realising there was only one way to know for certain, she flicked open her phone and found the app she needed. While it had only been two days since Jamie had installed the cameras, it still took her a couple of attempts before she recalled the correct password. Then, a moment later, her phone screen was filled with the interior of Just One More.

The image was incredibly clear. Jamie was currently weighing out sweets on the scales, while the other camera revealed Caroline retrieving something from the top shelf by the front door. Cinder toffee most likely, given the location. There were two customers behind her although, judging from the shadows that darted about, there were probably a couple more in the shop, too. Still, it all looked perfectly fine. *Looked*. That was the problem. As good as the cameras were, there was no way for her to hear what was going on. For all she knew, there could be a screaming riot happening just off camera.

With her toes starting to twitch, she turned off the camera and chewed on her bottom lip. She'd been gone for over two hours now, and in that time the only thing she'd heard from them had been a couple of smiley-face, emoji texts. Maybe she'd go for a walk down to the village and just happen to pass by. Not to spy or anything. Just to see if they needed help. She could get lunch. Or not, given that she'd just eaten. But she could take some of crusts she had in the bread bin and feed the ducks.

She packed these into her bag, along with a couple of apples and a banana, just in case she felt the need for a snack later. She would stroll back to the village as slowly as she could manage. She turned on the cameras again for one last, nervous look before she left the cottage and spotted that a full queue had now formed in front of the counter. Jamie and Caroline were here, there and everywhere. Customers were picking up jars of sweets they wanted weighing. Panic rose as she shoved her mobile back into her handbag. They were probably waiting for her to come and help. They probably wanted to call her but were too busy to even pick up the phone.

Forgetting how she had intended taking her time, she broke into a near sprint as she headed down the road and onto the High Street.

As she neared the shop, she slowed her pace to give herself the chance to catch her breath. When she arrived and gazed through the window, much to her surprise, the queue had almost gone. Several people were standing out front, munching on their newly purchased treats while, inside, Jamie looked utterly at ease, smiling as she took a young man's money. Caroline was straightening up the shelves, putting jars back in their right place.

Looking in from the outside, she saw the shop in a whole new light. The customers inside were all beaming and laughing. Was that how happy people looked when she served them? she wondered, almost with a pang of jealously, before quickly deciding, yes. Yes, it probably was. The sweet shop wasn't meant to be an extension of her or Agnes or anybody else. It was a whole entity in its own right. The thought made her stomach churn nervously, as she wondered again whether she would get the mortgage or not. There was no way she could let this place go to developers, to be turned into some soulless franchise. They would give it to her. They had to.

With her head still lost if all the *what ifs*, she was still daydreaming when a voice startled her.

'Are you spying on us?'

'Jamie? Oh, what? Um, no, no. I mean, not deliberately. I was going for a walk. That's all.'

'A walk that just happened to result in you stopping outside the shop and peering through the window?'

The heat of a blush flooded her cheeks.

'I was just checking you were all right. Sorry. It's not easy. It really isn't easy.'

Jamie chuckled. 'I guess it's better you do it this way then spy on us with your security cameras or something creepy like that.'

Holly avoided her gaze, and looked back through the window

into the shop, hoping she wouldn't be able to read the guilt on her face.

'But everything is going okay?' she asked.

'It's fine. Better than fine. Caroline is loving this. There's no way she's going to let you back inside today.'

A glance through the window confirmed it was true. Having moved away from the shelves, she was currently bagging up sugar mice while simultaneously ringing prices through the till, all with the addition of a baby strapped to her chest. Talk about multi-tasking.

'I think the baby's helping with sales. People love him,' Jamie said, refocussing Holly's attention back outside the shop. 'Now, as you can see that we are fine, you need to go and do something, go somewhere. Get out the village, if that helps. What would you normally do on a day off?'

What would she do? Holly considered the question. Given their frugal existence, she and Dan would have probably done some-thing cheap and practical. Until the mortgage was approved, she really wanted to avoid spending any more of her deposit. So, what could she do that cost zero money? There were probably some nice, little, local, art galleries around. Or she could always see if her parents were home.

'Why not go for a bike ride?' Jamie suggested, seeing her uncertainty.

'That sounds great, only I don't have a bike.'

'I do. Here.' She reached into a pocket and pulled out a keyring loaded with a dozen keys. 'It's parked inside the back gate. Just make sure you lock it up again, afterwards.'

Holly stared at the key. 'Are you sure?'

'Of course I'm sure. I wouldn't have offered if I wasn't. Now hurry up and go, will you? We've got a shop to run here.'

31

Jamie's house was in a prime, real-estate location on the outskirts of the village, towards the Fosseway. While the river was hidden behind an array of trees and hedges, the houses there were large, with gravelled driveways and hanging baskets ready and waiting for spring. Jamie's house was number thirty-four, a semi-detached with a blue door. It was easy to spot. With dormer windows and an extended porch, it was the type of place she dreamed about owning with Dan. Shaking off the thought, she set about finding the bike.

The side gate was secured with a large, brass padlock, exactly as Jamie had told her and, she guessed, required a large, matching key. Unfortunately, it wasn't as simple as that. On the keyring she'd been given, there were at least half a dozen that might fit the bill. She was busy trying the third one when a throat cleared behind her.

'Are you okay there?'

She twisted around to find the bank manager looking on, with an ever-so-slight smirk on his face.

'Ben,' she said, 'what are you doing here?'

'I live next-door,' he said, nodding towards the mirror image house adjoining Jamie's. 'Are you all right? It looks like you're struggling.'

She stared at the jumble of keys in her hand. The brief conversation meant she'd now lost track of those she'd already tried.

'I don't suppose you know which one of these works on this lock, do you?'

He stepped forward. 'Here, let me take a look.'

Rather than taking the keys from her, he went straight to the padlock, twisting it over in his hands so that he could view the top.

'You're looking for the one with pink nail varnish on,' he said.

'Sorry?'

'On the bow.'

'The what?'

'The bow. The round bit of the key.'

'That has a name?' Wow, she thought, momentarily staring at the keys in her hand. Twenty-nine years on the planet and this is the day that she learns that the top part of a key has a name.

'What's the other part of the key called, then?' she asked, still in awe of this new-found nugget of information. 'Does that have a name too? I'd always thought it was all just called a key.'

'The long bit's called the blade,' he replied, without a hint of condescension. 'Now, is there a pink one there?'

Only now that she was rifling through them with intent, did she notice that, yes in fact, there was a different-coloured blob of nail varnish on the bow of each key.

'That's a genius idea,' she said, finding the pink one, which she then handed to Ben. It went straight into the lock and turned without a moment's delay. 'I'm going to have to start doing that. Although why does she have so many keys?'

'Part of the job. Tool shed, tool boxes. She's got loads of cupboards with all her gear stowed away securely. It's her livelihood, so she has to keep it all safe.'

With the gate now open, he stepped back and handed her the keys and padlock.

'So, what are you doing here anyway? Shouldn't you be at the shop?'

'I've been given the day off. Well, forced to take it is probably more accurate. Jamie said I could use her bike while she had Caroline run the place.'

'Really?'

'Yup. Apparently, I spend too much time at work.'

It was only upon mentioning work that she noticed that, despite it being a Tuesday afternoon, Bank Manger Ben was in just jeans and a casual T shirt.

'You're not at work either,' she said.

'Well observed.'

'Is everything okay? I got the impression you were someone who was always at work, too. I assumed the bank was kind of, well, your thing.'

She then worried that he might take the comment as an insult, but he didn't seem bothered by it at all.

'Yes. Well, it appears we are in the same boat. According to Head Office, I have several days' holiday that need to be used up by the end of the month. Why it should bother them if I take them or not, I have no idea.'

'Why would you not take your holidays?'

'I do. I take them when I need them. When I want them. Anyway, you haven't had a day off since you started running the shop.'

'That's because I can't afford to employ anyone.'

'Then you'd be more than happy to let Jamie and Caroline take over like this again in the future?'

She'd been backed into a corner and she knew it.

'So,' Ben said, stepping back and most likely taking her silence as a win, 'you're taking her bike. Where do you plan on riding?'

It was a question she'd been deliberating during the walk over, although she hadn't yet made up her mind.

'I was thinking I might go up to Clapton. Test my fitness on that hill. Come back down Newbridge Lane.'

A furrow formed in Ben's brow.

'I wouldn't,' he said. 'They're redoing the roads there. Absolute nightmare to get up and down at the minute.'

'Oh.' She considered her other options. 'Maybe I'll just head across to Wyck, then. From what I remember, that was always a nice, gentle ride across the fields.'

'That's normally a good option,' he agreed. 'Although you won't be able to cut across the fields.'

'I won't? Why not?'

'Some land dispute, apparently. I've stopped following it, if I'm honest.'

'Right.' She was starting to wish she'd just gone back to the cottage and spent the afternoon sleeping.

'So, is there anywhere that I can get to that's nice?'

'There's always Lower Slaughter. That's where I tend to go when I just want to get out of the village. There's a place there that does the absolute best ice cream.'

'The Slaughters?' Holly considered.

Lower Slaughter and Upper Slaughter. Having grown up with the names of the quaint, country villages all around – even ones quainter than Bourton – she had never really considered how disturbing the names actually were. It was only when Dan had commented on it years ago that she had decided to look up the origins of the names. As it happened, they weren't in the slightest bit gruesome. It actually came from the old English word *Slohtre*, which meant 'muddy place'.

Etymology aside, Holly couldn't imagine Ben relaxing with an ice cream, let alone cycling somewhere specifically to get one. Before she knew it, words were spilling out of her mouth of their own accord.

'Well, if you know the best place to get ice cream, then you should probably come with me. Knowing my luck, at the minute, I'll probably get a flat tyre and trash Jamie's bike, too.'

A concerned look appeared on his face, which she was certain was about to be followed by a polite refusal. Instead, his chin dipped into what was most definitely a nod.

'I'll need five minutes to get myself changed,' he said. 'And don't forget to look in Jamie's shed for a helmet.'

Being on a bike felt like being a child again. The way the air made a whooshing noise as she peddled fast down the narrow country lanes. The way the bell tinged satisfyingly with its short, efficient ring. Racing and ringing bells. Why had she not done this more often? Probably because she'd been living in London and every few yards would have been forced to stop at traffic lights or a pedestrian crossing. Not to mention the air pollution.

'You know you're a menace,' Ben said, with not even the hint of a smile, when he finally caught up with her.

'I'm not a menace at all. I'm ringing my bell so people know I'm here. Besides, this is technically a cycle path. That's what the sign said back there.'

'Maybe, but you were still a menace as a pedestrian, in case you'd forgotten.'

'That was a one off,' she said, and rang her bell once again, this time veering off the path and doing a large loop in the field they were crossing. Cycling should be made mandatory, she decided. She hadn't felt this good in an age.

When the fields gave way to narrow paths that required them to go single file, both Ben and Holly dismounted from their bikes and walked with them instead. As much as she joked about it, the last thing she wanted was to hit someone on a nice afternoon stroll.

Just as they neared the village, instead of taking the lane towards the shops, he headed up a smaller one, running behind some houses.

'I thought you said we were going for ice cream?'

'We are.'

'But the shops are the other way.'

'I never said anything about going to the shops,' he said, continuing along the road.

Coming to stop a few metres later, he propped his bike against a tall, wooden fence, prompting Holly to do the same as he opened up the adjoining garden gate and headed up the path.

'I assume you know who lives here,' she said.

He didn't reply and she followed nervously behind. Along with beanpoles and a greenhouse, the space was full of raised beds and trellises. It looked more like a cottage farm than a house. Still, she drank it all in as he rapped his knuckles on the back door.

'Ted, are you in?' He opened the door by just a fraction and called again, before turning back to Holly. 'He wouldn't leave it open if he was out. Come on in, it's fine.'

The back door opened into a spacious utility room, whitewashed and immaculate, with a stone, farmhouse sink and two large, chest freezers against the walls.

'Hold on a minute,' a voice called from deeper in the house. 'I'm just in the kitchen, washing up.'

'Ted?' Holly made an educated guess.

'Yes, indeed.'

A minute later and the second door opened and there stood a small, rounded man. He wore thin, silver-framed glasses perched on the end of his nose and had not a scrap of hair anywhere on his face or head, other than eyebrows and tufts protruding from his ears.

'Benjamin,' he said, breaking into a smile and pumping his hand. 'Been a while since I've seen you here. Did they make you take a holiday again?'

Ben's face twisted, causing the old man to chuckle.

'So, I assume you've come for your usual?'

'I have, although, if it's all right with you, I'll take two cones now and come back for a couple of tubs later. I don't suppose you've got one of that beetroot and raspberry, have you? Jamie would never forgive me if I didn't bring her one back.'

'I'm sure I can sort that out. Now, excuse my manners, but I don't believe you've introduced us.'

He stretched out a hand to Holly. Already quite taken by the old man, she shook it, at which point he bowed his head and kissed the back of her hand, ever so lightly.

'Theodore Tobias Melbury,' he said. 'And you are?'

'Holly Berry.'

'Holly has taken over running Just One More,' Ben added to the conversation.

'Really. Wow, beautiful and a head for business. I am in awe.'

'Ted makes amazing ice-cream and is also a horrendous flirt. And by horrendous, I mean that he's terrible at it. Probably why he remains an *ineligible* bachelor.'

Ted sniffed in mock indignation. 'That insult would carry far more weight if it came from someone who didn't spend their nights fawning over compound interest rates.'

Holly snorted out a laugh and Ben scowled at her.

'Did you want ice cream or not, because I'm pretty sure I can get insulted anywhere?'

Stifling a giggle, she turned to Ted.

'Did I hear you say beetroot flavour?'

'Beetroot and raspberry. It's one of my most popular ones. Along with elderflower and gooseberry sorbet.'

'Right…'

She didn't think she had ever even heard of gooseberry- or beetroot-flavoured ice-cream. Mint choc chip was her usual go-to.

'What do you recommend?' she asked. 'What does Ben usually have?'

'Ben here always goes for the sloe gin and blackberry, but the elderflower and gooseberry is very popular.'

Hoping for something a little more conventional, she tried not to sound rude.

'I'll be honest. I'm not a great fan of gooseberries,' she said.

'That's what everybody says until they've tried it. I tell you what, I'll give you a cone and if you don't like it, then you can have a different one. No charge.'

'Are you sure?'

'Of course I am.'

'Well, that sounds too good to say no to,' she grinned.

'Excellent, I'll be back in a jiffy.' And with that he disappeared back into the kitchen.

Holly looked at Ben, who just gave her a knowing smile. A few moments later and Ted reappeared with a mug of steaming water and an ice-cream scoop.

'Right then, let's get you that cone,' he said, heading to one of the chest freezers.

* * *

'How on earth has he made gooseberries taste this good?' Holly said, as she and Ben strolled back towards the river. Given that he wanted to pick up more ice cream to take home – and, to be fair, so did she now too – Ted had let them shut their bikes inside his garden, so that they could head out for a walk, while enjoying his wares.

'I think the secret is excessive quantities of double cream and sugar,' he replied, to what had actually been a rhetorical question.

'But the gooseberries. I can taste them, but they're so much better than normal. I don't think I'll ever be able to eat regular, shop-bought ice cream again.'

'Welcome to my world.'

Hopefully Ted did something with chocolate in, too, she thought to herself. Then again, maybe she should give the raspberry and beetroot a try next.

'So where does he sell it?' she asked, as they crossed over a little, wooden bridge and took a seat on a nearby bench. 'Judging by the size of those freezers, he obviously makes plenty of it.'

'He does, but he won't sell it. Doesn't like the pressure.'

'Really? That's incredible. He could make a fortune.'

'Trust me, we've all told him.'

'Maybe I could sell it at the shop,' she thought out loud, wanting to go back and try a cone of every flavour. 'Maud always said she'd like a Mr Whippy machine, but Agnes thought they were tacky and vulgar. But this... even she would approve of this.'

'She did and wanted to stock it, but he wouldn't sell to her.'

'She knew him?'

'I think Agnes knew everyone.'

'Of course she did.'

The pair fell into a companionable silence, and whilst she had no evidence, Holly couldn't help but feel that Ben was thinking about Agnes too. Biting into his cone, he made a hesitant, humming sound.

'So, tell me about the shop. You've bought it now, right?'

'Not exactly. I am trying hard to, though. Essentially, it's mine. I've just got to wait for the mortgage to come through. Until then,

Maud's handed over the running of if to me, so I can treat it as if it's my own.'

'And when will you find out about the mortgage?'

'Hopefully in the next couple of days. I've already had to shell out a ton for repairs to the roof and the door, plus the new CCTV, scales and stock. But I still have a sizable deposit put by. I was going to buy a house in London, but well...' Her voice trailed off.

She worried that this line of conversation might lead him to ask more questions about Dan and what had happened, but it didn't. Instead, the pair just continued to sit amiably, enjoying their ice creams before heading back to Ted's to fetch their bikes and some tubs to take home.

* * *

This day off was giving Holly the chance to clear her head and was helping her state of mind more than she could possibly have imagined. On the return journey, she and Ben found common ground.

'I'm sure I'd remember if I was at school with you,' she said, in disbelief, when they'd worked out that they had been only two years apart.

'I kept myself to myself,' he said. 'Besides, it was a big school.'

'Not really.'

'Then I guess I'm just not particularly memorable.'

She suspected it wasn't just down to him. She had kept her head down during her secondary school years. She was the kid in the second-hand clothes, after all. The one who worked hard just to get away.

They continued their cycle ride, talking about old school teachers and what had become of them, not to mention a few notorious members of their year groups that they both remembered.

When she arrived back at the shop, Jamie and Caroline were cashing up the register.

'Please, take some sweets,' she said, when they refused all efforts to be paid for their work.

'The last thing my kids need is more sugar,' Caroline replied.

'Then have something they won't like. And Jamie, take some bits and pieces for the people at the nursing home.'

Holly had to practically beg them, but when they finally left, they did so with suitable amounts of confectionary.

When she arrived back at the cottage, she slumped down on the sofa with a feeling of utter contentment. While considering what to have for dinner, she flicked open her emails on her phone. In amongst the ads and spam, one stood out. The sender was Jennifer Smythe-Doyle, the mortgage broker. With a mounting sense of excitement, she tapped the screen to open it. Almost immediately, that feeling of euphoria turned to dread and then pure horror.

Dear Ms Berry,
I am sorry to inform you we have been unable to secure a commercial mortgage for the property you requested.

The message went on to give further explanation, referring to the limited net profit of the business and the surveyor's report, but she couldn't take it in. The sense of loss was exactly the same as she'd experienced a few weeks earlier, when she'd walked in on Dan and the girl.

Her whole world was spinning out of control. Again.

Holly felt terrible taking up even more of their day, especially given that Caroline would have only just got home to her family. But she was in need of friends, and today she and Jamie had shown themselves to be exactly that. She had also messaged Giles, but it was still not marked as read, and she wasn't holding out any hopes of him seeing it that evening.

So they were back at the Catherine Wheel, this time sharing a bottle of rosé.

'Explain again why they're not giving you the mortgage,' Caroline said.

'They said the books simply don't add up.'

'What does that mean, exactly?' Jamie asked.

Holly let out a long sigh. She couldn't blame them for all their questions. She had been exactly the same in her phone call to Jennifer Smythe-Doyle, trying to make sure she understood exactly what they were saying.

'Basically, the business doesn't make enough money to cover the mortgage I need to buy it. It's too much of a risk.'

'So is that it then? There's nothing you can do?' Jamie asked

'They did say if I can increase the revenue enough over a three-month period, then they will reconsider.'

'Increase it by how much?'

'It needs to be making twice as much as it did the same period last year.'

The two women let out low whistles, which did nothing to cheer her up.

'So can you do that, do you think?' Caroline asked.

'I just don't know. If I don't, then Maud will sell the place to the developers.'

* * *

'How many bags of sweets do you think the average person buys?' Holly asked Drey. Her first thought had been to open half an hour earlier on weekends and, as such, coax Drey out of bed a little earlier.

'I don't know. Two? Three?' Her hair was blue today. Very, very blue, although it went rather nicely with the apron. At least that was something.

'We need to know,' Holly said, jotting some numbers down on a note pad. 'And we need to get them to buy more. I've looked at the numbers. I reckon if we are open for an hour longer each day and we can make every customer spend just one or two pounds more, we'll have what we need. We just need an incentive to encourage them.'

'Like a buy one, get one free.'

'Exactly. Although maybe more like buy four, get one free.'

'You want me to make a sign for that? To put up by the jars?'

'Yes, I do. And we need to come up with a way of getting some of those customers over from the bakery in the morning. There's always such a big queue outside. How do we filter them over here?'

'How about an early morning offer? Ten percent off anything bought in the shop before nine.'

'That's a brilliant idea!'

'Oh, and what about loyalty cards? You know, like the type in coffee shops, where if you get ten stamps you get a free cup of coffee. You could do that, but give a free bag of marshmallows, instead.'

From the doorway came a loud meowing and a moment later four furry paws crossed the threshold into the shop.

'Oh no you don't,' Holly said, reaching for the broom, although Drey was quickly around the counter scooping the cat up in her arms.

'I've got him. I'll take him out,' she said, hurriedly. A moment later she returned without him.

'You're not still feeding him, are you?' Holly asked, aware that the cat had seemed far more confident with Drey was there. 'You know what I said about keeping him away from the shop and now we have the door open on warm days, we have to be really careful.'

'I know,' Drey said. 'I may have forgotten once or twice, but not inside the shop. Only outside.'

'Well you can't forget that,' Holly said, in her sternest, most managerial voice. 'I mean it.'

'I know. I promise, no more treats for Humbug at all. Now, how many of these signs do you want me to make?'

* * *

Holly spent the following week working on a marketing campaign. While putting any more money into the business with no guarantee of the mortgage was a hard pill to swallow, she had found an online printer that would make 1000 loyalty cards for thirty pounds, plus another five pounds for a custom stamp.

By the time Saturday came around again, she was pleased to tell Drey that she had given away nearly fifty of these and a handful of people had already returned, bringing them in for stamping again. Meanwhile, Drey revealed she had put her art skills to good use and created some promotional-offer posters for display. Over the weekend and for the rest of the next week, the four-for-three offer proved particularly successful with the tourists, several even splashing out on six lots of sweets, to get an extra two bags free. Holly asked Drey to pop in for a couple of hours on Friday afternoon to help restock the shelves, as they were getting so depleted.

'I had some more ideas,' Drey said, as she topped up a jar of liquorice allsorts. 'We could do sweet platters.'

'Sweet platters?'

'You know, for kids' parties. They have these whole tables filled with jars of sweets. The parents pay a fortune for them.'

'You mean they just buy loads of sweets?'

'Yeah, but it has to look great. Glass jars, big bowls.'

Holly quickly searched the idea on her phone. By the looks of things, that was definitely something she could manage.

'How would you advertise something like that?' she asked.

'Dunno. I guess you could put up some kind of sign in here. What you really need is a website.'

'Ah yes, a website.'

It was something she had already looked into. Unfortunately, the quotes she'd got were crazy and there was no way she could risk another expenditure like that now. It was already going to be touch-and-go as to whether she could turn enough profit to persuade the mortgage people to reconsider her application. There could be no more, sudden, big outlays that weren't absolutely necessary.

'We might have to put that on hold for now.'

'What about piñatas?' Drey asked, adding yet another sugges-tion to her list. 'Loads of kids have them at parties now. Although, at my cousin's, they got into a massive row over how many hits they'd each had and then started fighting over the stick thing. One kid ended up needing stitches. Not that you have to worry about that. You just want to sell the things. And they'd look really cool in the window, too.'

'I like it. We could definitely store some piñatas here. I'll see if I can order some. Any other ideas?'

In between discussing Drey's suggestions, many of which Holly had to agree were rather good, there had been a steady stream of customers, including quite a number she was starting to recognise.

'I'll have half a pound of—'

'—peppermint creams,' Holly finished for the gentleman. 'Chocolate-coated on the bottom, plain on the top. Is that right?'

'Well remembered, young lady.' The old man smiled at her. 'You're in a good mood today.'

'I'm feeling very optimistic,' she replied.

'Well, in that case, I hope whatever it is you're hoping for comes true.'

'Thank you, so do I,' she said, and stuck an extra sweet in the top for free. As she handed the tin and change back to him, her phone pinged with a message from Jamie, suggesting they go for a drink that evening. Ordinarily, she would have said yes in an instant, but Giles had got back to her earlier in the week and she'd promised that they'd have a catch up.

When it came to Giles and Jamie, she felt like she was stuck between a rock and a hard place. The last thing she wanted to do was offend Jamie over a guy, but she also wanted to be honest with her. In the end, though, she decided keeping her mouth shut would be the best idea. At least, this time, she would manage to be showered and dressed in clean clothes before Giles' arrival, unlike most of their previous meetings.

At ten to five, just before closing time, the bell above the door jangled again. Holly stopped wiping down the jars as Ben stepped into the shop.

'How's it going?' he asked. 'I passed by earlier in my lunch break, and it was packed, so I thought I'd come back later.'

'It's going well, I think.'

'Great.' Despite his positive words, there was that familiar air of awkwardness about him, a kind of rigidity, although that may simply have been the effect of his formal, business attire. There was no doubt Jamie wasn't lying when she'd said Ben ironed his socks. Most of Holly's clothes didn't look that smart hanging in her wardrobe, let alone at the end of a full day's work. After a moment of awkward silence, he shifted on the spot.

'I came to get some sweets, actually,' he said. 'I'm visiting my nephew this afternoon. He's always had a sweet tooth.'

'Oh, yes, great,' she said, still feeling on edge but not sure why. 'What would he like? Chocolate frogs are always popular with the children, for obvious reasons. And the sugar mice too.'

'Oh, no. He's a bit too old for those, actually. He's seventeen.'

'Seventeen, wow. Maybe not the chocolate frogs, then.'

'No. I mean if you had chocolate computers, that would be something. He spends half his life glued to a screen, designing one thing or another. Programs, websites. You name it. As long as it doesn't involve having to talk to anyone.'

'Sorry?' She put her duster down on the counter. 'You have a seventeen-year-old nephew who can build websites?'

'Yes. Apparently, that's something kids do nowadays.'

'I don't suppose there's any chance he'd work for sweets, is there?'

34

'That's fantastic news, Hols. I'm so pleased for you. We should go out and celebrate properly. Maybe go back to the restaurant in Bibury again? They change the tasting menu every month and I haven't tried this one's yet. You know it'll be exquisite,' Giles said, as they sat enjoying the fine evening in Maud's garden.

'Business is up, but it's not there yet,' she replied. 'I need the profit over these next few weeks to be really strong, otherwise I won't make the target they've set. Not to mention one more mishap, leading to another dip into my savings, could mean I won't have enough left for the deposit. Trust me, I'm not having a single, frivolous outing until the deal is done and dusted.'

It had been over two weeks since she and Giles had last met up. Part of her had begun to think that between accusing him of sabotage, her friendship with Jamie and *the kiss*, maybe she'd scared him away for good.

'In that case, you'll just have to cook for me,' he said.

'That I will.'

She sat back in her chair, continuing to soak up the last rays of the sun.

'Have you thought about advertising?' he asked, leaning forward. 'If you're as close as you say to hitting this target, it would be devastating to just miss it. Some good publicity might be just the thing.'

'Like I said, no extra spending at the minute. Not until I'm through these next few weeks. Besides, I've got a website in the offing now, thanks to Ben and his nephew.'

The young man had turned out to be a real star, agreeing to a payment of a large supply of jelly beans and sour worms, plus a written reference when it was time for him to apply to college.

Giles seem to bristle slightly at the mention of Ben's name, but she decided to ignore it.

'I'm mostly worried about this place right now, if I'm honest.'

'This place?'

'The cottage. I know Maud will give me as much warning as she can, but when she gets a buyer, I'm going to have to find somewhere else to live. And we all know how much rental deposits cost.'

'I'm sure that won't be a problem for a while. Sales take an age to go through. Have you had many viewings?'

'Only two this entire time.'

'Well, there you are then; everything is completely fine. Nothing to worry about.' Giles paused for a moment, seeming to be mulling something over in his mind. 'Just so you know, I've got contacts on the editorial teams of all the big countryside magazines: *Cotswold Creatives*, *Country Days* and suchlike. An article in one of those could be just the thing you need. And I'm sure I can get you mates' rates on an advertorial.'

'Thank you. That could be an idea.'

'Well, don't wait too long. It could make all the difference. Anyway, I'm heading off to Marseille tomorrow,' he said, drawing the conversation away from the shop for the first time since he'd arrived. 'I should probably head home and pack. Maybe, when I get back, we could do that dinner?'

'That sounds lovely.'

'And think about the advertising. Some opportunities are worth the risk.'

'I'll definitely think about it.'

A few minutes later, when she was on her own in the house, she considered the turn her life had taken. From a standard nine-to-five office job in London, to this... whatever this was. Some days she really did have to pinch herself.

* * *

The next day was annoyingly grey for a Saturday, but the steady stream of regulars served to not only keep the till busy, but also to brighten up her mood.

'Here, Mrs Brown, let me take that for you. You don't want to be lifting things with that arm of yours.'

'Oh thank you, Holly dear. You are a gem. The doctor says the cast will be off in two weeks. I'll be honest, it's been a nightmare. An absolute nightmare.'

'Well let me know if there's anything I can do to help. You could leave your shopping list with me and I'll pop to the Co-op for you at the end of the day. I don't mind. I don't want you to risk having another fall, carrying all those bags.'

'You are lovely, Holly, but no thank you. Nadia, my granddaughter, is over this weekend. She's doing a shop at the big Tesco for me before she comes.'

'Okay then, if you're sure, but you know where I am if you change your mind.'

The old woman smiled, deepening the wrinkles around her eyes.

'What a kind thought. You're an absolute blessing to this village, Holly Berry. An absolute blessing.'

This was what had been special about working here before, Holly remembered. This was why Agnes and Maud had bought the place. A chance to make the world just a little bit sunnier.

Over the next few weeks, business steadily improved and things really seemed to be picking up. Ben's nephew, true to his promise, had set up an attractive website and she'd had several online orders. Nothing big – no party platters or anything like that – but, little by little, it was all adding up. She'd been going out with Caroline or Jamie in the evenings, too, being introduced to new people and making more friends and, hopefully, a few new customers.

One evening, as she sat down with a steaming mug of tea to go over the books, she realised just how utterly settled she felt; as strange as it sounded, even more so than she had with Dan. Even with the impending deadline edging closer. The whole time they had been together, she had been thinking about the future, about what house they were going to buy, what suburb they were going to live in. Even what they would name their children. She'd spent so much time concentrating on the future that she'd never made the most of the present. That's what was so different about her life now, she realised. Whether it was an occasional glass of wine with Giles, or an evening spent with Jamie and Caroline, she was taking each day as it came and enjoying the little things. That was why everything felt so good. She finally knew what it meant to be living in the moment and she was loving it.

Then the telephone rang.

35

During the two-and-a-half months Holly had been living in Maud's cottage, the land line had rung exactly zero times. There was simply no need for it. On the two occasions that Maud had telephoned to see how things were going, she had rung the shop and Holly had insisted that everything was just fine and hung up as quickly as possible. She felt guilty about those non-conversations and the last thing she wanted was another one now. She hoped not to hear from Maud again until after she'd got the mortgage approved.

As for other calls, if they didn't come through to the shop, they went to her mobile. The estate agent that Maud had signed on with had her number, too, as did pretty much everyone else. Which was why, tucked up on the sofa reviewing her finances, it took her a solid minute to not only realise what the sound was, but to then find the telephone again, tucked away on a shelf behind her.

'Oh, Holly love, I'm so glad you're in. I was worried you'd have gone out for the night.'

'Maud, how are you? Where are you? Is Scotland okay? I saw you've been having terrible weather.'

'Oh, I'm not in Scotland, dear. Did I forgot to tell you? I'm in Austria.'

'Austria?'

'I know, I know. I arrived about three weeks ago. It was all quite sudden. Eleanor has a friend who needed a house sitter here for her four cats, while she and her husband are on holiday for a month in the Caribbean. Well, I thought, why not? It's a beautiful cottage, a bit like mine only right by a lake. There are lovely walks around here, too. Such a shame that Agnes never saw this. She'd have loved the place.'

The change was plain to hear. This was the Maud she'd been used to in the old days – the way she looked for the good in everything, not how she'd been when Holly had returned to Bourton.

'It sounds like you're having a great time.'

'Oh, I am, I am. And, honestly, I have you to thank. All the pressure you took off my shoulders. How's it going? Have you got that mortgage approved?'

'Not long now, just a few more bits and bobs of paperwork to sort out,' she said, crossing her fingers as she spoke and feeling bad about misleading her old friend. She was so close to success; she couldn't risk her getting cold feet and calling the developers.

'Well, I think it's fate. And I just can't thank you enough.'

'Don't be silly.' She was starting to feel quite emotional and, judging by the pause on the other end of the line, Maud was feeling exactly the same way.

'Agnes would be thrilled. You know she would. I can't imagine anyone she would rather have had taking over the shop.'

Now tears were starting to well up. She had to make it work. She would keep the shop open twenty-four hours a day if need be. Not that it looked like it would come to that.

'Now...' Maud said, her voice suddenly stronger, 'the reason I called. You'll never guess what. It's only gone and sold.'

'What has?'

'The cottage. I really hadn't expected it to go so fast. I mean, two months on the market's nothing these days, is it?'

'No. No it's not. That's really great news.' She hoped the catch in her voice was less noticeable to Maud than it was to herself. 'I'm so pleased for you.'

'You should be pleased for both of us. No more living in that dusty, old place any more. And – wait for the best bit – they're cash buyers!'

While Maud was absolutely delighted, Holly was struggling to see how this was the best bit.

'Cash buyers? What does that mean?'

'Well, it means there's no chain. They can move in as soon as the contracts are signed.'

A wave of nausea hit her.

'Which will be when?'

'Well, they're getting the papers out to me here tomorrow by express delivery. So, I think it might all be sorted out by the end of next week.'

'Wow. The end of next week.' She could barely breathe now.

'That'll be all right, won't it? I thought you'd want to be out of the place as soon as possible. I know that doesn't leave you much time, though.'

'I'll be fine. That's no problem at all.'

Her mind was racing. Just as she was feeling settled, the carpet was being pulled out from under her feet again – literally, this time.

'I'm so pleased for you,' she repeated, unable to come up with anything more convincing.

'Isn't it funny how life turns out? I don't want to be rude, love, but I'd better go. The marching band's just going up the street and I do like to watch it. They look ever-so lovely in their uniforms. Take care, won't you?'

'Of course.' Her lips were moving of their own accord. 'Of course. And you too.'

And with that, she hung up the phone.

Ten days to find somewhere to live.

* * *

There was no point in wasting time, particularly as she didn't have any to waste. Feeling almost dizzy, she opened her laptop and started searching for properties to rent in Bourton-on-the-Water.

'You have to be kidding,' she said, her eyes almost watering at what she saw displayed on the screen. Only three properties were available in the village, one of which was an astronomical, four-thousand pounds a month. Four thousand pounds? The others were more reasonable and closer to what she thought she could afford, but they all came unfurnished. The place she and Dan had rented had been fully furnished. If she rented one of these, she would need to buy herself everything: fridge, freeze, sofa, bed, the lot. How much was that going to cost? Surely regular people couldn't afford this lifestyle, she thought.

Expanding the search radius, a few more properties appeared that were maybe do-able. But there were still other factors to take into consideration, like the month's rent up front and the security deposit. Taking more money out of her savings would definitely reduce the chances of the mortgage on the shop being sufficient, even if it was approved. But what other option did she have? The only other thing she could think of was to move back in with her parents. Twenty-nine and moving back home? She wasn't even sure she could stomach the thought.

She sighed, shut the lid and headed upstairs to bed, although she didn't expect she was going to get much sleep.

* * *

'Are you all right there, Holly?' Bernard asked as he placed the jar of sherbet lemons on the countertop ready for her. 'You don't seem quite yourself this morning.'

'Sorry.' She forced a smile. 'Just a few things on my mind, that's all.'

'Well, don't fret too much. You never know, it might never happen.'

It already has, was what she wanted to say, but she didn't think that burdening him with her troubles would be particularly good customer service. Besides, it went against Agnes' golden rule. So, instead, she bagged up his sweets, stamped his customer loyalty card – which was only one purchase away from a free gift – and bid him a good day.

Deciding there was no point beating about the bush, she'd already rung an estate agent about one of the properties in a nearby village. At just under eight hundred pounds a month, it was the cheapest there was. But it was a shoebox. The single-roomed, studio flat looked like there'd be just about enough room for a sofa bed. That would be it. No separate bedroom. No spare room for guests. Probably not even enough space to store her few belongings. Eight hundred pounds. The down payment alone would make a big dent in her shop-deposit funds.

Unfortunately, when she'd finally steeled herself enough to make the call, it had already gone. They did have another, about to come on the market, she was told, this time at a thousand a month and not even that much bigger. There was no garden either, which would have put paid to her ideas of summer barbecues and home-grown tomatoes. It had a minimum twelve-month lease too, meaning that once she'd signed on the dotted line, she would be stuck there for at least a year.

She told the woman she'd get back to her soon, and got the reply that, if she was really interested in the place, she should book an appointment to look at it that day. Rental properties didn't hang around long. Holly suspected she was telling the truth.

Around midday, her phone pinged with a message from Jamie.

Going to a scrumpy tasting. 7 o'clock. The Beagle's Nose.

She looked at the message. She had no idea where the Beagle's Nose was, although it seemed safe to assume it was a pub. Not that it mattered. Scrumpy tasting was probably like wine tasting, well out of her price bracket right now. She messaged back:

Sorry. I've got stuff to sort out.

Jamie's reply was instant.

Stuff can wait. Too good to miss. Caroline's coming too, and you can't say no… it's free!

Free events were very definitely her favourite. But still, she wasn't in the mood for socialising.

I'm not sure I'll be great company.

That's fine. Pick you up at seven.

In spite of everything, she found herself chuckling.

Tonight, it appeared, she was going out.

36

The difference between scrumpy and cider, Holly learned that evening, was subtle but distinct. Cider is a sparkling, carbonated beverage made by the fermentation of only the most select apples. Scrumpy, while also made from the fermentation of apples, is far rougher, with little-to-no specific selection of the fruit involved, and the process, which takes place in far smaller batches, results in a generally cloudier drink, which is typically far more alcoholic.

'Every one of us here is on the judging panel,' Jamie told her, as they took their seats in the corner of the pub. Ben had also joined them for the evening, although his demeanour, as usual, was far more subdued.

The Beagle's Nose, which was situated between Bourton and Stow-on-the-Wold, was a small pub which Holly had previously not even known existed, although, judging from the decor, it had been there for a very long time. That night it was absolutely rammed.

'So, what is it that we're judging, exactly?' she asked, as groups of locals dressed in an unnatural amount of tweed, laughed and slapped each other on the back.

'It's all the homebrews. There are dozens of small farms and smallholdings around here and, every year, there's a competition to see who's produced the best scrumpy. Mainly, it's the brewers themselves here judging, but since I did some work on the place a couple of years back, I always get an invite, too. It's a blind tasting. Every drink is numbered and only the landlady knows which is which. So it means you can't vote for your friends.'

'We're going to try a dozen different scrumpies?' Holly asked, wondering how she was going to feel in the shop the next day. Not to mention the fact that she still had to remember to ring the estate agent again to make an appointment to view the flat, provided it was still available.

'Probably more. And it'll just be the three of us drinking,' Caroline said. 'Ben is our designated driver.'

Ben raised an eyebrow, and she couldn't help but feel a tad guilty.

'Are you sure you don't mind?' she asked. Designated driver was a job she was happy to do, provided the passengers didn't get too inebriated. She couldn't help feeling that tonight was going to get messy.

'Don't feel sorry for him,' Caroline said. 'It's his turn. Besides, I drove last year, even though I was seven months pregnant, and he got so drunk that he threw up in my car.'

In no possible way could she ever imagine him getting into that state although, from the embarrassed look on his face, it must be true.

'I will admit,' he said, 'it was not my finest hour. So, I am more than happy to stay sober tonight. I have also brought a notepad and will record any comments you might pass on a particular offering.' The three women rolled their eyes.

It wasn't long before the first drink came out and then the second. Whilst Holly couldn't remember drinking scrumpy before, she'd had a fair-few ciders. As such, she expected the taste to be similar. How wrong she was.

'It just tastes like apples. Like the best apples.'

'That's why it's so dangerous,' Caroline said. 'Trust me. Just take a few sips of each one.'

Given how delicious it was, following this advice was far easier said than done. Hopefully, she thought, there would be a few she wouldn't like and therefore wouldn't be so keen to finish. By the time the fifth one arrived, she realised that was unlikely to be the case.

'I don't really think this is a fair way of doing it,' she said, her mood lightening as her housing problem slipped further and further to the back of her mind. 'I mean I can't actually remember what the first one tasted like now, apart from the fact that it was delicious. But then they all are, so how are we supposed to choose?'

'It's a flaw in the system,' Caroline agreed. 'To be honest, I think the landlady just picks one at random. I'm not complaining. It's pretty much my favourite night of the year. So, tell us, aren't you glad you came now?'

'You know what? I am. I really am.'

'So,' Jamie asked, scribbling something onto Ben's notepad. 'Do you want to tell us what put you in such a grump earlier, or is it a no-go area?'

She sighed. Now that the subject of the cottage and been brought up, there was no way she could avoid thinking about it. And there was no point hiding the truth, either. It wasn't like it was something that she could change.

'It's the cottage. Maud's sold it.'

'Really? That's fantastic.'

'Yes, for Maud,' she agreed. 'I'm happy for her. Unfortunately for me, it's a cash buyer who wants to be in by the end of next week. Which means I've got to find somewhere else to live, pronto. Rental prices in the village are extortionate and the only things available require a twelve-month lease and a deposit that's going to bleed me dry. Not to mention all the furnishings. As far as I can see, the only option is to move back in with my parents, which is not what I want to do. I'm not even sure they'd want me back, either. Honestly, I sometimes feel I should just give up, move back to London and be done with the whole thing. I mean, really, what is the point? Maybe not getting the mortgage was a sign.'

Silence followed her outburst, as three, stunned faces stared at her. She could feel pity radiating from them all. Now she'd done it. Ruined Caroline's favourite night of the year. They'd stop inviting her out if she kept bringing the mood down like this.

Wishing she could take back the moment, she was about to open her mouth to apologise, when Jamie spoke.

'Well, that's easy then. Just move in with me.'

'What?'

'It's the perfect solution. The house is way too big for me on my own and I've been thinking about getting a lodger for at least a year, haven't I Ben?'

'She has, indeed.'

'It's just I'm fussy about people, that's all.'

'You mean people are fussy about living with you,' Caroline interjected.

'Hey, that's not fair. I'd be a wonderful housemate. For starters, you'd know you never have to worry about anything breaking down on you.'

Now Holly was the stunned one, as she struggled to decide if Jamie's offer was genuine.

'I mean it,' Jamie said, reading her face. 'I've got two bathrooms, three bedrooms, a massive garden and you'd be helping me out with the rent money. I wouldn't need a deposit either, so that would sort out that little problem, too. From what I can see, it would be the perfect solution. I'm really easy going. I mean, you can have people over.'

Holly laughed. 'Who would I have over? I only know you three. Well, and Giles.'

'Okay, just let me make a correction to that. You can have people over, as long as they're not Giles Caverty.' Her faced hardened. 'That man will not step foot in my house.'

The Secret Diary of Sarah Chambers

37

With all the time that had passed, Holly had pushed the issue of Giles and Jamie to the back of her mind, but now Jamie had brought it up. The idea of moving in with her seemed like the solution to all her problems, but her issue with Giles – this seemed more than just a just casual animosity, which was a real bind. To say no to Jamie's kind offer of somewhere to live would leave her right back where she'd been before: completely screwed. But how could she move in with someone who felt that way about one of her few friends in the village? There was nothing else for it.

'Can I at least ask what happened between you two?' she asked. 'I mean, I know he told me that you had a thing once.'

All three of her companions seemed to be struggling not to choke on their scrumpy at this point.

'He told you what?' Jamie managed at last. 'What *exactly* did he say?'

Holly could feel their eyes boring into her, waiting for an answer. She picked up the nearest glass to her and downed a large mouthful before she replied.

'He didn't say much, really, just that you had a thing. And that maybe you wanted more than he did...?'

The last line came out tentatively, as she feared the response, but by the tears of laughter building in both Ben and Caroline's eyes, her comment was a source of amusement rather than anger.

'Seriously, where the hell does that guy get off?' Jamie demanded. 'The reason I hate him is because he's an arsehole.'

Holly looked to Caroline and Ben, both of whom nodded.

'I know you like him and everything and I know you think he's your friend. But seriously, the guy is sly, underhand and downright dodgy.'

'Dodgy?'

'Well, there was the thing with the nursing home to for starters.'

'What thing?'

Holly didn't mean to sound like she was badgering Jamie for answers, but so far, Giles had been nothing but lovely to her. If someone was going to make accusations like that, she at least wanted to know the basis for them.

'It's a long story, but basically a couple of years back, when I thought we were friends, he spent a few months coming to the nursing home with me. It seemed great at the time but I find out later that'd he'd been asking the staff all sorts of questions, like the number of residents they had, what the fees were and did they cover their costs. That sort of thing. The next thing you know, the Council has sold up to his uncle. He had just been getting inside information to strengthen his hand.'

'You can't be serious?'

'Oh, I admit I don't have any proof. But do you know how many times he visited between the sale being agreed and the old folks being turfed out? Zero. That's how many. Zero. I wouldn't trust him as far as I could throw him.'

'So, what he said about you and him being a thing?'

The anger left Jamie's face. 'I will confess that, perhaps, one evening not too dissimilar to this, I may have got a little bit drunk and there may have been a short fumble in a pub car park. But that was it. And I can assure you that it's something I have been trying to forget ever since.'

By this point, Caroline and Ben were nearly wetting themselves. Holly, on the other hand, was completely torn. She had no doubt that Jamie was telling the truth as she saw it, and the others weren't disagreeing, but she had misjudged Giles herself, until he'd explained his side of things. Could he really have been that unscrupulous? Maybe it was just a clash of personalities, pure and simple.

'What about if he only comes round when you're not there?' Holly asked, not wanting to push things too far with her potential landlady, yet not quite ready to entirely condemn Giles over something no one could prove, either.

Jamie sniffed. 'I suppose I could deal with that, but you'd have to air the place out afterwards: open the windows, hoover down the sofa or wherever he'd sat.'

Holly laughed. 'Okay, I think I can manage that.'

'Well, in that case, it sounds like we have a deal.'

Holly experienced a strange fluttering that was half caused by nervous-excitement and half scrumpy-fuelled.

'You're sure you want me living with you?'

'Can you cook?'

'I'm a very good cook. I can also darn socks and sew buttons on clothes extremely well.'

'Then it's a deal.' Grinning, Jamie lifted her glass. 'To housemates,' she said.

'To housemates,' they toasted. Although, as Holly went to clink hers with Ben's, she noticed a small twitch on his lips.

'And to new neighbours, as well,' she offered. And, all of a sudden, she felt even more excited by the prospect of her next move.

* * *

Jamie had wanted a little time to get the room in order – a fresh lick of paint, that kind of thing – and so it was four days later that Holly shoved her clothes in the same duffel bag that she'd left London with, plus a few bin bags, thanks to Caroline's donations. Funny the way things had a habit of turning out, she thought as she dropped the keys off at the estate agents by the river, before stopping to watch some children paddling in the freezing water. Was this constant roller-coaster section of a life nearing its end? She felt it might be. Provided there were no more major calamities, she was going to reach the profit target the mortgage company had set. Then she'd be a fully-fledged business owner, living with a new friend in a part of the country she loved.

'It's taken me a few years to get it exactly as I wanted it,' Jamie told Holly when she arrived. 'In hindsight, you probably should have seen other places before you decided to live here, but the contract's signed now,' she winked.

The contract she was referring to, was a slip of paper torn out of Ben's notepad at the scrumpy tasting, upon which was written the words *House Contract*, in drunken scrawl, underneath which both women had signed their names. Said piece of paper was now attached by a magnet to Jamie's very impressive fridge. In fact, from what Holly could see, everything about the house was impressive. The open-plan kitchen-diner was a beautiful mixture of stained wood and white-washed walls. The two bathrooms upstairs were fully appointed and the spare bedroom, that was now hers, was at least as big as the bedroom she'd shared with Dan.

'It's the garden that really needs working on,' Jamie continued. 'I want to put in a water feature, but I can't decide whether I want a standard fish pond, or a more Zen-type thing. I'd also like a veg patch, one day.'

'I can help with that,' Holly offered, finding another way she could contribute, particularly as the rent she was being charged was outrageously low. 'Mum and Dad had me growing tomatoes and courgettes from before I could even walk.'

'Great, then we have another housemate job assigned. You, Holly Berry, are in charge of the vegetable garden, cooking and all clothes repairs.'

'Sounds good to me. How about I start tonight?'

*　*　*

'What is that amazing smell? Please tell me there's some for me,' Jamie said, as she came into the kitchen the next morning. 'You didn't have to make breakfast too, you know. Dinner was amazing.'

'It's nothing. I hope you don't mind; I raided the cupboards. And it is only French toast with a blackberry compote. Frozen blackberries, I'm afraid, but you've got a hedgerow with brambles in outside, so in the autumn we can have them fresh.'

Jamie reached past her and tore off a corner, straight out of the pan. How the hell it didn't burn her fingers, Holly had no idea, but a moment later the food was in her mouth, and she was groaning with pleasure.

'Oh my God, that's so delicious. You are definitely staying now. And cooking every meal, too.'

Grinning, Holly turned off the hob and slid the French toast onto plates, before Jamie tried to eat it all out of the pan

'You can reheat it later if you want. There might be a bit too much to finish now.'

'Are you not eating?'

Holly looked out the window before shaking her head.

'I need to get to the shop before it starts to rain. It's looking pretty horrid outside. I just hope it doesn't put the tourists off.'

By the time she'd grabbed a coat and found her umbrella, it was already starting to spit, although fortunately she managed to get into the shop moments before the storm broke. It was a relief not to have to worry about the roof, although she couldn't stop herself going up to check once or twice, just to make sure there were no drips. Old habits die hard and it was one she suspected she would have trouble breaking.

The grey day wore on and, as eleven o'clock approached, it became clear that even the regulars weren't going to come out in this weather. Knowing that there were only two options – continue staring out the window, hoping that some brave soul might venture out to buy some sweets or busy herself with other jobs, leaving Drey to man the fort – Holly had just gone upstairs when her phone pinged. The title of the email alone was enough to make her heart flutter: *Enquiry about birthday sweet platter.*

Excitement flooded through her as she read the message, which explained how the gentleman had found her website and wondered if she would be able to do something for his daughter's eleventh birthday.

'Drey, we have our first sweet platter order,' she called down the stairs.

After they had composed themselves, Holly typed a professional yet friendly reply in which she stated the various options she could offer, although saying that she was willing to work within any budget and accommodate specific requests.

'Oh Drey, you are a genius.'

'It has been said before,' she replied.

Unfortunately, that was the highlight of the day. The weather refused to break and the whole village was as quiet as a graveyard.

Any tour-coach visitors that arrived were ushered straight into the warmth of the various cafés, only to hurry back to their vehicles afterwards. When Holly finally closed up for the day, she had taken less than half of what she'd expected to.

* * *

The next day was the same, as was the rest of the week. The weekend brightened a little, but then Monday picked up right where the previous week had left off. By Thursday, she was getting quite despondent.

'The sweet platters have helped,' she told Jamie that evening. 'But the next three days have to pick up big time. If they don't, I'm not going to make enough to hit the target.'

'Well maybe Maud could give you another few weeks. Surely, when summer arrives, business will really pick up.'

'I can't ask her to do that. She has already put off the developers for three months. If she has to leave it any longer, she might worry they'll lose interest.'

'The weather forecast promises sunshine tomorrow. Let's pray they're right for once,' Jamie said, with a hopeful smile.

Before Holly could respond, her phone pinged with a message. She pursed her lips at the name. An action Jamie immediately noticed.

'Let me guess: Mr Caverty is requesting your company? I thought he'd been absent for a while.'

Holly had thought the exact same thing. It had been a couple of weeks since she'd last heard from Giles and she was starting to think he'd ghosted her for good this time. She was pleased that this wasn't the case.

'He wants to head out for a drink tonight. You don't mind if I disappear, do you?'

'Of course not. Actually, I've got an Ann Summers party organised. I was going to ask if you'd like to join me. You could start running them yourself, if you want?'

'Perhaps next time,' she replied, a definite note of scepticism in her voice.

Jamie smirked. 'I'm going to hold you to that,' she said.

38

They arranged to meet at the river and decide where to go from
there. While they were lucky enough to be enjoying some fine,
spring weather and a fair few people were milling about, Giles was
easy to spot in his salmon-pink shirt, sweater draped over his
shoulders.

'How was Marseille?' Holly asked, as she moved in to kiss him
on the cheek. She'd never really thought of herself as a cheek kisser.
It always struck her as somewhat affected. He was still chewing
gum. How long was it going to take him to quit smoking?

'Marseille is overrated,' he replied. 'Have you been?'

'To Marseille? No.'

'It's worth a visit, but I think I'm just tired of it now. I find I get
that way with places. You reach a point where you've seen it all,
don't you think?'

'Given that I've only been on a plane a dozen times, including
the return journeys, I don't think I'm in danger of that just yet.'

'Ah, humble Holly.' With a slight narrowing of his eyes, he tilted
his head and studied her. 'You look happy.'

'Do I?'

'Yes, I have to admit, I wasn't expecting it.'

'Were you not?'

'I'd heard a rumour although, by all appearances, I suspect it isn't true.'

'Oh, what rumour was that?'

At some point they had started walking along beside the river. Where they were heading, she had no idea. Not that it really mattered. The evening was warm enough, and there was something a little romantic about the darkening skies, although she wasn't going to fall into that trap again. Friends was absolutely fine. Friends was what she needed. She just hoped the clouds weren't still there tomorrow. She needed the next two weeks to be absolutely perfect.

'I heard on the grapevine that Maud had sold the cottage and you were going to be turfed out onto the street next week. I wanted to message from France to check, but my signal's been just terrible. And, judging by how well you look, I guess it's not true.'

Holly was once again amazed at the speed of the village gossip mill.

'Actually, your sources were quite correct. She has got a buyer. And it was all a bit worrying for a day or two there. Fortunately, Jamie came to the rescue. I moved into her spare room last week, as a matter of fact.'

'Jamie?'

'She's got a wonderful home. Loads of space. To be honest, she's been a complete life saver. I have no idea how I could have managed to put a deposit down on a place without digging into the mortgage deposit money, and I really didn't want to go back to my parents with my tail between my legs. It probably sounds cheesy, but it feels like it was fated.'

'It really does sound that way, doesn't it?'

They had reached the last bridge. In a few metres, grass gave way to road. There was still plenty more to see in that direction during daylight hours: the model village, the maze, Birdland. But none of them were open at this hour, and there didn't seem much point in them continuing in that direction.

'So, what do you fancy doing?' she asked. 'Are you hungry? Do you want to go for dinner? Or just get a drink? As long as it's not scrumpy. It's going to be a while before I can look at another glass of that.' Pausing on the path and taking her hand, Giles squinted as he considered the question.

'Do you know what? To be honest, I've had a real sweet craving all day. Actually, while I was away too.'

'So you just want to get dessert somewhere?'

'No, I think I want sweets.'

'You're not serious?' She arched an eyebrow.

'I am. All day I've had a massive hankering for those pink shrimp things: the foam ones. You know the ones I mean?'

'Of course, I do. I run a confectionery. What kind of sweet shop owner would I be if I didn't sell pink shrimps?'

A cheeky smile slanted one side of his face. 'I don't suppose you've got your shop keys with you, have you?'

* * *

'For crying out loud, not again,' Holly exclaimed as they reached the shop.

'What is it?' Giles asked.

'Another little gift from our feline friend,' she said, pointing to the dead mouse in front of the door. 'Drey promised she'd stop feeding him here but if this doesn't improve soon, I'm going to have to start throwing water on him.'

'Don't worry,' Giles said, pulling a handkerchief from his pocket.

'I'll get rid of it.' With that he scooped it up and turned towards the bin while Holly unlocked the door.

There seemed something inherently mischievous about being there together in the shop at that time of the evening. Of course she'd pulled late nights before, when she'd needed to restock the shelves, et cetera, but that had been work. She'd never gone into her own premises for the sole purpose of late-night nibbles.

'Pink shrimps,' she said, pulling the jar off the shelf and placing it on the counter.

'I don't think I ever noticed what a treasure trove this place is, before,' he said, turning full circle. 'You've done amazingly. You must have every sweet imaginable.'

'I'm not sure I've got every one but hopefully I'm pretty close.'

'Flying saucers? '

'Of course.'

'What about pineapple cubes? And cola cubes?'

'Yes and yes. Like I said, it's a sweet shop.'

As he peered from one shelf to the next, he really did look like the proverbial kid in a candy store, she thought. It was one thing seeing strangers fall in love with the place, but there was something even more special about seeing friends do it. After scanning every jar, he stopped at an empty one and turned to her.

'No lemon bonbons?' he said with a mock sad face. 'I love those.'

Holly let out an exaggerated sigh. 'Let me go check upstairs.'

* * *

When they left the shop, he was cradling several bags of sweets. The inner child was very definitely out.

'Well, this definitely goes down as the best date night ever.'

The word *date* hovered in her mind for just a moment. A month ago, she would have probably fixated on it, read far more into it than he'd intended. But she knew the truth. They were just two friends having a bit of fun. Just like that non-date with Ben, cycling around the Slaughters and eating ice cream. That had been a really good day, too.

Back where they had started, they took a seat together on one of the benches by the river. Holly's mind was occupied with thoughts of the upcoming weekend. She'd kept a close watch on the finances, diligently filling in the spreadsheets, and she was set to meet the all-important target – just. Then she'd send them through to the broker next week and all this stress would be gone. Or at least, a large part of it.

Next to her, Giles munched on yet another pink shrimp, unusually quiet, probably still tired from his trip.

'I should be heading back,' she said, after a minute of watching the street lights reflecting off the surface of the water in tiny, golden sparkles.

'Sorry, what was that?'

'I've been opening the shop early. Getting customers in first thing. And Fridays are always busy, so I should really get an early night.'

'Are you sure? Shall I drop you back at the house? I brought the Porsche; it's parked just up the road.'

'It's fine. It's not a long walk and, to be honest, I quite like it. But I'll see you soon?'

'I hope so.'

A kiss on each cheek followed, and she realised she was starting to feel a chill in the air. Still, a brisk walk would help alleviate the cold.

Ten minutes later and she was standing on the driveway. Judging by the dark windows, she had arrived home before Jamie. Next door, there was only one light on. She smiled to herself. Of course, Ben wouldn't waste electricity by leaving extra lights on. As she slid the key into the lock and opened the front door, she paused for just a second.

A permanent place to live, a business that she could keep afloat and friends. This was exactly what she'd been after when she moved here. Life was pretty great.

39

For once, the weather forecast was spot on. The next day was glorious.

Normally, busy days like this one only happened on weekends or bank holidays, when Drey was there to help. But it didn't matter. Holly was in her element, gathering one jar then another, making suggestions and selections, even giving away lollipops to well-behaved children and one or two who looked like they just needed a distraction. This was what she needed. As long as the weekend stayed like this – as the forecast assured her it would – then she would hit the target. She could do it. She could definitely do it.

Even Humbug made her laugh as he stood outside the window meowing for a stroke.

'At least you've learned to stay there now,' she said to him through the glass. 'But don't think I've forgiven you for yesterday's present. You need to mend your ways if you think you're going to get anywhere with me.'

With a disgruntled mew, he looked up pleadingly, before turning around and sauntering off, leaving Holly to her customers.

With the afternoon quickly upon her, she was busy adding a stamp to another loyalty card when a man approached the counter. Dressed in a suit and tie, beneath a rather depressing-looking raincoat, he wore a blue lanyard around his neck that she couldn't quite make out.

'Miss Holly Berry?' He had waited until the previous customer had left before speaking.

'Yes, can I help you?'

'I hope so. My name is Victor Martinez. I'm here from the Chartered Institute of Environmental Health.'

'Environmental Health?' Her heart momentarily skipped a beat, before quickly settling down again. Of course, how long had it been since the last visit? One month? Two? Obviously, time for the developers to try their luck again with more scare tactics. Well, she knew better than to let some faceless creeps get the better of her now. Her body stiffened and her jaws locked as she looked the man up and down.

'Unbelievable,' she said.

'Sorry?'

Her previous feeling of contentment had evaporated and well and truly been replaced with outrage. They may have exchanged the long-nosed stooge for one who looked more convincing, but she wasn't falling for it again. No chance. This was almost hers, and she was hanging on to it.

'Get out,' she spat.

'Excuse me?'

'When are they going to give up?'

The man cleared his throat. 'I don't know if you heard what I said, Miss Berry, but I'm from Environmental Health.'

'Oh I heard exactly what you said. And I normally work at the Folies Bergère. Now listen to me. You can go straight back to the people who hired you and tell them it's not going to work this time.

I'm not going to roll over. These bullying tactics aren't going to work on me any longer. Did you get all that?'

'Miss Berry, I am very concerned...'

'So you should be. Maybe you thought you could intimidate me before. But that's not happening again. Not when I'm *this* close. Now please, get off my property before I call the police.'

His face was growing more and more shocked by the second. Good, she thought to herself. He should be put out. It was school-yard bullying, plain and simple.

'Miss Berry, I would urge you to listen to me. I don't think you understand the gravity of the situation. These allegations are quite serious. Unless you co-operate and we work together to address them, particularly as the shop has had prior issues...'

'Allegations? Work together?' Of course, a different ploy. Obviously outright intimidation hadn't worked, so he was going for a nicey-nicey routine. 'Nope, I'm done with you. Out. Out. Get out now.'

If the broom had been handy, she would have used it, but as all she had was her hands, that was what she used, coming around the counter to shoo him out the door. She would have got him there too, if it hadn't been for Ben's sudden appearance.

'Hey Holly,' he said, before his eyes widened in surprise at the state of her unwanted guest. 'Victor, what are you doing here?'

'I'm supposed to be doing an inspection,' he replied, as he clung to his bag.

'Well, I don't need any more phoney visits from so-called health inspectors or Trading Standards,' she spat.

'She doesn't seem to be in a rational state of mind,' the Inspector said to Ben.

'What you mean is, I'm not falling for your lies again. Tell him, Ben. Tell him I know what they're up to and I'm not going anywhere. Not now, not ever,'

Knowing that Ben – apart from their first encounter – tended to have the habit of thinking carefully before speaking, the speed of his response took her by surprise.

'Holly, is this Victor Martinez, and he works for the Institute of Environmental Health. This is a real inspection.'

40

Holly had made mistakes before: said the wrong thing, put her foot in her mouth and wound up being embarrassed. But it was nothing compared to how she felt at that precise moment. Mortified. No, even mortified didn't cover it. Never before had she so desperately wished that the ground would open up and swallow her whole.

'I'm so, so sorry.' she apologised for the umpteenth time, as she locked the door and turned the sign around to *Closed*. 'I've just had quite a few problems. Somebody impersonating a health inspector. Actually, he may not have actually been impersonating one. We think that somebody was maybe paying him. In fact, we're almost positive. And I'm under quite a lot of pressure. You see the mortgage company need to know that I can turn this place around and make a profit, and the deadline is this weekend.'

'Miss Berry.'

Her name was said as a statement that very much meant it was time for her to stop talking. And she did, although a moment later she wanted to start explaining all over again. Silence was bad. She didn't like silence.

'I have to say I am very concerned. Normally when people act so... *defensively*, it's because they have something to hide.'

'No, no, no.' She shook her head as fast as she could. 'I don't have anything to hide. Nothing at all. Please, help yourself. Look around.'

From the look on his face, there was a very good chance he thought she was utterly out of her mind, and, to give him his due, she wasn't entirely sure that she wasn't. She certainly felt like she was going crazy. To think of how she'd behaved; she must have looked completely insane.

'I can vouch for her,' Ben said, in a firm, supporting manner. 'She's had a lot of stress trying to get this place up and running. And it does appear that people have tried to make life particularly difficult.'

'Well,' he seemed only mildly reassured by Ben's words. 'I should tell you that I've not arrived here on a random visit. I've actually had a complaint.'

Holly's heart sank.

'What do you mean? A complaint? Why? What did they say? What was the problem?'

He wrung his hands together. This was different from her previous 'inspections'. This chap looked almost apologetic.

'Miss Berry, perhaps it's easier if I carry out my inspection first? See if there is any weight to these claims.'

'Of course. Whatever you need.'

With a quick nod, he placed his briefcase on the counter, opened it up and pulled out a pair of plastic gloves and a face mask. By the time these were in place, he looked more like he was about to do a dental inspection than a shop one.

'Over here, is this the only place in the shop that you have chocolate hedgehogs?'

'Chocolate hedgehogs?' she queried, taken aback by the peculiarly specific question. 'Uhm, yes. There's some more upstairs in the store room, I think.'

'But only here on the shop floor?'

'Yes.'

'Okay then. Thank you.'

If Holly had been surprised by the question, it was nothing compared to what happened next, as the Inspector pushed items aside, and slid a hand all the way to the back of the shelf. A moment later, he stood back up, pulling the glove inside out over his fist and holding it up.

It was Ben who spoke first, stepping forwards, a frown etched on his forehead as he peered at it.

'Is that a mouse?' he asked.

'It is,' the Inspector replied. 'It's a dead mouse. Miss Berry, I'm afraid this is an extremely serious health violation.'

41

If felt as though somebody had sucked all the air out of the room. She was trying to stay rational, trying to think straight, but the shop was spinning around her. The sweet smell that she adored so much was now making her feel sick. Resting her hand against the wall, Holly tried to steady herself.

'Is there somewhere you can take a seat?' Mr Martinez asked. 'Maybe a glass of water? A cup of tea perhaps?'

'There's a kettle upstairs. I'll do it,' Ben said.

'Shouldn't you be getting back to work?' she asked. 'You must have appointments. People you need to see.'

'It's not a problem, honestly. There's only twenty minutes left until closing time, anyway. I'll stay as long as you need me.'

Still reeling from the turn of events, she noticed the two men exchanging a fleeting glance, although what this meant, she had no idea.

'Miss Berry.' Mr Martinez started speaking, as Ben disappeared upstairs. 'I can see you're very upset by this.'

'You think?' A tear ran down her cheek. 'I would never... I just...'

The Inspector nodded solemnly.

'Miss Berry, in cases like this, I'm afraid it is rarely a one off. Have you seen any other mice on the premises? It's likely there will be a nest.'

'A nest?' She shook her head. 'No, I've not seen any mice here. Not any, except... oh God, that damn cat!'

'Cat? You have a cat in the sweet shop?'

'Not deliberately, no. But sometimes it would come in. Before I took over, that is. Drey used to feed it treats. But I told her she wasn't to do that any more, and it stopped coming in. But the mice... once or twice... only outside, though. Only outside...' She couldn't even bring herself to manage full sentences. 'What do I do?' she asked. 'What do I do?'

'I know the cat she means; the whole village does.' Ben came to her defence far more passionately than she'd ever seen him act before. 'Honestly, you can ask anyone. The thing's a nightmare. It brought a bird into the bank once. A fully grown, live bird into a bank full of people. And then let it go.'

'That may be the case, Ben, but Miss Berry here has a duty of care when it comes to the health and welfare of her customers.'

'So, what does that mean?' she asked. 'What about the shop?'

'My heart goes out to you, Miss Berry. But I can't let you reopen the shop. Not until I can sign off on a full inspection.'

'What does that mean?' she asked again.

'Well, obviously, you will need to get pest control in, and carry out whatever procedures they require. After that, we can make an appointment for me to come back. Hopefully, if you can get every-thing underway immediately, you may be able to reopen in a couple of weeks or so. Subject to the full inspection, of course. If you fail that, then the closure will be permanent.'

A couple of weeks. It felt like someone had kicked her in the stomach.

'So, I'm done,' she said. 'That's it. If I can't open the shop this weekend, I won't be able to show the mortgage broker the profit she wanted. Which means it's game over. All that work. All that time. And it's just going to go to the developers.'

'Victor, please. You and I go back a long way. You can take my word, there's no issue here apart from a scruffy, village cat.'

'I can't, Ben. I wish I could. I'm so sorry, Miss Berry. Really I am.'

Closing his briefcase, he straightened up and offered one more solemn nod.

'I'll be in touch,' he said, sadly.

All the warmth had drained from the shop. It was more than just the cool of the evening. It was as though it had evaporated from the very bricks of the building, along with the laughter, the sweet innocence. Sucked clean away. And it was her fault; that was what hurt so badly. All the other things: the shoplifting, the debts, even the roof caving in, had been – for the most part – beyond her control. But this. This was entirely down to her. She had been too soft hearted.

'I made you a cup of tea,' Ben said, holding out a mug. 'But I didn't know how you take it.'

She could hear the question, but she couldn't find it within herself to respond.

'Do you need sugar? Milk? I should have added milk. Of course you'd want milk. I'll go and put some in.'

'No, no it's fine.' She reached out to take the mug, but grabbed his arm instead. The moment her fingers touched him, every emotion she had been holding in for the last hour came roaring to the surface.

'I thought I was doing it right. I thought I could do this. But I can't. I can't.'

'Yes, you can. It's just a hiccup.'

'It's not a hiccup, Ben. I've got so close. Without this weekend's sales, I can't meet the target.' The juddering breaths turned into angry sobs that spilled out as great, gulping wheezes. 'It's over. It's all over.'

'It's fine. It's fine. There, there.'

Trying to hold onto a steaming mug, while offering words of comfort to a borderline hysterical woman, was no mean feat, but Ben was managing rather well, manoeuvring himself to place the tea on the counter, while still keeping an arm wrapped around Holly. Her snivels continued for a minute or two longer, before he spoke again.

'Do you want the tea?' he asked, breaking away. 'Or do you just want to head home?'

Realising the words were probably meant as a polite way of saying it was time to get herself together, with one final sniff, she wiped her nose with the back of her hand.

'There's no point hanging around here. I can't sell anything.'

After collecting her coat and bag from upstairs, she switched off the lights and closed the front door. From behind her came a sad meow.

'You have to be kidding me,' she snapped.

42

Angry wasn't even close to how she felt. She had been back home for a full hour and was on her third cup of tea and still her blood was boiling.

'All the times I told her not to feed that sodding cat.' Holly forced herself to take slow, deep breaths in and out. 'I told her not to let it into the shop.'

'I can't imagine she deliberately ignored you,' Jamie said. 'I've only met the girl once or twice, but I don't believe she'd do anything to intentionally jeopardise the business. She loves it there.'

'I know that. Believe me I do. But this is on her. All of this. I told her the very first day I met her. She knew exactly what the rules were. The truth is, there's no way it would have carried on coming into the shop if she hadn't kept feeding it. And what else would one mouse being doing in the shop like that? The fact that Drey didn't listen to me...'

It hurt, was what she wanted to say. True, the girl was over ten years younger than her, but Holly had seen so much of herself in Drey. She had trusted her. Now she had lost her shop and any sense of trust with it.

When they had seen the cat, standing outside the front door, waiting for snacks, she had been so furious that it was all Ben could do to stop her ringing Drey there and then and firing her. Never in her life had she been so furious.

'I need to ring her. I need to speak to her.'

'That's probably not a good idea until you calm down a little,' Jamie suggested.

'Well, I have to tell her not to come in tomorrow. Or any day in the future, for that matter.'

'I can ring her for you, if that would be easier?' Jamie said, her face still full of concern.

'No, I have to do this.'

Leaving her in the kitchen, Holly took her phone up to her room. Not that it would be hers much longer, she thought. Without the sweet shop, there was little point staying in the village, and it wasn't as if getting a job here would be an option. At least she still had most of her house deposit money. That would see her through until she found a new one.

Her fingers hovered over Drey's name, before she finally plucked up the courage to hit *Call*. It was answered on the second ring.

'Hi Holly, everything okay? I was going to come in early tomorrow. Make sure we're super ready. I was thinking seven-thirty? Is that all right?' she paused, waiting for Holly to reply, but she couldn't. 'Holly, is everything all right?'

'The shop will be closed tomorrow.' Her voiced sounded detached, as if it wasn't even part of her any more.

'What do you mean? Have you already hit the target? It's a Saturday. I'm still happy to come in.'

Holly was finding it hard to speak.

'The shop won't be opening again,' she said, in an oddly business-like manner.

'What? What do you mean?'

'We've been shut down. By Environmental Heath. We won't be able to open again. Without this weekend, I've lost my chance with the mortgage broker.'

Saying it out loud, caused an ache to spread through her chest.

'How? I mean, why? What happened?'

A thousand responses ran through her head. *You happened*, she wanted to say. *You and that bloody cat.* It was the truth. She should say it, she thought. But Drey loved the shop. She was going to be heartbroken enough as it was. Could she really do that to her?

'Best of luck for the future, Andrea,' she said, finally, then hung up.

* * *

The next day dawned and nothing had changed. Her heart was still just as heavy. And all the crying the night before had left her with red eyes, a sore throat and a headache. Even the old standby of coffee, painkillers and junk food couldn't shift it.

'I've got a job on this morning, but I can come back for lunch if you'd like?' Jamie said from the doorway

Holly had relocated from the bedroom to the living room, but brought her duvet down with her. Sometimes a duvet on the sofa was the best you could hope for.

'Don't worry, I'll be fine,' she said, as she munched on another biscuit from the packet she'd found at the back of a cupboard.

'Just ring me, okay? If you need anything at all, ring me.'

'I will,' she said. They both knew it was a lie.

Although Jamie had to go out, it didn't stop her from sending people to check in on Holly.

Caroline was the first. After calling her mobile several times, then messaging to say she was popping over, she spent a solid minute ringing the doorbell. Short rings, long rings, syncopated ones, she tried them all. No response. Holly squirmed with guilt. She was a terrible person, leaving her friend outside while she hid with the curtains drawn and pretended she wasn't in. But she couldn't face people. Not now. Not yet.

Unfortunately, her ruse didn't work so well on Ben. First he knocked on the front door, then on the back and finally called through the letterbox.

'Holly, I know you're in there. Caroline's not been able to raise you and Jamie wants me to check on you.'

She sank deeper under the duvet.

'Fine, then,' he called. 'I'll just let myself in.'

It was too late. By the time she realised he wasn't joking and did, in fact, possess a key, he was already in the house and standing in the living room doorway. She went to get to her feet then, suddenly conscious of her crumpled and, worse, stained pyjamas, sank back under the duvet.

'So you are in,' he said. 'That's good at least.'

'I need some alone time.'

'So I can see. And how's that working?'

A venomous scowl was her only response.

'You would probably feel better if you didn't stay cooped up. We could go for a bike ride,' he suggested. 'It's a beautiful day.'

'Brilliant,' Holly replied with a sneer. 'A beautiful day. I'm sure the village is packed.'

She didn't say any more. He knew what she meant.

'Well, if you change your mind, I'll be home next door, all day.'

'I won't,' she said, picking up the remote and flicked over to another channel. A moment later, she heard the front door go and she flopped back, feeling even more guilty than before.

* * *

'You need something to take your mind off things,' Jamie said, when she returned at lunchtime. 'How about I take you for a drink? Or an afternoon tea. They do a lovely one at a café in Stow. I could ring Caroline, too. You know she'd be up for it.'

'I wouldn't be good company.'

'Who said you are normally?' Jamie fired back. The joke fell completely flat and she bit down on her lip and tried again. 'I can't imagine how horrid you must feel. I really can't. But I hate to see you like this. Maybe just go for a walk. I can come with you, or not. I don't mind. I'm just worried about the brooding. Have you even had a shower today?'

Holly was about to reply that brooding could sometimes be a very therapeutic and worthwhile pastime, not to mention showering every day was bad for your skin and the environment, when her phone buzzed on the table. Giles' name flashed up. The accompanying message read:

I saw the shop was shut. Is everything okay?

Somehow, even from across the room, Jamie sensed who it was.

'For once, seeing him might actually be something I approve of,' she said.

'I'm not sure.'

'I'd even pay you to go and see him. How about that for a turn around?'

Holly really didn't want to move but suspected she was right. Sitting in the same spot so long had already brought on a severe bout of pins and needles, and as much as she didn't want to admit it, a full morning's moping had done absolutely nothing to improve the situation. Maybe she could ask Giles for a job polishing his sports cars. It would be better than nothing, which was exactly what she had now.

'Fine,' she said, tapping in,

Fancy a drink?

'Although you might want to think about getting out of your pyjamas first.'

While the shower helped her feel a fraction more human, the walk to the pub had done nothing to shake her out of the doldrums.

Giles was already waiting inside, drinks poured and a wine bottle in the cooler.

'I ordered. Is that okay?' he asked, as she sat down opposite him.

She picked up the glass in front of her and gulped down half the contents.

'Maybe you'd like something stronger,' he suggested.

'You have no idea.'

After another sizeable swig, she put the glass down and he immediately topped it up.

'Come on, it can't be that bad.'

'Well, it depends if you call failing an Environmental Health inspection and having to shut up shop not that bad. If you don't, then I guess it isn't.'

'How on earth did that happen?'

'He found a dead mouse in the shop.'

Holly opened her mouth to continue, but even thinking about it caused tears to well up again. As silly as it sounded, the guilt was overwhelming. Guilt for the pain she knew Drey was going to feel if she ever found out what she'd caused. Guilt for having let Maud and Agnes down. Guilt for making her drama the centre of Giles and Jamie and Caroline and Ben's lives, yet again. She thought back to what he had said to her, all those weeks ago, about some people just not being cut out to run their own business. She had dismissed it out of hand. Seen it as nothing more than cocky, male arrogance.

Now she had to face facts. She, Holly Berry, had been out of her depth all long. She swallowed the tears back down.

'How about we don't talk about it now, if that's all right with you? Tell me what you've been doing. What exciting trips have you got in the offing?'

Thankfully, he moved the conversation on to his next travel plans. Apparently, he was considering investing in some holiday properties in Thailand but was having trouble deciding exactly where.

'Phuket has a reputation,' he told her. 'But if you head to the south of the island, there are some incredible beaches. Then again, Koh Lanta has always been underrated.'

She nodded along, only half-listening, mind still on what on earth she was supposed to do next. She could probably go back to her old job. They were always recruiting and she'd worked there for years with no complaints. But could she face doing that?

Finishing the last of her wine, she lifted the bottle for a refill, only to find it was empty.

'I'll get us another,' he said immediately, standing up.

She shook her head. 'No, it's okay. Actually, I think I've probably had enough. I should head home.'

'Are you sure?'

'I am.'

'All right then. Just let me settle up and I'll walk you there, if you'd like?'

'That would be nice,' she said, with a smile.

The blue sky was transforming with hues of purple and tangerine, casting the village in an almost ethereal light while, on the river, a family of ducks was heading downstream. The whole scene was perfectly serene and only served to deepen her sense of loss. She dug her hands into her pockets. Giles wrapped his arm around her in a tight squeeze that pulled her against his chest. She let her body slump into his. This was what she needed, she realised, as the tears began to surface yet again. A hug. For the longest moment she stayed there, absorbing the warmth of his body and wishing that life could put itself on pause for just a minute, so that she could delay facing it a little longer.

Clearing his throat, he released her and combed his fingers through his hair.

'Holly Berry, you are one determined woman, you know that don't you? Don't worry about all this. You've got your whole future ahead of you. Think of all you can do without the stress of the shop. Maybe travel, like you said you've always wanted to. Perhaps even get a job abroad. Take this as a chance to seize all the opportunities that are out there for you, rather than focus on what you've lost.'

'I know. You are right.' The truth was, she'd thought the same thing at least a dozen times that very afternoon.

'In a couple of years, you'll look back on this and laugh. It sounds crazy, I know, but you will. You'll have a great story to tell all your friends about the mouse hiding amongst the chocolate hedgehogs.'

Holly tried to smile, but it would take more than a couple of years to laugh about this, she thought and was about to say as much, when a thought struck her like a thunderbolt.

'How did you know the mouse was in with hedgehogs?'

43

Her question was met with silence. She could hear the water lapping gently beneath the bridge, the rustle of the evening breeze shaking the leaves on the trees and the noise of distant chatter, drifting over from outside the pub. Come to think of it, she could probably hear dozens of things, but not a sound came from Giles.

He stood there stunned, as if frozen to the spot. He finally shook his head with a laugh.

'It was the first thing you told me when you arrived.'

'No. No I didn't. I said there was a mouse. I didn't say where it was. I certainly didn't mention the chocolate hedgehogs. So why would you say that?'

'Well, but... it's an obvious assumption to make, anyway. They're close to the door and I think I read something about mice liking chocolate once, not that it would matter to them if it was hedgehog-shaped, of course. Assuming you didn't tell me, that is. Are you sure you didn't?'

He was rambling, just like she always did when she was nervous. She stepped further away from him and looked him straight in the face.

'Yes, I'm sure I didn't. And, given all the sweets in my shop, guessing the exact place where the mouse was found is pretty incredibly, really. More than incredible.'

'You just don't remember what you said.'

'Just stop Giles. Please, stop. It all makes sense now. It was you all along. You're the one with the health inspector in your pocket, and when that didn't work, you had to resort to an even dirtier trick to get me out of my shop.'

'Holly, I don't know what you're on about. You're just very upset and emotional.'

'You think I'm upset? I'm not upset. I am... bloody furious! You will pay for this. I mean *really* pay. There will be legal consequences for what you've done, I can promise you that.'

'Legal consequences?' Giles' smile was gone, his charming, relaxed demeanour replaced with one that dripped pure venom. 'Come on, Holly, I've done you a favour. I've been trying to do you a favour the whole time. You don't know the first thing about running a business. And you're obviously emotionally unstable, or else why would you consider buying one with no experience and no money to back you? You were destined to fail. You swept in and messed up. That's all there is to it.'

'You're the developer. You've been planning this all along.'

'That's right, for three years. For three whole years I have been putting together planning proposals, business constructs, working out how to turn that derelict little shack into something with a decent profit. Trying to persuade that miserable, old woman to part with the place. And you just turn up and everything falls into place for you. She rolls over without you even having to break into a sweat. It's not that I don't like you, Holly. Maybe, in different circumstances, there could have been something between us. It was obvious you wouldn't kick me out of bed in a hurry.'

'You horrid, vile man. You won't get away with this.'

'Away with what? Honestly, weeks without a day off have taken their toll on you. It would just be your word against mine. And the thing that people – people like you, at least – don't realise, is that money can't buy you happiness. But it can buy power. And, Holly Berry, I have an awful lot of that around here. Face it: you're done.'

With a sneer that made her want to punch him in the face, he started to turn away from her. Then, out of nowhere and before she knew what she was doing, she shoved him as hard as she could. It was no more than he deserved. Far less, in fact. But it was all that she had to give at that moment. Giles clearly wasn't expecting it and made matters worse by tripping over his own feet.

The splash, as he went tumbling into the river, sent all the ducks flapping and squawking into the sky.

'You crazy bloody woman!' he spluttered as he picked himself up, water running off him. 'Do you know how much this jacket cost? And oh God, my sodding phone.' He pulled it dripping from his pocket.

'Serves you right.'

'That was assault, pure and simple. You're lucky I can't call the police right now, but I bloody well will.'

'Well, I don't see any witnesses, so I guess it's just your word against mine.'

'There are CCTV cameras all along here.'

'Well if there are, then I hope it gives the police a good laugh when they watch it back.'

She really didn't care any more.

It was at that moment that it hit her. *Watch it back.* The cameras. She began to laugh. A chuckle at first, but it quickly grew into a full-on belly laugh.

'You think this is funny?' he literally spat at her from the water. 'Great, laugh away. I've got the last laugh Holly. You're ruined.'

'Thank you,' she spluttered out through the tears that were now streaming down her cheeks.

'Sorry?'

'Thank you. Thank you so much.'

He had now managed to climb up the bank and stood there, dripping on the grass. Which only made her laugh all the harder.

* * *

'I can't believe it. I honestly can't believe it. That devious little...' Ben said, as he and Jamie peered over Holly's shoulder to get a clear view of her phone screen.

She'd already watched it at least a dozen times, just to make sure her eyes weren't playing tricks on her and had needed a second opinion. She was replayed the part of the video with them in the shop together, her flitting in and out of shot, before disappearing up the stairs. Giles could be seen immediately heading straight to the chocolate hedgehog display, pulling his handkerchief from his pocket and carefully opening it up. He lifted the dead mouse by its tail and pushed the boxes aside and then his hand disappeared amongst them. Next he readjusted the display. A moment later and he was back by the counter as Holly came down the stairs.

No matter how many times she watched it, the betrayal cut through her like a knife. Once again, it was like the moment she had walked in on Dan in their bedroom all over again. It may not have been years of her life that Giles had taken from her, but in some ways, it felt even worse. This was her shop and, as ridiculous as it might sound, she was starting to think that it had always been the true love of her life.

'So, what does this mean?' Jamie asked as she slumped down the sofa, her eyes still wide with shock.

'I don't know,' Holly said, honestly. 'I mean, I still failed the inspection.'

'No,' Ben said firmly. 'You were sabotaged. That's entirely different. Can you email me that video?'

'Umm...' Holly tapped the screen. 'I think so, why?'

'Because I'm taking this straight to Victor Martinez. That guy owes me a favour. I think it's time I cashed it in, don't you?'

The next two hours went by in a blur. Ben darted in and out of the house, mostly on his phone, but occasionally with a hand free to grab a drink.

'Do you think he'll manage it? Do you think he'll get the Inspector to allow me to open up tomorrow?' she asked Jamie

'I'm not sure,' she replied, wringing her hands as she spoke. 'But if anyone can make it happen, he can.'

'He's sent him the video, right? He'll have to watch it, won't he?'

'Maybe, but it's Saturday night. He might not look at it until Monday morning...'

Jamie didn't need to finish what she was saying. It was the same thought Holly had been having: Monday morning would be too late.

At ten-thirty, Ben returned to the house. She had no idea how it was possible to become so dishevelled just talking on the phone. Well, by Ben's standards, at least.

'So?' she asked, her heart drumming so loudly she was sure it was going to crack a rib. 'What did he say? Did he look at it? Did he watch the video?'

'He did...' Ben's voice was breathy.

'And...'

'And there will need to be an official investigation before the report can be quashed, but... you can reopen the shop tomorrow, as long as the area has been fully sanitised. Which I suggest we go and do right now.' With that, he pulled out a pair of rubber gloves and a cleaning spray from behind his back, grinning.

Never had she experienced quite such a blend of euphoria and panic.

'How much money do you need to take?' Jamie asked, as Holly rushed to get her shoes on.

'A lot. It needs to be the best day we've ever had. By a long chalk.'

'But it's doable?'

'If every person in Bourton and the surrounding villages decides that tomorrow is going to be their day to by sweets, then it is.'

'Okay, so how are we going to make that happen?'

While Jamie got on the phone to Caroline to tell her about the sudden turn of events, Holly had a different call to make.

'Holly, what time is it? Is everything okay?' The sleepy teenager's voice crackled down the line.

'Drey, I need you to be at work for seven-thirty tomorrow, like you offered before, can you still do that?'

'What? Work? I thought you said the shop was closed.'

'It's a long story.'

'Okay.'

'And Drey?'

'Yes?'

'I'm sorry.'

'What for?'

Holly knew she had nothing to apologise for; after all, she'd not actually accused her of anything to her face, but she'd believed the worst, all the same. Believed that a person who loved the sweet shop almost as much as she did could have jeopardised it.

'I'll tell you tomorrow,' she said, instead.

44

'Drey, can you run upstairs and get another bag of the coconut mushrooms?'

'I just need to restock the rock first.'

'Okay, well grab them both at the same time. And pick up a bag of strawberry bonbons while you're there, too. We're running really low on those.'

Their voices were barely audible over the constant chatter and laughter that filled the little shop. It would appear that Holly had got her wish, although it hadn't happened by chance.

'These are all ladies from my first NTC group,' Caroline said, as she swept in bringing a dozen similarly aged women with her. 'Of course, we've all got birthday parties coming up at the same time, so decided we'd stock up on sweets for the party bags now. I can do some weighing, if that would help?'

'That would be amazing. Thank you.'

Caroline slipped behind the counter next to her, as one of them requested two hundred grams each of strawberry laces, flying saucers and jelly babies.

'I think I'll take the same,' the woman behind her said. 'But I also want some of those fried eggs, and the fizzy fish sweets.'

'I knew this would be a good idea,' Caroline whispered in Holly's ear, with a sly smirk. 'They always try to outdo each other, particularly when it comes to spending money on the kids.'

She was right, and by the time they'd left, every flying saucer in the building was sold and the marzipan animals had taken an impressive hit.

'I'll come down with Michael and the children later, too,' Caroline said, preparing to leave. 'Unless you need me to stay now?'

'I think we'll be okay,' Holly replied, still trying to weigh and serve at the same time. 'But can I ring you, if I need you?'

'I think you might want her to hang on,' Drey said, appearing next to them, arms laden with bags for top ups. 'I told all my college friends that I'd give them a five percent discount if they spend over ten pounds today. That's okay, isn't it? I think a load of them are coming.'

Five percent, Holly thought, that was definitely something she could cope with, especially if they were all spending that amount of money. But college students...

'Don't worry,' Drey said, reading her expression. 'These are good guys. Besides, none of them would want to get on the wrong side of me.'

'Brilliant,' Holly replied. 'I trust your judgement.'

And she did. In fact, she'd promised herself she would never doubt Drey again, although she'd not yet told her the reason behind the shop's closure. There simply hadn't been time.

She turned back to Caroline. 'Are you sure you're okay to stay?'

'Too right I am. I'm just hoping you start doing well enough to bring me in permanently.'

'One step at a time. Let's get enough for the mortgage first.'

While the three women were busy working away, Ben, having taken liberties with the bank's photocopier and printed a hundred of Drey's four for three posters, was currently distributing them on the Green in front of the shop. Holly took a moment to watch him awkwardly move from one tourist to another, her heart overflowing with gratitude. Of all the things he hated doing, she was certain talking to strangers was pretty high up on the list, and yet there he was, doing it for her.

'Holly Bear. Oh, this is magnificent. Absolutely magnificent.'

'Mum?' Her attention brought back inside, Holly gasped in excitement before dashing around the counter to give her mother the quickest of squeezes. 'Thank you so much for coming.'

'Don't be silly. I'm only sorry I hadn't come down earlier. This looks fantastic, and you're so busy.'

'I just hope we're busy enough. Did you manage to tell anyone else about today? Has anyone said they'd come down? What about Aunt June? Or Uncle Henry?'

'I'm afraid I couldn't get hold of either of them.'

'Oh, never mind,' she said, continuing to smile despite the disappointment she felt. True, it was only two people, but today every single person mattered.

'I did manage to rustle up this lot, however,' her mother said. Holly frowned. There was no one else walking into the shop at that precise moment and no-one she could see outside, although that was mainly due to the large bus that had just pulled up. As her mother continued to grin like an insane, Cheshire cat, one person, then another slowly stepped off and headed towards the door. That was when she read the name on the side. *The Cotswold Community Choir*.

'Mum...' She could barely find the words.

'We can't all fit in the one vehicle, but the mini bus and a couple of cars are going to bring the stragglers down in half an hour or so.

Now, tell me, are there any sweets you would recommend for singers?'

Everybody who could step up, did so that day. Jamie not only convinced a few of the guys from the site she was working on to swing by but also volunteers from the retirement home, half the patrons from the scrumpy tasting contest and several people she knew from her Ann Summers parties. Drey's classmates turned up, as did her family and even a couple of her teachers. And all of this on top of one of the busiest tourist days Holly had ever known. By the time they closed the door at five-thirty, the shop was in a complete state but in the best possible way. Many of the jars were empty, and there were gaps in the shelves where they had sold clean out of many different lines.

'Do you want me to start sorting this out now?' Drey asked, as she sat on the stairs, massaging her feet. 'I just need a couple of minutes.'

'No, don't be silly. I can deal with all this in the morning. Besides, I need to cash up.' She was awash with nerves and excitement. Without a shadow of a doubt, it had been their best day ever, but that didn't guarantee it would be enough. Now it was time to find out.

45

Six hundred and fifty-six pounds, twenty-four pence. That's how much short she was. She had taken the money home to count, so she could go over the figures with her laptop to hand. After checking and then double checking, she had come up with the same answer.

Jamie placed a cup of tea down on the table in front of her.

'What about if I lend you the money?' she asked. 'Would that help?'

'That's really kind of you but it all needs to be in the books, as sales. They need to see the numbers.'

'What if I buy six hundred and fifty quid's worth of sweets?'

Holly gave her a sad smile.

'But it's close. It's really close. Surely if you explain to them what happened with Giles, about having to close the shop...'

'They're mortgage brokers. They don't care about sob stories. They gave me a target I had to reach, and I didn't make it. It's that simple.'

Maybe it was the fact that she'd already thought she'd lost the place once that was making this easier to swallow. Then again, it was more likely that she was just numb. Completely and utterly numb. At some point, she was going to have to ring Maud. Tell her she couldn't do it. But that wasn't a job for tonight. She just couldn't face it right now. She would call her tomorrow. Tell her to sell to the developers. Giles had won: a very bitter pill to swallow.

'Are those your final figures?' Ben asked, peering over at the screen. 'Can I take a look?'

'Be my guest, but trust me, there's no extra six hundred and fifty-six pounds hiding on any of the tabs. I've looked.'

She got up to allow him to slip into her seat in front of the laptop, silently shaking her head.

'And does this have all the previous data on here too? All of Maud's takings?'

'Everything that I've got. But, like I said, there's nothing else there that's going to help. Still, knock yourself out. I'm going to have a bath.'

By eight o'clock, she was tucked up in bed. Her arms and legs ached, and her eyes were stinging from staring at the computer screen, but her mind still felt numb. It was the unfairness of it all. The fact that Giles would win, even after the supreme effort she and all her friends had put in. But, at the end of the day, he'd been right. Money bought power and he was the one with all of it.

* * *

The next morning, she stayed in bed until nine before dragging herself down to the shop for just before ten. It didn't matter any more. It didn't matter how many sales she made, or how well stocked the shelves were. As soon as she spoke to Maud, her old friend would contact the developers and that would be it. The end of this chapter of her life.

'Morning, Holly. Everything all right? You're very late opening up this morning.'

'Morning, Mrs Brown,' she replied, rummaging in her bag for the keys. 'Just a bit of a slow start, that's all.'

What was the point in telling them? She thought. She didn't want to burden anyone else with her troubles.

'Well, I hope you're taking care of yourself. Can't have you getting sick. I don't know what we'd do without you.'

Holly's smile was watery and weak, but it was all she could offer as she unlocked the door and flipped over the sign to *Open*.

'Now, what can I get you today?' she asked.

As much as she'd wanted to get the phone call to Maud over and done with, the morning was full on, with regulars and visitors alike. It wasn't as busy as the previous day, of course. Not a patch on that, but it did mean that it was nearly midday before she actually had the time to pick up her phone.

It was a conversation she didn't want interrupted, so she crossed to the door and flicked the sign to *Closed*. But just as she stepped away, the little bell jangled again.

'Sorry, we're closed for... Ben? Is everything all right?'

His tie was slightly askew, which was very unlike him although, apart from that, he looked as professional as ever in his smart suit, briefcase at his side.

'Have you rung her? Have you rung Maud yet?'

'No,' she sighed. 'I'm just about to do it now.'

'Well don't.'

'Sorry?'

He lifted his briefcase onto the counter, flipped it open and pulled out a bulging, brown envelope.

'Here,' he said. 'Take it.'

She frowned, staring at the envelope, which obviously contained something substantial.

Sighing again, she shook her head. 'It's really kind of you but I already told Jamie, money's not going to help. I needed to make enough profit.'

'It's not money. Open it up.'

Still hesitating, she took it from him and pulled out a wodge of papers. She unfolded them.

'What is this?' she asked, seeing the official letter head of the bank.

'It's a mortgage offer. For you.'

'What?' She blinked rapidly as she scanned down the first page. There was her name and the name and address of the shop and, at the bottom, a very large number in words and digits.

'I don't understand. The mortgage broker...'

'Is a person. Just like I am a person. But I'm one who looked through your figures in detail. And who knows you. The turn-around you've achieved here in such a small time is astronomical. I didn't want to say anything yesterday, not until I'd run the numbers through our system, but it's all legit. My bank can do it. We can offer you a mortgage, Holly Berry. All you need to do is sign on the dotted line and Just One More is all yours.'

EPILOGUE

Two months on and it was still hard for Holly to believe how much she had gone through and survived. High season was upon them now. The blue skies and summer warmth brought day visitors from up and down the country. Caroline had officially come to work at the shop, only two days a week, plus every other Sunday, but it was enough to give Holly a regular break and Caroline some sanity back in her life (her own words). Drey was working full time now she was off college, and the website was starting to take off, with regular orders for the party platters. It wasn't going to result in early retirement, but it would see her through the quieter months, later in the year.

October gave way to November and, somehow, she had been running the shop for nine months. Three quarters of a year. Bourton-on-the-Water was, after all this time, home again. She visited her parents fortnightly, on her Sundays off, for a family roast. She'd settled in well at Jamie's, and had successfully constructed a series of raised beds in the back garden.

As she locked up one Thursday evening, she noted a distinct

chill in the air and the scent of wood smoke. It wouldn't be long until the first frost and then Christmas, and then a whole new year would begin, with a thousand, positive things to look forward to.

'You ready to head home?'

Ben was wearing a winter coat over his smart suit, with a deer-stalker hat pulled down over his ears. They'd got into a routine now, walking back and forth to work each day together. Normally, he would just listen as she talked about one customer or another, but sometimes they discussed things, like bike rides they were planning for the weekend or how Jamie's latest project was going.

'Ready and waiting,' she said, dropping the keys into her bag.

That evening, he was particularly quiet, barely speaking until they were off the High Street and only a hundred or so metres from home. When they reached the gravel driveway shared by the two semi-detached houses, he stopped.

'I wondered if you might like to do something different this weekend,' he said, as the soft, orange glow of a street lamp flicked on above him. 'Maybe go to the cinema, then out for food?'

'That sounds good. I'll check what's on. You know we can't let Jamie pick the film. She has terrible taste.'

Even in the dusky light, she noticed that his cheeks had coloured by just a fraction. He lowered his gaze.

'Actually, I meant just you and me. You know, on a sort of, kind of, well, a date, I guess.'

'A date?'

His complexion went from pink to red.

'You're right, silly idea. Forget I asked. Just...'

'That sounds nice,' she said, cutting him off.

'It does?'

'It does.'

When he raised his eyes to meet hers again, she noticed a

twinkle there and felt a butterfly tingling in return. A date with Ben. The idea *was* nice. More than nice, actually. It felt right

'A date it is, then,' she said with a smile.

ACKNOWLEDGMENTS

I want to start by saying a massive thank you to my team at Boldwood, particularly Emily for your belief in my books. A huge thank you also belongs to Carol for her endless help, although she has now moved firmly from the spot of colleague to family.

My eagle-eyed beta readers Lucy and Kath, who have stayed with me through many series, not to mention genres, thank you for your speedy responses when I give you literally days to read through, usually because I am very far behind schedule. Then of course Jake. Sorry. If I had listened to your advice, this book would have been finished a lot sooner!

Lastly, it wouldn't be right not to give a final mention to my beloved sweet shop boss. I thank my stars frequently that you said yes to giving me a job all those decades ago. This book is a homage to that time in my life that I will never forget.

MORE FROM HANNAH LYNN

We hope you enjoyed reading *The Sweet Shop of Second Chances*. If you did, please leave a review.

If you'd like to gift a copy, this book is also available as an ebook, large print, hardback, digital audio download and audiobook CD.

Sign up to Hannah Lynn's mailing list for news, competitions and updates on future books.

https://bit.ly/HannahLynnNews

Why not try *Love Blooms at the Second Chances Sweet Shop*, the next instalment in the Holly Berry Sweet Shop Series...

ABOUT THE AUTHOR

Hannah Lynn is the author of over twenty books spanning several genres. As well as signing a new romantic fiction series, Boldwood will be republishing her bestselling Sweet Shop series inspired by her Cotswolds childhood.

Visit Hannah's website: www.hannahlynnauthor.com

Follow Hannah on social media:

facebook.com/hannahlynnauthor

instagram.com/hannahlynnwrites

tiktok.com/@hannah.lynn.romcoms

bookbub.com/authors/hannah-lynn

Boldwood

Boldwood Books is an award-winning fiction publishing company seeking out the best stories from around the world.

Find out more at www.boldwoodbooks.com

Join our reader community for brilliant books, competitions and offers!

Follow us
@BoldwoodBooks
@BookandTonic

Sign up to our weekly deals newsletter

https://bit.ly/BoldwoodBNewsletter

Ingram Content Group UK Ltd.
Milton Keynes UK
UKHW042028130723
425110UK00004B/138

9 781805 495833